THE LAST OASIS

BOOK 13 THE THAW CHRONICLES

TAMAR SLOAN

HEIDI CATHERINE

SEQUEL HOUSE

FYVE

*F*yve needs to blink, but he can't bring himself to. There's too much to take in. Too much to process.

He's trying to understand the violent arrival of the eleven men and one woman who've corralled the teens into a corner of the deck, even as he realizes he and Halo now have the ultimate answer they were looking for. The man standing at the forefront of the group smugly said it himself.

We are the real Terra.

These are the people who've been controlling the threads of their lives. Pulling when they feel like it. Twisting on a whim. Severing them when they want.

What's more, Jiro is one of them.

Fyve struggles to tear his gaze from the man he was stupid enough to trust. Jiro helped him. And yet, he's standing at the rear of the group, holding one of the metal weapons that throw flames.

Pointedly looking at every teen but Fyve.

Anger suffuses Fyve's limbs, then his chest, then his thoughts. It's slow at first, hampered by disbelief and shock. But as reality refuses to be denied, the fury fires with the same explosive speed it did from the weapons. It injects itself into every sinew, every tendon, every cell. It pulses with two words.

No.

More.

Halo slips her warm hand in his. "Not yet," she whispers.

Fyve draws in a calm, cooling breath. She's right. If they fight now, people will get hurt. He eyes the dangerous weapons their captors are holding, the scent of burned flesh and toxic fumes still coating the back of his throat. They need to bide their time.

The man without the beard, the one who's clearly the leader, glares at the girl clinging to Halo. "Return to your father," he says, his voice hard.

Terra shrinks behind Halo, looking terrified. A faint whimper stains the air.

"Now."

The word isn't shouted. It's little more than a sharp bite. But it's undeniably an order. One that's expected to be obeyed.

Or there'll be consequences.

In fact, Terra immediately releases Halo and stands to attention. Her face turns blank, all emotion instantly wiped away. Almost robotically, she walks toward the man, and Fyve has to suppress the need to stop her. It's like she just tucked all her humanity, her ability to feel, into a place no one can touch.

But when she walks past the leader, Fyve stills. He'd assumed the man was her father. Instead, Terra walks past the others, her body ramrod straight, reaches Jiro, then stands behind him.

Fyve loses the ability to breathe. Jiro is Terra's father?

Mentally shaking himself, Fyve tells himself it doesn't matter. That's an answer to a question he never even had. Instead, he decides to do exactly what Halo would—gather information. "What do you mean?" he calls out. It's clear the girl who they've all been calling Terra isn't who they were led to believe she is. "That you're the real Terra."

Especially when it was a scared little girl who was clinging to Halo. One who's been able to speak this whole time.

The man at the front puffs out his chest until it's almost as inflated as his middle. "Let us go to the ballroom. We shall talk there."

The teens shuffle and glance at each other. The words are said amiably, like an invite. Yet the men holding the weapons tense, their hands tightening on the guns. Jiro's gaze finally lands on Fyve, clearly trying to communicate something. Fyve can practically hear the words as if Jiro can still talk to him in his mind.

Do as they say. It's the only way.

Then again, Jiro also told him he'd keep him safe, and Fyve barely survived the final Trial. The man even pretended to care. Fyve looks away, suppressing a sound of disgust. Jiro is nothing to him now. Their connection was a lie, just like everything else on this ship.

The man who spoke steps back, waving an arm with a flourish. "Shall we?"

Two men and the woman walk to the door, although it only opens when they hold their wrist over it.

Halo stiffens. "The doors are locked again," she whispers.

Probably every last one on the ship, too. The Oasis just became a monstrous, floating prison.

Fyve registers the man and woman are both wearing bracelets, and it reminds him of the chip that still sits in his pocket. The one Jiro gave him. He keeps his gaze far away from the man who tried to pretend to be an ally as he mulls it over. They may have an advantage. He squeezes Halo's hand, hoping to convey some reassurance even though he can't give her any details.

The man and woman pass through the door, clearly expecting the teens to follow. Except the group of fifty contract closer together. For some reason, going below deck feels far more dangerous than being up here. Although they're trapped, no matter what, the stifling confines of The Oasis will be physical proof of it.

The leader narrows his eyes. "Go to the ballroom. Immediately."

The veneer of civility is gone. These words are said as the threat they are, with barely concealed menace.

There's a creak of metal as one of the other men hefts his flame throwing weapon. It's the same man who fired at Sica, inadvertently burning the girl who's now tucked beside Iva, shivering as she stares at her charred and peeling hands in horror. And his expression suggests he's looking forward to doing it again.

Fyve and Halo glance at each other, already knowing what they need to do. Simultaneously, they step forward, following the man and woman. Justice is quick to join them. Then Cloud, holding her babies tightly to her chest. That's all it takes. The teens are either desperate for someone to make these decisions or they don't want to be separated, because they shuffle to catch up.

Halo moves a little closer so they can pass through the door, then stays glued to Fyve's side once they're inside. It feels like they just stepped into the jaws of a leatherskin. The walk to the ballroom is accompanied by the muted sounds of dragging feet and shallow breathing. It's like everyone is half holding their breaths, half trying to calm the fear that's a living parasite in their chests.

No one knows what the reveal of these adults, who have obviously been on the ship the whole time, will mean.

Inside the ballroom, Fyve and Halo walk to the center before they stop and turn around. To his surprise, the other teens file past and congregate behind them, leaving Fyve and Halo at the front. Their appointed leaders. Or a flimsy buffer.

The man and woman they followed circle back to join the

other captors, and they spread out in a proud line before the teens. Under the artificial light of the ballroom, they look even more pasty, their waists round but also saggy, as if their skin can't hold the weight of their excess.

The man without the beard smiles, once more congenial and gracious, as if he's hosting friends rather than prisoners. "I can understand why you're all nervous. Let me introduce us. We are the Echelons. My name is Nole, and I have always been your Terra."

The woman frowns a little. "We all have been."

"Yes, we have," Nole agrees, not glancing at her. "You owe your lives to us. We've watched over you since Treasure Island."

A round of soft gasps ripple through the teens.

"We're the ones who orchestrated the Trials so you could be chosen for Tomorrow Land."

Fyve's gut clenches painfully. These are the people who watched his siblings die, one by one. They're the ones who killed Coal in their brutal games.

Nole beams even wider. "And now, we're the ones who chose you to accompany us to Tomorrow Land."

Halo shifts her weight. The motion is subtle, but Fyve notices it because they're standing so close. Or possibly because the words also made him uncomfortable. Being chosen has come at an unimaginable price. And Tomorrow Land feels as attainable as freedom right now.

"You must be curious about us," Nole continues, his gaze roaming over the teens with pride. Fyve tenses when the man's eyes seem to stay for a second too long on Halo. "And we want to give you the opportunity to get to know your generous benefactors. To ask any question you like."

A couple of the teens grunt assent. A quick glance over Fyve's shoulder reveals they're all watching the Echelons with guarded intensity. Most have layers of confusion twisting their brows. A few have their arms crossed. One or two look cautiously hopeful.

Fyve doesn't trust any of this. Or any of the Echelons.

Including Jiro.

Nole turns to his comrades. "Let us take our Treasures so they can begin to understand how wonderful their future is going to be."

The woman steps forward. "I am Rhina." Her gaze lands on one of the teens and stays there. Fyve's not certain, but he's pretty sure it turned hungry. "Ajax, come with me."

Halo gasps, as do a few others behind them. Ajax shrinks back, looking as if he wishes he was invisible. "Me?" he squeaks.

Rhina's face softens. "Yes, my Treasure," she purrs. "I won't hurt you. I want to take care of you."

Ajax straightens. "You do?"

"Very much so," Rhina says, her eyes softening in her pudgy face. "Come, let me show you."

Fyve watches as Ajax willingly walks toward Rhina, not sure why he's surprised. Halo's brother has always been both exceptionally stupid and unbelievably selfish. The promise in both Rhina's words and eyes are all he needs to see where this will go. To ensure he survives another day.

The moment he's within reach, Rhina takes Ajax's hand. "So strong," she murmurs as she tugs him toward the door.

Another Echelon steps forward, indicating toward a girl at the back. "Come. You're with me."

The girl glances at the teen standing on her right, then her left, but no one's sure what the right thing to do is. Refuse? Fyve doesn't think the Echelons will use those flame throwing guns inside, but he's also not ready to find out. The only alternative is to comply…

The girl must reach the same conclusion, because she drops her head so her hair curtains her face and shuffles forward.

The Echelon beams. "Good girl."

"Sica," grunts the Echelon beside him. "You're mine."

"I don't belong to anyone," Sica growls back, obviously choosing the first option—reject this abhorrent order.

The Echelon steps forward, a scowl drawing down the folds of his face. "Do you not remember what happened the last time you refused?"

Somewhere in the crowd, the girl who was burned whimpers.

Sica lifts her chin. "You won't use those things inside. One out of control fire and we'll all end up at the bottom of the ocean."

The Echelon slips his hand in his pocket and brings out a small, black object. Glaring at Sica, he squeezes it between his thumb and finger.

She drops to the ground with a cry, her hands clasping her head. A thin trickle of blood seeps from her nose as she writhes on the ground, her screams filtered through gritted teeth.

The Echelon walks over, the teens around her stepping back in fear. He kneels down, making a show of releasing the trigger he's clearly holding. "I'm going to enjoy us getting to know each other."

He scoops Sica up with a grunt, ignoring her moan of protest. Without another word, or a glance at the shocked teens around him, he turns and leaves the ballroom.

Fyve watches as one by one, the Echelons pick a teen and walk to the door. Even Jiro selects someone. He calls on Cloud, his face impassive as she whimpers, holding Miracle and Marvel to her like she plans on dying before they're hurt. Fyve glares at Jiro as he pulls Cloud to his side, disgust a bitter film on his tongue, but Jiro never looks at him. Terra remains his impassive shadow, the screaming girl of not long ago buried so deep, it's as if she never existed.

Apart from Rhina and the Echelon who took Sica, the others stay, their Treasure—as the Echelons call them—standing mutely by their side. Fyve quickly realizes it's to maintain a show of numbers. To keep the teens subdued.

It means the Echelons know the teens they've captured have an advantage—their numbers.

Fyve grips the chip in his pocket, letting it dig into his palm. The Echelons are clueless that the teens aren't as helpless as they think.

Rebellion is inevitable.

It's only a matter of time before war is waged.

They just have to wait for the right moment.

Nole steps forward, the final Echelon to collect his Treasure. His gaze settles unerringly on Halo. "Come with me."

Halo recoils against Fyve, stunned. "N-no."

Impatience tugs at the corners of Nole's mouth as he steps forward. "You'll soon understand how lucky you are." He reaches out and clamps a hand around Halo's arm. "Now, let's go."

The growing uneasiness as Fyve's been watching this disturbing turn of events is instantly washed away. He can't stand by and let this happen. Not when it comes to Halo.

He shoves himself between Halo and Nole, breaking the hold the man has on her. "She's staying here," he grinds out.

Nole's nostrils flare as he inflates like a puffer fish. "You obviously don't understand how lucky you are, either."

The threat in the words is unmistakable, and it has Fyve thinking of the way the plank shook when he stood on it, trying to topple him into an ocean swirling with leatherskins.

Nole pushes his face closer. "Or that luck can run out."

Fyve glares back. "Leave Halo alone."

The smile that curves up Nole's face sends chills down Fyve's spine. The fleshy man steps closer and snaps an arm out, but rather than grab Fyve, he reaches around and grasps Halo once more. "She's mine," he whispers, only loud enough for Fyve to hear. "She always has been."

Disgust and fury are a hurricane in Fyve's gut. The possessive glint in Nole's eye speaks of far more than a benevolent benefactor. Like hell he's taking Halo away from him. And he doesn't know that Fyve no longer has his chip. He can't be claimed. He can't be subjugated by pain like Sica was.

It seems the time for rebellion came much sooner than even Fyve expected.

Knowing he needs to move fast, that the first strike has to count, he coils his muscles. Draws every drop of energy into them, prepared to explode.

Without warning, agony detonates along Fyve's temple. His head snaps to the side with the force, dragging his body with him as he crashes into the ground. He lands with a grunt and rolls onto his side, willing himself to get back up.

But the connection to his legs is gone.

All he can feel is pain. It clamps around his mind, excluding all else.

Half-groaning, half-gasping, Fyve looks up. Darkness crowds the edges of his vision, creating a tunnel that focuses on one thing.

Jiro's standing above him, breathing hard as he lowers the butt of his gun back to his side. His face is impassive in a way that reminds Fyve of Terra.

"No," he moans, although there's no sound. His voice is as disconnected as the rest of his body.

He fights as the blackness contracts, cutting off his consciousness, but he can stop that as much as he could stop the events in the ballroom. The world turns to night as Fyve's final thoughts filter through the pain.

The Echelons have each taken a teen. Nole has taken Halo.

To who knows where.

And to do who knows what.

HALO

"What have you done?" Halo throws herself at Fyve who's sprawled on the floor. But before she can reach him, she's hauled back by the man who calls himself Nole.

"Leave him, my Treasure," he growls in her ear, his breath warm and far too intimate for her liking.

She struggles to free herself, but her depleted body is no match for the vice-like grip he has on her arm and she's dragged backward.

Fyve groans and while it's a noise that means he's in pain, it's also sweet relief. He's alive, having survived that massive blow at the hands of the man who little Terra had indicated is her father. Which means that not only is Fyve in danger, but so is Terra.

Terra's father steps away from Fyve and returns to Cloud, taking her forcibly by the arm. Bile builds in Halo's throat. Cloud and the babies are in danger, too.

And there's nothing Halo can do about any of this. Not while she's being dragged away against her will.

"Give me a flamethrower," Nole barks at one of his men,

taking a weapon and looping the strap over his shoulder. He hauls Halo from the ballroom.

"Why are you doing this?" she asks as her feet move down the corridor in the opposite direction to where she wants to go.

"It's for your own good," he replies. "You'll see."

Her legs collapse as she tries to fall to the floor, feeling like this is the only way she can protest. Nole swings his flamethrower over his shoulder and scoops her up, holding her tightly against his chest. She blanches, not wanting to be in such close contact with the man who's responsible for the sea of misery she's been surrounded by ever since she got on this ship.

"I'll walk," she hisses, needing her own space as much as she needs the stale air inside this corridor to hell.

"I knew you'd come around, my Treasure." He sets her down, keeping hold of her arm in case she tries anything else. Taking her to the staircase, he indicates for her to walk up. She begins the climb with him panting far too close behind her. They pass the seventh floor and Halo adds levels to the map she's been keeping in her mind.

"Here," growls Nole, stepping past her to slide open a door on the landing. They leave the stairwell and Halo eyes his weapon, wondering if now's the time to make her move. It's hard to tell how strong Nole is. Can muscles sit underneath layers of fat? She's never seen anyone with such excess on their body before and it's disconcerting. Kind of like a picture she once saw of a hoofed animal that had a hump on its back that could keep it alive for weeks without a drop of water. Except Nole carries his hump on his stomach...

He notices her gaze and moves his flamethrower to the front of his body.

"It's easier if you do as I tell you," he says. "Just like the way you always obeyed your father back on that pile of trash you call home."

"You killed my father." She crosses her arms as she walks. "He always did what you told him and look where that got him."

"Hmm." Nole scratches at his chin. "That's true. Only until recently though, when he became quite disruptive. I wouldn't recommend you follow in his footsteps. You have a far more pleasant future ahead of you. If you behave yourself..."

She glares at him, not willing to make any such promise.

He presses his bracelet against a square thing next to a door and it slides open. Halo's eyes bug at what greets them.

The room before her is the most lavish place she could ever imagine. It's so unlike the rest of this decaying ship, giving the impression of only having been recently constructed.

Her feet sink into fluffy black carpet that's nothing like the threadbare remains in the ballroom as she steps forward. The walls have been coated in velvety patterns of swirling purple and blue with thick golden curtains hanging from the windows. There are round tables with surfaces so shiny they look like mirrors and seats padded with plush purple cushions. Crystals hang from the ceiling in glittering arrangements, sending shadows and sparks flickering around the room.

A sound fills the opulent space and Halo blinks as she tries to take it in. There are high notes and low notes that shift and change as they blend and merge, then fly apart without warning, shattering in every direction as they create what can only be described as dancing inside her ears.

"What is that?" she asks, pointing at one ear as she tilts her head, trying to drink in more of the hypnotic sound.

Nole smiles. "It's called music. Do you like it?"

Halo nods before she can stop herself. The sounds are doing strange things to her insides as they take her on a journey through valleys of sadness, then send her soaring to the sky, buzzing with overwhelming joy. Tears run down her face, and she wipes them away, trying to understand how the sense of sound alone can possibly spark this kind of emotion.

"Music," she says, turning the word over in her mouth. It reminds her of her tree back on Treasure Island. Something created with no purpose, other than to inspire.

"I forget you've never experienced such things." Nole widens his smile, revealing a set of straight teeth that are too white to be human. "I have so many more pleasures to introduce you to."

These words snap Halo back to reality, and she notices the teens who were taken from the ballroom are also here. They're already seated at the small tables, each with an Echelon beaming at them. Sica is cracking her knuckles and scowling deeply. Other teens are shaking as they listen to words Halo can't quite make out. Ajax is laughing at something the female Echelon has said.

Nole leads Halo to a vacant table and pulls out a chair. It takes her a moment to realize he wants her to sit down.

"A gentleman always seats his lady," says Nole, as she sinks into the plush cushion.

"I'm not your lady," she replies, wanting to make the situation abundantly clear.

Nole sits down across from her, and a terrified Cloud enters the room with Terra's father. She doesn't have the twins with her, and Halo can only hope Iva is looking after them.

"Eyes here," says Nole, his tone clipped with harshness. "I've waited a long time for this day."

Halo bites down on her tongue to stop the words that are trying to cascade from her lips. This is the man who's responsible for all this fear and misery. And the deaths. The first chance she gets, she's going to kill him so he can experience the same misery he's inflicted on so many others. But for now, it's best she sits and learns everything she can. She may not have a weapon strapped to her back, but knowledge is a source of power all on its own.

A man wearing a feathered mask and long black robes steps into the room via another door, holding a tray of tall glasses filled with golden liquid. He makes his way around the tables, depositing two on each.

Halo is unable to take her eyes off the intricate detail of the man's mask. The black feathers fan out to cover his face with a long, dark beak positioned where his nose must be. There are two holes for his eyes and as he gets closer, Halo sees his irises are the color of night. His head has been shaved in the same way as Terra's, with dark bristles coating his scalp.

"Is he one of you?" Halo asks.

Nole seems to find her question funny. "No, he's a Raven."

"What's a Raven?" she asks, watching the man place a glass on the table where Cloud is seated.

"They help us," says Nole. "You can't possibly think we've been serving you all those meals by ourselves."

"So, they're your slaves." Halo nods, thinking she understands the situation now, and not liking it one little bit. "Is that what you're going to turn us into?"

Nole laughs again. "Not at all. You're too precious for that. You're our Treasures."

The Raven approaches their table and sets down a glass.

"Careful, Raven," barks Nole. "Do it slowly! Like I taught you."

The Raven nods his apology and Halo sees his hands begin to shake. He takes another glass and puts it in front of Halo. The liquid sloshes due to the jerkiness of his frightened movements and Halo darts out her hand to take the glass.

"Oops, sorry," she says. "I think I spilled a little bit."

The Raven looks at her and it's impossible to miss the way his pupils widen.

"What's your name?" Halo asks him.

"Ravens don't talk," Nole snaps. "Nor do they have names."

The Raven returns his hand to his tray and his sleeve slips back, revealing the tanned forearm of someone who's spent his

14

life in the sun with a narrow, fair band of skin around his wrist. This nags at something in the recesses of Halo's memory, telling her it's important, but she can't bring it to the surface just now. If he's spent his life outdoors, why hasn't she seen him on the deck?

"Be gone." Nole clicks his fingers impatiently, and the Raven moves to the next table.

Halo fixes her gaze on the glass in front of her, not wanting to look at the awful man demanding her attention. An infinite supply of bubbles rise in the glass, and she stares at them in fascination, wondering where they're all coming from.

"Drink up," says Nole. "Good champagne is one of the pleasures of life I was talking about."

Halo takes a sip, certain she hadn't been taken all the way up here to be poisoned. The bubbles tingle on her tongue and she savors the taste, trying to decide if it's bitter or sweet. The music picks up pace with a drumming sound marching to the foreground and she can feel it vibrate in her chest.

"We made this room to enjoy with our Treasures." Nole sweeps out his hand. "Do you like it?"

"What I'd like, is to know if Fyve's okay." Halo sets down her glass and lifts her gaze.

Nole waves his hand dismissively. "He's fine. Just learning an important lesson."

"And what would that be?" Halo leans forward on her elbows.

Nole lets out a long sigh. "Treasure, can't you see we've done all of this for your benefit?"

Her eyes widen as she sits back in her chair. "Are you kidding me?"

He blinks at her in full seriousness. "No, Treasure. I am most certainly not."

"Let me get this right," she says. "You murder us at random, force us to participate in dangerous Trials, put us on a ship and kill half of us, all the while making us take part in even more dangerous Trials. Then you knock us unconscious when we try to resist being taken away. And we're supposed to be grateful for some kind of important lesson you've been teaching us?"

Nole tuts. "You're seeing it all wrong, Treasure! We've been watching over you all your lives, caring for you in the same way a mother protects her child. We handpicked the very best of you to take you to a miraculous place where you have the unique opportunity to build a brand-new world."

"Coal was the very best of the lot of us," says Halo, pushing her drink away. "Where's his unique opportunity?"

"For every achievement, sacrifices must be made." Nole reaches across the table and pushes her glass back to her.

"Coal was my friend," says Halo. "Not a sacrifice. He was a living, breathing human who never hurt another soul."

Nole doesn't even flinch at this. "Mother Nature can be random in her acts."

"But this wasn't Mother Nature," Halo snaps. "It was you."

Ajax's laugh filters over the music and she turns to see him reaching over the table to stroke the female Echelon's face.

"Your brother is grateful," says Nole. "He can see what Rhina is offering him."

"What is she offering him exactly?" Halo narrows her eyes.

"The world, my Treasure." Nole leans back in his chair and slurps the last of the bubbling liquid from his glass. "She's quite literally offering him the world."

Knowing a world without Fyve isn't something she wants, Halo drains her glass, trying not to wince as the bubbles find their way up her nose. She scowls at her captor, not caring to continue this conversation any further.

Sensing her shutting down, Nole leans forward. "Oh, Treasure—"

"I'm not your Treasure," she bites back as the Raven

approaches their table to take their empty glasses. "I'm not some shiny possession you can put on your shelf. And he's not a Raven, or any animal that you can claim ownership of. We're people, just like you."

The Raven takes her glass, his eyes wide behind his feathered mask as he subtly shakes his head in a warning. His sleeve slips up, once more revealing the pale band of skin on his wrist and Halo realizes who this is.

It's Dargo. It has to be. The guy who wore a leather strap made for him as a symbol of love, never once removing it—not until he'd been taken by the Echelons and was desperate to send Iva a message.

Halo's heart swells with hope as she remains silent, not wanting to endanger him any further. If Dargo's alive, then so might be some of the others.

Their army of fifty just got bigger.

Dargo scurries to the table Sica is seated at, just as she throws her drink all over the Echelon facing her. Her captor seems to find this amusing and chuckles heartily as he takes a cloth from Dargo to wipe his face.

"Let's continue this chat somewhere else," says Nole, pushing to his feet.

Halo's heart picks up pace, not wanting to go anywhere with his man. Especially if it means being alone with him. "I'm fine here."

"I don't think so," he says, coming to her side of the table and putting out his hand. "There's something I've been looking forward to showing you."

"Do I get a choice?" Halo asks, even though the answer is already obvious.

"You always have a choice," he replies. "Can I remind you that nobody made you enter the Oasis Trials? You *wanted* to be here. You fought hard for your place."

He grabs her arm once more, forcing her to stand, and she

17

winces, having no idea what he wants to show her. All she knows is that she doesn't want to see it.

She may have fought hard to be here.

But she's going to fight even harder to find her way out.

FYVE

*T*he first thing that Fyve registers is crying. Sobs large enough to choke whoever is being wracked by them. The sound has him leaping to his feet before he can remember why he's lying down in the first place.

"Halo!" he calls in a panic, wondering why she's crying.

Then it all hits him in a rush.

The Echelons.

Jiro's callous blow.

Halo's not here. Because Nole took her.

The ballroom spins for nauseating seconds and Fyve grips his head as if that will stop it. It takes far longer than he'd like, but he starts lurching toward the door, anyway. He has to save Halo.

"It's locked, Fyve," someone says behind him. He thinks it's Justice, but he ignores them. Nothing will stop him from getting to Halo.

He reaches the door and grabs the handle, growling when it doesn't budge. He yanks hard, making it rattle, but it still doesn't open. Wrapping both hands around it, Fyve grits his teeth and pulls with everything he has, trying to slide it open.

It most definitely stops him from getting to Halo.

Yanking the chip out of his pocket, he swipes it over the door, his muscles coiled as he prepares to step through and break into a sprint.

The door doesn't move.

Fyve tries again, this time waving the chip frantically over the entirety of the door, and even a two-foot border around it.

Nothing.

"Ah, I don't think an interpretive dance is going to help."

Fyve spins around, confirming it's Justice who's speaking to him. Her crutches are leaning against her as she has her arms crossed.

"I'm trying to open the door," he growls.

"And you don't think we've all tried it while you were taking your enforced nap?" she asks archly. "The only way in and out of this place is locked."

The sobs that had halted start up again, quickly morphing to a wail. "We're all going to die." Viney collapses to her knees, her face falling into her hands as she continues to cry in big, gulping heaves.

Justice rolls her eyes. "I'm going to fight a little harder before I give up."

Fyve turns back to the door, scanning its outline as if he'll find a weakness. "I'm going to help Halo."

"Sure thing." Justice snorts, another eye roll evident in her tone. "Even if you manage to break out, they'll claim you the moment they find you've escaped."

"I can't be claimed," he snaps, once more waving the chip around.

The sound of sharp footsteps reaches him, then a hand is gripping his arm and spinning him around. "What do you mean, you can't be claimed?"

Fyve jerks away, wishing he'd kept his mouth shut. "I'll explain later."

When he's found a way out of this prison.

"No, Fyve." This time it's another voice and he sees Iva approaching. "We're all worried. We've all lost so much already. We deserve answers."

Justice nods sharply. "Damn right we do."

He pauses, recognizing the truth in their words. Even Viney quiets down to a few hiccupping gulps. His gaze scans the group of teens, now missing the dozen the Echelons took. Every eye is on him. It looks like every breath is being held as they wait to see what he'll do.

As they wait for him to lead this fight.

Except they don't realize his strength, his purpose, is Halo. Without her, there is no fight.

Iva takes another step forward. "Why can't you be claimed?"

Fyve's gaze once more roams over the expectant faces. They're all looking at him as if he not only has that answer, but *all* the answers. Like how to get them out of this.

Justice clenches her fists. "They've been controlling everything, us, from the start."

She has no idea how right she is. And now they have a name for them. The Echelons.

"They've been watching us all along," he says, acknowledging they have a right to know. "They use cameras and watch us on screens. Even back on Treasure Island. The Trials were rigged from the start."

Someone gasps. "There is no Terra."

Fyve winces. Losing Terra for some would be the same as losing hope. And the belief there's a reason they've been through everything they have.

"The Echelons used the idea of Terra to manipulate us." He thinks of Jiro and the lump at the back of his head throbs. "They've been using us all along."

Viney moans. "My poor Ajax."

Fyve resists the urge to glare at her. Ajax managed to twist every Trial to his advantage like the snake he is. "They're probably watching us right now."

The teens look around, shuffling uncomfortably.

"So, they'll see you leave?" Justice asks, her eyes narrowing.

Fyve's gaze darts around the room, wondering if Jiro is watching him right now, or worse, whether he's hurting Cloud. "Probably."

Viney moans. "If you escape, they'll kill us. Every last one."

Fyve pauses, wondering if that's true. Nole spoke of choosing them. Of working together. Killing them doesn't make sense. At the same time, they're now trapped in the ballroom with twelve of them taken, most against their will.

His stomach sinks. He can't take the chance. As much as every shred of his being wants to find Halo, he can't do it at the risk of these people's lives.

Yet he refuses to be stuck. To just sit here and wait to see what the Echelons plan to do with them next. Fyve steps away from the door, his gaze scanning the walls. "They won't have a reason to kill us if they can't see us," he growls.

He strides to the nearest corner, finding what he's looking for. It's a small, black square with a round piece of glass in the center, like a fathomless eye. Watching them. Always watching them.

A quick lap of the ballroom reveals there are eight cameras, four in the corners of the room, four more halfway along the walls. Each one is several feet off the ground, out of reach even if he were to jump.

Iva plants her hands on her hips. "We need to destroy them."

Viney claps her hands over her ears as if she can stop the words reaching her. "If we do that, they'll claim us for sure," she moans.

"The Echelons are busy with their Treasures," Justice spits in disgust. "Now is the time to do this."

Fyve's stomach churns at the way Nole called Halo his Treasure, but he quickly pushes the thought away. Justice and Iva are right. They need to destroy the cameras, and now is their chance, while the Echelons are preoccupied.

The question is how. The ballroom is empty, meaning there's no way of climbing up to reach the cameras. There's nothing to throw. They have no weapons. Fyve executes a slow turn, his hands on his hips as he thinks. They had a lot less on Treasure Island and that never stopped him.

Justice hobbles to a corner, glaring up at the camera there, looking as if she's considering scaling the wall, despite her injury. She leans against a crutch, scowling.

Instantly giving Fyve an idea.

He strides over to her and takes hold of the other crutch leaning loosely against her. "May I?"

Her eyes light up. "You may."

Fyve grips it as he walks back to his corner, flipping it over so he's holding it by the tip. The Y that slots under Justice's arm now rests on the ground as he holds the other end. He looks up at the camera above him, judging the distance. Then, with a smooth leap and a wide swing, he slams the top of the crutch onto it.

There's a *crunch*, a shattering sound, and pieces of black plastic and glass rain down on him. A satisfied smile climbs up Fyve's face. That felt good. He stalks to the camera further down the wall and repeats the process. This strike misses, but all that does is fuel the next one. When the crutch hits this camera, it explodes with such force that plastic scatters almost as far as the teens watching all this unfold with wide eyes.

The sound of more smashing has him turning around, finding Justice destroying the camera above her. It falls to the ground, and she stomps on it before looking up with a grin. "I haven't really needed the crutches for a little while now. But I had a feeling they could be useful."

Fyve finds himself smiling back. "They're quite versatile."

23

They move around the room, methodically smashing the remaining cameras until they're nothing but broken plastic and glass. A couple of teens even cheer as they destroy the final ones.

Fyve steps back as the last camera shatters, finding he's breathing a little heavily. With each camera he smashed, more adrenaline fired through his blood. It felt good to destroy them.

To show Jiro he won't be beaten.

To take some power back.

And now he can go after Halo.

Fyve returns the crutch to Justice, deciding he needs to swipe the chip slower and more carefully. His frantic panic had fueled the fear he wouldn't be able to get to Halo. He spins around, only to find Iva standing in front of him, her arms crossed.

"So how have they been claiming us?" she asks, frowning.

Fyve pauses. The need to get out of here, especially now that the cameras are destroyed, is overwhelming. Yet, he'd be abandoning these teens. Taking the knowledge he carries with him.

The knowledge that was kept from them in the same way it was kept from him. With the intent to manipulate and use.

Halo, wherever she is, would hate the thought as much as he does.

"We all have a chip in our head. It was placed there at birth. It's how Terra—the Echelons—have been communicating with us. It's also how they claim us." Fyve doesn't add that it was Elijah and his mother who put them there. He still doesn't understand how that all happened, nor does he want to tarnish Elijah's memory. He may have blindly followed Terra, but he was the beloved leader of every teen in this room. "Mine was removed, and I took Halo's out."

The teens glance at each other as if they're seeing each other anew. A few run their fingers over their skulls, trying to find the alien piece that's been living inside of them.

Justice straightens. "How do you get rid of the chip?"

Fyve's gut tightens, thinking of what he had to do to Halo. "You cut them out."

A few teens shrink back, the fragile courage they were trying to cultivate quickly withering.

Iva nods resolutely. "Then that's what we do."

She's right. That's what they have to do. And Fyve knows that Halo would say the same thing, no matter how much he wants to go to her.

Every teen on this ship deserves a fighting chance.

He removes the knife from his pocket, swallowing hard. "It's only a small cut," he says, wondering if he's reassuring himself or them.

Justice passes her crutches to Iva, then steps forward with an obvious limp. "I'll go first."

Fyve nods, conscious of how quiet the other teens are. It almost felt like Justice's statement was a shout. He points to the floor a few feet away. "It's probably best if you sit down."

Justice does as she's told, looking a little pale. Fyve can't blame her. He's feeling a little pale himself. There are over thirty teens in this room. And he's going to have to cut out each and every chip from their temple.

He kneels beside Justice, brushing her hair back and carefully feeling for the chip. The small, raised bump is there, making his stomach turn, and not just because he has to get it out.

The Echelons have a lot to answer for.

"This will sting a little," he mutters, remembering that Halo was unconscious for this part. In fact, so was he when his own was removed.

Justice glances at him. "I've had worse," she says dryly.

Acknowledging that's sadly true with a brother like Zake and the father they shared, Fyve focuses on getting this done quickly. Drawing in a steadying breath, he presses the tip of the

25

knife to the skin at her temple. Working on keeping his hand steady, he presses down, suppressing a grimace when the skin splits and blood balloons in a red globule. Pinching his fingers, he can't help the twisting of his features as the chip slides out, lubricated by more blood.

Justice doesn't flinch once.

Fyve pauses, his eyes widening slightly when he realizes that, just like with Halo, he started this without thinking of how to mop up the blood. There's a tearing sound behind him and he turns to find Iva holding out a patch of cloth, the hem of her trousers now shorter on one leg than the other.

"Thanks," he says, taking it and pressing the wadded material to Justice's temple.

"Put pressure on it," Iva says over his shoulder. "It'll slow the bleeding."

Justice nods, taking over the pressing of the cloth to the side of her head. She gets up, her jaw set even if her cheeks lack color. She holds out her other hand for the chip and Fyve passes it to her.

She glares down at it, then looks up at the teens who've been watching this all in silence. Justice grips the chip in her fist and lifts it. "I'm one step closer to freedom."

Ten or so teens rush forward, while a handful take an uncertain step back. One or two have their fingers at their temple, covering the area protectively.

"They'll be fine once we've done a few more," Iva says in a low voice. She turns to Fyve. "I could do it, if you like?"

He doesn't hesitate before passing her the knife.

Iva didn't once look like this is the grossest thing she's ever seen. It's certainly the grossest thing he's ever done. "It's all yours."

A young man is already standing beside them, holding back the hair at his temple. "Get the thing out of me."

"Tear some cloth off your trousers," Fyve says. "Then sit down."

"The name's Antic," the guy says, sitting down as Iva kneels beside him. "And I just wanted to say thanks. We needed someone to be strong."

Fyve nods, not entirely sure how to respond to that.

Iva bites her lip as she focuses on her task, moving quickly. Her hands are steady as she slices the skin, the cut just big enough for the chip to slide through on a bead of blood. She passes it to Antic, who exchanges it for the cloth, which she presses on the small incision. Antic stares down at the chip, frowning.

Such a small thing.

Such momentous consequences.

"Next," Justice calls.

Fyve steps back, watching as Justice has the teens lining up and tearing strips from their trousers, then Iva efficiently removes chip after chip. Once the first ten are done, the ones who were apprehensive step forward and join the line, still looking nervous, but willing to do this.

Most are stoic. A few gasp, blinking rapidly at the sting. One or two yank back at the first sign of pain, but Iva talks to them in a reassuring voice Fyve's never heard her use before. It seems to calm the entire room.

Viney's last, and she whimpers throughout, even clasping her hand over her mouth to hold back a cry. The whole time, she acts like a martyred soldier having their leg amputated.

"It's okay," Iva tells her. "Do it for Ajax. You want to see him again, don't you?"

Viney nods and the procedure is over as quickly as the others.

Justice limps over to Fyve, the crutches now lying on the ground. She stands beside him, surveying the thirty-strong teens, all holding blood-stained cloth to their temples. "Now what?" she asks, sounding determined.

Hopeful.

The same two emotions that are stamped on every face now turned to him.

Fyve blinks, realizing he's done two things.

Made these teens believe he has some idea of what they're supposed to do next.

And sown the seeds of rebellion.

HALO

$\mathcal{N}$ole keeps his fingers clenched painfully around Halo's arm as he leads her down the staircase. At first, she thinks he's taking her back to the ballroom, but they continue on and she quickly realizes where they're headed.

The engine room.

She hasn't been back there since Terra almost claimed her on her first night on the ship. Well, not Terra, she knows now. She's nothing but a frightened child. So, who then? Nole?

"Why are we here?" she asks as he opens the thick metal door, and the hum of the machinery gets instantly louder. Nole turns to close the door, spinning a large metal handle until there's a loud thud. Only then does he give her some space.

"It's a treat," Nole says, smiling. "A treat for my Treasure. I know you like it here."

"You almost killed me last time I was here," she reminds him, refusing to return his smile.

He shakes his head. "That was to keep you safe. I'd never have let you die."

"Why me?" she asks. "Why should I be safe?"

"Because you're *my* Treasure." He reaches out a hand like he's about to stroke her face, and she moves abruptly back. "I chose you."

An old man steps out from behind one of the generators and Halo tilts her head in surprise. He wasn't one of the Echelons who'd stormed the deck. He smiles at Halo, warmth radiating from his eyes. It feels like he knows her, even though she's certain she's never seen him before. She's never met anyone with so many wrinkles on their face.

"Get back to work, Raven," Nole snaps, and the old man scurries back behind the generator.

"He's a Raven?" Halo asks. "Where's his mask?"

"They don't all wear one." Nole waves his hand dismissively, but Halo thinks she's already answered her own question. Nobody here knows this old man, so there's no need to disguise him. She's convinced now, more than ever, that it was Dargo she'd seen in that strange dining room. Why else would he need to cover his face?

"Is he driving the ship?" Halo asks, hearing a *clunk* from the direction the old man had disappeared, wondering if he has more people with him. She takes a few steps to follow him, but Nole grabs her and pulls her back.

"Don't wander off without permission," he snaps. "It's not safe."

"What about the teens left in the ballroom?" Halo asks, desperate to return to Fyve. "Are they safe?"

"Let's have a look." Nole grins proudly and takes Halo over to a glowing screen. He types something into a keyboard below it and she watches him closely. She'd found computers washed up on Treasure Island, but she'd never been able to get one to actually work. As much as she really doesn't want to be impressed, she can't help but be in awe of what she's witnessing. Nole is controlling the screen with the letters and numbers he's typing on the keyboard. It's like magic.

Images inside The Oasis pop up on the screen as Nole

takes her on a tour of all the corridors and rooms that have become familiar in her time on this ship. The dining room lights up the screen and she sees the Echelons seated at their tables with their chosen teen for company. Ajax is still laughing at everything his Echelon says, while Sica remains scowling at hers.

Nole presses more buttons and the image changes to the engine room and Halo sees herself standing beside Nole, bent over slightly, staring at a screen.

"Wave." Nole turns and raises his hand, the action reflected on the screen.

Halo lifts her hand, keeping her eyes glued to her image as she sees the tiny version of herself mimic her movements.

"Look at this," says Nole, pointing at the image of the computer where she can see an even tinier version of herself staring at yet another screen. "It goes on forever."

Halo emits a tiny gasp as she sees what he means, then reminds herself of what she really needs to see here. Or rather, who.

"The ballroom," she reminds Nole. "I want to see the ballroom."

"Eager little thing, aren't you?" Nole chuckles and presses some more buttons. "But anything for my Treasure."

The screen goes black and Nole frowns, typing in more combinations of letters, his fingers moving too quickly for Halo to decipher the words. The screen flickers but goes black again.

"How dare they," Nole breathes, stepping back from the keyboard like the letters have scalded him. "Ungrateful swines. That's destruction of property."

"What is?" Halo asks, not understanding.

"They've destroyed the cameras," he says. "All of them."

For the first time since she was dragged from the ballroom, Halo smiles. Fyve would have been the one to do that. She's certain of it. Justice likely helped him, too. There's no way they'd be sitting in that room all meek and mild, waiting for the Echelons to make their next move.

"This is not good news," Nole growls, noticing her pleasure. "Insubordination will not be tolerated. It will not go unpunished."

Halo lets the smile fall from her face and realizes she hasn't been very smart in her interactions with Nole. She'd been too scared and too angry to think logically. But this revolting creep clearly likes her—more than likes—which means she can manipulate him, just like he's been manipulating all of them, all their lives.

"Take me back to the ballroom," she says, trying her best to inject some softness into her voice. "I'll talk to them. They'll listen to me. I'll tell them you're only trying to look after us. That without the cameras, you can't make sure we're safe."

He reaches for her, taking hold of her hand and running his thumb over her palm. "You're so beautiful, Halo."

She pushes down the bile that builds in the back of her throat. "Thank you."

"Your skin is so clear," he continues, using his free hand to stroke her cheek in the way he'd been desperate to earlier. "Clear eyes, strong nails, a family history of good fertility."

She gives him a small smile, using every cell in her body not to pull away from his touch. His hands are warm and slightly moist and his breathing raspy as he moves in closer. She can't do this. She really can't!

But she has to.

If she wants to survive this. If she wants to get back to Fyve. If she wants to find a way off this ship that was forged in the fires of hell...

"It was your brains that caught my attention at first," Nole says, so close now that his soft belly is skimming the front of her tunic. "So smart, even from a young age."

She nods, considering which of her knees she's going to slam into his groin if he gets any closer.

"Sevin was smart, too," he continues. "Which was why I almost allowed her to pass the Trials. I really wanted to, but…"

Halo waits for Nole to continue, trying to look past him so she doesn't have to look into his watery eyes. "But, what?" she asks, glad now that whatever it was had prevented Sevin from getting on this ship.

"It was her eyesight." Nole grimaces like the memory of the struggles Sevin had with her eyes is repugnant. "Coal was the same. Those aren't genes we want to pass on. If Tomorrow Land is going to thrive, we need the best of the best. Like you, Halo."

It's all clear now. The Echelons have chosen them as breeding stock. They're no different to the rats they tried to breed back on Treasure Island. And it's not each other they'll be breeding with.

It's the Echelons.

Halo swallows down the fear that's building in her belly. She has to get back to Fyve and as far away from Nole as possible. But how does she do that without angering him? Whatever plan they come up with has got to be easier if Nole thinks she's on his side.

He leans in closer, licking his lips as his face hovers only an inch from her own.

There's a loud *clunk* from behind the generator and a jet of steam billows out.

"Raven!" Nole shouts, stepping away from Halo to march toward the disruption. "You'd better not have broken anything."

The old man appears, holding up a spanner, bringing Nole to a stop.

"It was an accident," he says, his voice croaky like he hasn't used it in a while. "I'm sorry."

"Well, fix it then," barks Nole. "We don't exactly have access to spare parts out here."

The Raven nods. "I'm on it."

Nole turns back to Halo, and the Raven winks at her. It's a gesture so subtle she almost misses it, but she's certain he's letting her know that noise had been no accident. He'd given her just the distraction she'd needed to put some distance between herself and Nole's advances.

"Now, where were we?" Nole asks, stepping closer again.

Halo walks quickly to the door. "You were taking me back to the ballroom so I can explain the situation to everyone."

"I don't want you near Fyve," says Nole firmly as he follows her. "He's not even supposed to be here."

"He listens to me," says Halo, trying to keep the emotion out of her voice. "And he's strong. We can use his muscles when we get to Tomorrow Land. It's wise to keep him around."

Nole grabs Halo by each arm and forces her up against the door. "You think I'm a fool. You think I don't see how repulsed you are by me? You think I don't know how you feel about that boy? You think you're playing me. But you're not..."

"You're right," says Halo through gritted teeth, unable to play his sick game for a moment longer. "I hate you."

He pushes himself hard against her and now she can feel every inch of his sweaty body. She turns her face and squeezes her eyes closed, thoughts of Zake attacking her on the beach plaguing her. This cannot be happening again.

There's a loud *thump* and Nole slumps to the floor.

Halo's eyes spring open to see the old Raven standing behind him with the spanner still clutched in his hand.

"Is he...dead?" Halo stares down at Nole.

The Raven shakes his head. "Would you like him to be?"

"I don't want anyone to be dead." Halo squats down and removes Nole's bracelet, slipping it onto her own wrist. "I just want to get back to the ballroom."

"Take me with you," says the Raven. "I can help."

Halo stands and opens the door. "Who's going to steer the

ship?"

The Raven shrugs, giving Halo the smallest of smiles as he pokes Nole with his foot. "I suppose that's his problem."

"Let's go then," says Halo, deciding that having this Raven on their side will make an excellent bargaining chip, especially if he's the only one who knows how to steer this ship. "Hurry."

They run to the stairwell and begin to climb.

"What's your name?" Halo calls over her shoulder.

"Abacus," he replies. "My family called me Abe. Although, that's been a while."

"Pleased to meet you, Abe." She steps out onto the landing. "I'm Halo."

"I know," he replies, following her down the corridor to the ballroom. "Nole's been watching you for years. I've seen you grow up. I've come to think of you like a daughter."

Halo's steps falter as she tries to decide how to feel about this. The invasion of her privacy is massive. But this man just saved her from whatever evil Nole was about to inflict. Which means he's more friend than foe.

They reach the ballroom and Halo uses Nole's bracelet to open the door.

As the door slides back, the scene inside isn't anything like what she expected to find. Every single teen is lying on the floor, deathly pale and perfectly still. Bloodied cloths are scattered around, their tunics stained with crimson.

"We're too late," she whimpers.

Abe puts a steadying hand on her back as they walk forward. The door slides closed behind them and clicks.

She knows without trying that Nole's bracelet won't be able to unlock it this time. And she doesn't care. She has nothing left to live for. Every person she had left in this world is dead.

Then a baby cries out, and hope lights in her chest.

"Fyve," she calls across the sea of bodies. "Where are you? It's me."

FYVE

*F*yve launches to his feet, already running before he's finished calling out Halo's name. The same emotions tumbling through him flash across her face as she also breaks into a run.

Relief.

Joy.

The overwhelming desire to touch and make sure this is real.

They crash into each other's arms, holding on tightly. Fyve's hands roam over Halo's hair, shoulders, back, then come up to cup her face. "Are you okay?" he chokes.

She nods, tears glistening in her shimmering eyes. "I'm fine. You?"

He presses a kiss to her forehead, drawing in a deep breath. It feels like his lungs are actually working again. "I am now."

Halo sinks into his arms, pressing her head against his chest as if she's listening to his heartbeat. "Me, too."

Fyve finds himself smiling at the fervent way she says those two words. Would any of this be possible if Halo didn't feel the same as he did for her? He doubts it.

Someone clears their throat and Fyve realizes that Halo

didn't return with the others, but despite that, she didn't return alone. An older man is standing a few feet away, arms crossed. "You destroyed the cameras. The Echelons won't be happy about that."

Halo keeps an arm around Fyve as she turns to face him. "Fyve, this is Abe. He saved me from Nole."

Fyve studies the newcomer, conscious that no one has been what they seemed on The Oasis. "Thank you," he says, meaning it despite the distrust.

Abe grunts. "The Echelons won't accept rebellion without punishment."

Halo looks up at Fyve. "You really destroyed the cameras?" she asks, a proud twinkle in her eye.

"We had to," he says with a shrug. "To take out everyone's chips."

Halo steps away to look at the other teens in the ballroom, who are now all standing, too. "That explains the blood."

"Sorry for scaring you." Fyve frowns. "We were trying for the element of surprise in case it was the Echelons."

She smiles, shaking her head. "The whole playing dead thing was quite convincing."

He presses a kiss to her temple, grinning a little. "Seeing you brought me back to life."

Halo's answering smile lights up every corner of his chest. How he wishes they could have more than a few moments to honor these feelings. To revel in them.

As if to prove exactly how unlikely that is, Abe grunts again. "Destroying the cameras was smart. And also really stupid."

Justice appears beside Fyve and Halo. "And who exactly are you?"

Abe arches a wiry brow. "I'm a Raven. One of the Echelons' servants." His mouth twists. "Whether we like it or not."

Fyve frowns. That sounds very much like a slave.

"And I'm the one who's been keeping this ship going."

"I met Abe in the engine room," Halo says. "He knows how to drive The Oasis."

A low murmur ripples through the teens as they digest this. Abe could be an ally that changes everything. Assuming they can trust him...

The old man's gaze sweeps over them. "I'm just as much a prisoner of the Echelons as you are. I have been for most of my life."

Halo presses her hand to Fyve's chest. "Abe hit Nole over the head with a spanner when he tried to...when he cornered me in the engine room."

Fyve's gut constricts as he realizes what Nole probably had on his mind. The bastard. He holds Abe's gaze. "Thank you."

"You knocked out the leader of the Echelons?" Justice asks incredulously. "And you reckon destroying the cameras was a bold move?"

Iva appears on Halo's other side, gently rocking one of the babies. "We all did what was necessary. We need to focus on what's next."

"Iva's right. What are we going to do?" asks a girl, raising her chin even as she clasps her shaking hands.

Fyve glances at Halo, conscious that courage is trying to be born, but it's fragile. Tremulous. Unsure whether it will survive.

She stares back at him, the same quiet knowledge settling in her gaze.

War's already been declared.

Their hands wind together, fingers interlinking tightly as they turn to face the group of teens looking at them expectantly. "The Echelons have lied to us. Manipulated us." The familiar anger bubbles in Fyve's gut. "They want to use us."

"To breed," adds Halo, eliciting gasps from the teens. Even Fyve blanches a little. "They chose us to help them repopulate Tomorrow Land."

Uneasy murmurs and glances shift through the teens. Fyve

thinks of Jiro and how he took Cloud, and the disgust only burns hotter. Cloud's proven her fertility. It's probably why she was allowed to stay in the first place, even though Elijah snuck her onto the ship. How could Fyve have ever thought Jiro was an ally?

His lip curls. "And they killed anyone else."

Their culling started back on Treasure Island, with good people like Coal. Then continued with cold-hearted calculation.

Fyve's gaze drops to the bundle Iva's holding. Little Marvel or Miracle. The other is being held by another teen beside Iva. This is their future they're fighting for.

"No more," he says, his voice carrying throughout the ballroom.

"No more!" Justice echoes.

Halo nods resolutely as she straightens her spine. "They will not hold our lives or our futures in their hands."

Iva holds the baby closer to her chest. "Never again."

Fyve lifts his and Halo's clasped hands. "From now on, we choose our own tomorrow!"

A rousing cheer erupts from the teens as fists are thrown into the air. Hope surges through Fyve with the same fervor. They easily outnumber the Echelons. They have youth and strength on their side.

And a drive for justice the Echelons themselves created.

Now, they need to decide what that future will be. Fyve turns to Abe. "The ship is sailing toward Tomorrow Land?"

He snorts as he shakes his head. "No one knows where Tomorrow Land is. All we're doing is heading further into uncharted waters than anyone has before."

Halo looks up at Fyve. "Then we go back to Treasure Island."

He draws in a sharp breath. "We go back?"

To Sevin?

To their home?

She nods. "We should never have left. Every promise made to us was a lie."

Fyve turns to Abe. "Can you do that? Can you turn this ship around?"

The old man scratches his bristly chin. "The engine room will be guarded. But if you can get me to the wheelhouse, yeah, I can turn this rust bucket around."

Fyve's gaze settles on the teens again. Whatever a wheelhouse is, they can get Abe there. "We're going back! We'll share the food, the beds, the riches that have been kept from us!"

The second cheer is even louder and Fyve finds himself smiling. So is Halo. And Justice and Iva and every other teen in the ballroom. For the first time since they all boarded The Oasis, there's a sense of control. Of their fates being their own.

It's time to forge every one of their tomorrows.

"We are very displeased."

The sharp bark has a series of gasps puncturing the air. Fyve spins toward the door, expecting to see Nole standing there with the rest of the Echelons, wielding the deadly flamethrowers.

But the door remains closed.

"After everything we've done for you!" Nole shouts, the sound falling from above. "This is how you repay us?"

"He's talking through the speaker," Fyve says, pointing to the mesh circle in the ceiling. "They can't see us."

The teens glance between each other. Iva and Justice move closer to the babies. Halo, on the other hand, glares up at the speaker, fists now clenched. "You've done nothing but take from us!"

The Echelons can't hear them, either, but Halo knows that. Those words were for the teens.

"You obviously don't realize who's in control," Nole continues, his voice hard and clipped. "Who's always been in control. Our generosity will not be taken for granted."

Fyve clenches his jaw. "We've had enough of your generosity," he spits.

"You are now locked in the ballroom. There will be no food until you surrender. We will wait as long as it takes." A thud echoes through the speaker as if Nole just hit something, making a couple of teens jump. "Knock three times on the door when you're ready to show your appreciation."

The silence that follows reveals the energy in the room has changed. It's heavier. More foreboding. The elation of rebellion has already been dampened.

Justice indicates with her chin toward a doorway to their right. "We have a bathroom and water. That'll buy us some time."

"To do what?" Viney asks, eyes wide as they dart around. "Have clean faces as we starve to death?"

"Enough," Fyve snaps. "This is exactly what the Echelons want—for us to panic. For us to give in without a fight."

"Well, that's not freaking happening," Justice growls.

"No, it's not," he promises. Which means they need to find a way to stay alive.

Halo grips his arm. "We'll get our own food. No more depending on their generosity," she says, the last word drenched in disdain.

"But how?" Viney wails. "We're trapped in here."

Halo frowns, glancing at Abe. "My chip won't work anymore."

The old man nods. "They would've disabled it the moment they could."

Before Viney can start wailing that all is lost again, Fyve pulls Jiro's bracelet out of his pocket. "We have this."

Halo's eyes widen. "You have one, too?"

"Long story," he says, winking. "But yes, I have one, too."

Her gaze turns thoughtful. "We need to destroy the rest of the cameras on this ship. Then we can get everyone out of here."

Fyve grins, imagining Nole's face when he discovers the ballroom empty. "Good thinking." He turns to Justice and the others. "Stay here. We're going to show the Echelons exactly how in control they are."

Justice's lip curls as she passes one of her crutches. "Take out every last one of those silent spies."

Fyve clasps it with a nod. Then he and Halo are at the door and he's holding his breath, wondering if the chip will even work. It certainly didn't when he was trying to go after Halo, but he was panicked at the time. All Jiro had to do was tell the Echelons that Fyve has one, too...

A single swipe is all it takes to get the answer. There's a faint *click* and the door jolts open an inch.

"It worked," Halo breathes.

Fyve's just as astounded. Jiro must've forgotten. "We'll be back as soon as we can," he says over his shoulder, registering the crowd of frightened faces watching them. "And we'll bring food," he promises, even as he's not sure whether they can.

"Why do we have to wait in here?" asks Viney. "We should get out while we can."

"Because then they'll know we *can* get out," says Fyve. "We'll lose our element of surprise and they'll attack. Let's be smart about this. We can eat, rest, then make our move."

Fyve slips through the door, senses alert as Halo joins him. But the corridor is empty, revealing exactly how arrogant the Echelons are.

"There," Halo whispers, pointing to the far corner.

Another camera, the silent spy of the Echelons, is staring at them.

Fyve runs and leaps, smashing it with one blow. Black plastic and shattered glass fall to the floor, and he stomps on it for good measure. "This is going to feel good." He turns back to Halo. "You lead the way."

She looks one way, then the other, no doubt consulting her

internal map and considering the most efficient way to scour the corridors. "Come on."

Halo guides the way as they navigate their way through The Oasis. They pause at each set of stairs, at each new turn, listening and looking. Each time they discover they're alone. And that the ship is infested with cameras. They're on every floor, every set of stairs, they would've been in every one of their rooms, out on the deck, probably in their bathrooms. Although the destruction of each one is a small victory, Fyve and Halo look a little paler with each time.

Every broken lens is proof of how deeply and insidiously the Echelons have been a part of their lives. And they had no idea.

Which quickly makes Fyve mad. On the next floor, he smashes the cameras with more gusto. Teeth bared. Almost grunting with the effort. Soon, Halo's smiling as each and every one is destroyed.

They're taking back control. They're making their lives their own.

They've combed all of the floors that they've used during their time on The Oasis, when Halo pauses. "We should get back, but we have no idea how many cameras there are."

Fyve's about to agree when he remembers something. "There's a way we can find out." Taking her hand, he turns back the way they came.

"Where are we going?"

Wishing there was more time to explain this, Fyve does the best he can as he leads Halo through the corridors. Without cameras to smash, he tells her everything.

About Jiro talking in his head. How Jiro pretended to help him.

That he showed him parts of the ship no one else knew about.

And as they walk, Halo fills Fyve in on what happened when Nole took her. Turns out she's also seen the dining hall. And although she skims over what happened in the engine room, even a hint of what Nole intended has fury firing through Fyve's veins.

The Echelons are disgusting. Selfish.

Evil.

They reach the room that has all the screens and Fyve raises his finger to his lips. Halo tenses, realizing they're somewhere significant. One swipe of the bracelet and the door opens. Fyve leaps in, fists raised, ready to fight.

But the surveillance room is empty, and far darker than the last time he was here. Most of the screens are now black, apart from a few. And the handful of images still being projected from Treasure Island.

"Fyve," Halo whispers in awe. "It's home."

He tugs her forward, smiling at her wide-eyed expression. "This is how I knew Sevin's still alive."

Halo's hand brushes over the screen displaying her tree. "She planted more of them."

"And she's started the waterfall," Fyve adds proudly. He presses a kiss to Halo's temple. "You were right. She's not only survived, she's thrived."

Halo smiles up at him. "Because you taught her how to." Her gaze falls back on the screens, scanning them hungrily. "I can't wait to go back."

"You will never go back."

Halo spins around with a gasp. Fyve leaps in front of her, lip curled as he faces the one man who's lied the most.

Jiro.

HALO

"*W*hat have you done with Cloud?" Halo marches toward Jiro, her entire body shaking with rage. "Where is she?"

"She's back in the ballroom," he says. "Where you should be."

Halo points at the images of Treasure Island that Fyve just showed her. "That's where we should be. Home."

"You chose to take part in the Trials," Jiro says, his voice seeming to float from beneath his sagging jowls.

"You tricked us into getting on this ship," she sneers. "Why don't *you* go back to the ballroom. We've had enough of taking orders from you."

Jiro crosses his arms over his protruding belly. "My orders kept Fyve alive during the Trials."

Fyve lurches forward at these words. "Liar! Your orders nearly had me fed to the leatherskins."

Jiro reels back. "What do you mean? You were approved to be kept safe in the final Trial."

A deep laugh erupts from Fyve's throat, even though no part of him appears amused. "If wobbling the plank, then letting it collapse is keeping me safe, then yeah, I was fine. Just fine."

"But…" Jiro scratches at his beard, then starts typing furiously on one of the keyboards. "You were approved."

An image of Fyve springs to life on the screen directly in front of Jiro. He's standing beside Terra at the foot of the plank in the final Trial.

Halo shakes her head, not understanding.

"How can he be there, when he's here?" she asks, tilting her head to study the image. When Nole had shown her the screens in the engine room, the images had moved in time with what was happening right now.

"It's a recording." Jiro rolls his eyes, making Halo feel just as foolish as he no-doubt intended. "Of something that happened back in time."

She watches as the image of Fyve steps onto the plank and walks out above the raging ocean. Even though she knows he survived, it's difficult to witness. The real Fyve slips an arm around her shoulders, and they stare at the recording of him walking slowly out on the plank in the same way Halo had been forced to. As he reaches the end, the plank unmistakably wobbles.

"See!" Fyve points at the screen. "You were trying to kill me."

"This can't be," breathes Jiro as they watch Fyve turn around and increase his pace, desperate to get back to the ship. But a large wobble has Fyve falling to the hard surface. He throws out his arms and clamps them around the plank, shuffling forward while the plank mimics the movements of a thrashing leatherskin as it tries to shake him free.

There's a dark flash at the bottom of the screen where a giant shark leaps an impossible distance and snaps at Fyve's feet. Then the plank swings down in a long arc and Fyve yanks a knife out of his pocket, slamming it into the timber to save himself.

"Fyve," Halo whimpers with a hand pressed to her mouth. She knew what had happened, but seeing it is so much worse.

He'd come so close to death. Her walk on the plank had been easy in comparison.

Then she sees a small image of herself leaning over the side of the ship with her arm extended as she grips his hand and hauls him to safety while Terra watches on.

"It's okay," the real Fyve whispers, seeing her distress. "I made it."

Wrapping her arm around his waist, she breathes in his essence, thankful that she'd been there at the right time to help him.

"Jiro?" Fyve's voice is filled with confusion.

Halo turns and sees what has caught Fyve's attention.

Jiro has tears running down his face and his shoulders are heaving like he's trying to hold back an entire well.

"You were approved," he sobs. "That can't have happened. You were approved."

"Approved to die," Fyve says, coldly.

Halo can't blame him for being angry. Jiro claiming to have kept Fyve alive was far-fetched. The only reason Fyve's standing here beside her is because of his own strength and initiative. And a little help from her.

"That wasn't supposed to happen," says Jiro, pulling himself together as he drags his eyes from the screen. "I don't understand."

"I understand perfectly," says Fyve. "None of you can be trusted. Which is why we refuse to take orders from you. Or listen to your *helpful* advice."

Jiro spins around and grips Fyve on the arm, his face leeching with desperation. "But you must listen to me, Fyve. Do as you're told. It's the only way to keep you safe. Both of you." He shifts his gaze to Halo as if acknowledging her presence for the first time.

"Why do you care about me all of a sudden?" Halo asks,

balling her hands into fists. "Fyve told me you tried to keep us apart."

"You …" Jiro lets go of Fyve and runs a hand through his hair. "You saved Fyve. On the plank. Which means I owe you."

Halo's brows shoot up as she looks to Fyve, who seems equally as confused.

"But you must stay apart!" Jiro adds before she can get any further with this thought. "You're Nole's Treasure. You belong to hi—"

"She belongs to nobody but herself," Fyve roars, shoving Jiro backward.

Jiro steadies himself. But instead of retaliating, he points at the wall of screens. Most of them are blank now, but a few cameras are still running. Halo takes images of them in her mind so they can destroy them later. One of them shows Nole and the female Echelon walking down a corridor.

"Quick!" says Jiro, pointing. "They're coming here. You have to leave."

Halo plants her hands on her hips. "Fyve already told you, we're not taking your orders."

"Then take our food instead!" Jiro pulls back the wall of screens, revealing a hidden door. "Go! Take as much as you can. Just don't let Nole see you."

Halo and Fyve remain where they are, which panics Jiro more.

"Be smart about this," Jiro says desperately. "It's suicide to confront Nole now."

"Maybe he's right," says Halo, knowing the importance of choosing their time carefully. "We can take out the rest of the cameras, then decide our best move."

Fyve lets out a deep sigh and slips his hand into Halo's. Together, they disappear through the hidden door and Jiro closes it behind them.

But instead of going to look for food, they both press their ears to the back of the door, hoping to hear something that will give them an advantage in a situation that's felt nothing but helpless since they first arrived.

As they wait, Halo thinks about Jiro. He's an interesting person. It's no wonder Fyve hasn't been able to work out if he can trust him. He seemed genuinely upset that Fyve had almost died in the Trial. Although...was that grief? Or was it fear? If Nole had gone against his *approval* then he may be fearing for his position of power within the Echelons. Jiro really hadn't struck Halo as someone who cared about anyone except himself.

"Jiro!" says Nole's voice through the wall, and Halo shudders to think of the slimy words he'd said to her earlier. "What are you doing in here?"

"Checking what surveillance we still have in place," says Jiro, sounding matter-of-fact. "We still have a few cameras left."

"Nole, sit down," says the female Echelon. "That's a nasty wound on your head. Let me take a look at it."

"I'm fine, Rhina," he snaps. "Don't fuss. It's only superficial."

"Suit yourself," says Rhina on a huff.

"I usually do," he replies, and Halo blanches. He might be used to getting his own way but there's no chance that will happen when it comes to her.

"My Treasure would never hurt me like that," purrs Rhina. "Did you see how enamored he was with me?"

Halo remembers only too well how Ajax had been playing up to Rhina in the dining room. Is she really so foolish to believe the way he was blinking at her across the table was genuine?

"He's divine," Rhina continues. "So handsome, so fertile. I really thought I'd missed the chance for my genes to be passed down, but I'm certain my Treasure can give me a child. He's so virile."

Fyve makes a strangled sound and Halo touches him on the arm to keep him quiet.

"My Treasure didn't hurt me," growls Nole. "She was too busy fawning over me."

Halo's mouth pops open to defend herself, but she quickly sees there's no need. The anger vibrating from Fyve's every pore is being directed straight through the door.

"Who hit you then?" asks Jiro.

"The old Raven," says Nole. "The old *dead* Raven when I get my hands on him."

"That might not be wise." Jiro speaks in a cautious tone. "He's the only one who knows how to keep the ship running."

"Pfft!" says Nole. "It can't be that hard if a stupid Raven can figure it out. Besides, you forget how clever my Treasure is. She could work it out with her eyes closed."

"Pretty sure it's not her brains you're interested in," quips Jiro, making Halo certain he doesn't realize they can hear him. And that he really doesn't care less about her, whether he believes he owes her or not.

"Why do you say that, little brother?" asks Nole.

Halo's hand flies to her mouth. Nole and Jiro are brothers? She supposes they have the same pasty skin and watery eyes. But Nole is so much more revolting than Jiro. Is that just because of what he tried to do to her?

"If you really value brains so much, you'd have chosen Sevin," says Jiro, bitterly. "She's smarter than Halo."

Halo couldn't care less about this insult. Maybe Sevin is smarter than her. Hopefully she is, given the difficult life she has ahead. Fyve shuffles his feet and Halo can see just how much he wants to burst back through the door and shake some answers out of these awful Echelons about his sister.

"You know exactly why I couldn't choose Sevin," says Nole.

"She was approved," sneers Jiro. "Not that it mattered to you.

Fyve was approved, too. I know what you tried in the final Trial, but he was too strong to fall for your tricks."

"So, that's what you were really doing in here." Nole chuckles. "Checking the footage. Wasn't it enough that your *precious* Fyve survived? Does it matter now how it happened?"

"Of course, it matters!" shouts Jiro. "But given the size of that lump on your head, I'm going to let it slide for now. Seems what your Treasure lacks in brains, she makes up for in strength. She sure knows how to leave her mark."

"I told you it wasn't her!" Nole booms. "She's into me. She might even be pregnant already."

Halo shakes her head at Fyve, hoping he'll believe Nole never got the chance to touch her like that.

"Brothers!" says Rhina in a tone that's unable to be ignored. "Enough bickering! We have bigger issues to focus on right now. Save your family squabbles for when we get to Tomorrow Land."

"If we ever get there," huffs Jiro. "Our fuel is getting low."

"We're almost there," grunts Nole. "We don't need more fuel."

"You don't know that." Jiro takes up the role of disgruntled brother to perfection. "We've used up more than half our fuel, so we can't turn back. If you're wrong, we'll all die out here."

"I'm not wrong," says Nole. "We're close."

Fyve pulls on Halo's arm and leads her away from the door.

"I've heard enough," he says, keeping his voice low. "Those idiots have no idea what they're doing. We can outsmart them."

They make their way to the dining room, entering cautiously to find it's now empty.

"There's a kitchen back here," says Fyve. "Let's see what's there. We'll bring some food back to the others and take out the other cameras on our way back. Once everyone's been fed, we can storm the ship. We outnumber them. We can take their flamethrowers. They won't know which way we're coming from."

"Slow down." Halo pulls him to a stop. "We need to make careful moves. Don't you want to talk about what we just heard?"

His face fills with uncertainty. "I'm not sure. It's…a lot."

"He never touched me," says Halo. "I mean, he wanted to, but Abe saved me. He's just talking it up."

Fyve nods. "I know. If I believed him, nothing would have stopped me getting into that room and knocking him out—permanently this time."

Halo doesn't doubt that. "I think Jiro really is on your side. He was genuinely shocked at what happened to you in the final Trial."

"He's just scared," says Fyve. "About what it means if Nole overrules him, like he did with Sevin."

"I thought that, too." She lets out a sigh. "But it's more than that. He seems to care about you. Nole called you Jiro's *precious.*"

"You think he wanted me as his Treasure?" asks Fyve, seeming surprised. "But because we can't breed together, it wasn't allowed?"

"Possibly," says Halo carefully. "I mean, it would explain why he chose Cloud as his Treasure. She's only just had a pregnancy, so it buys him a bit of time."

Fyve throws out his hands. "I don't know. Maybe. Maybe not. But Jiro wanting me as his Treasure is no less wrong than Nole wanting you. We're not possessions for them to pick and choose between. Which is exactly why we need to take control of this ship."

"You heard what they said about the fuel." Halo pushes down the sense of dread that's been building in her stomach since she heard that news. "We can't go home. And they don't even know where Tomorrow Land is."

"Then we figure it out." Fyve takes a step toward the kitchen, clearly having had enough of the conversation. "And we have Abe on our side. Once we have control of the ship, we'll find a solution. We always do."

Halo swallows as she nods. He's right. They can't do anything until they have the upper hand. It's time to wipe out any remaining cameras, feed their people, and make a plan.

The Echelons don't know it, but their very own Trial is just about to begin.

FYVE

*F*yve looks one way down the corridor then the other, breathing hard. Surely, it's not possible that he and Halo just smashed the last of the cameras and returned to the ballroom without seeing or hearing another Echelon?

Yet, here they are, standing on either side of the door, blinking in disbelief at each other.

They even found a jar of some shiny, black straps that taste exactly like they smell—sweet, pungent, and weird. Fyve loved the unique flavor. Halo had scrunched up her nose as she chewed, but still swallowed.

The success of their mission gives Fyve a heady sense of hope.

He pulls Halo to him for a fast and fierce kiss, and he can still taste the strange sweetness on her breath. "We did it," he says with a grin.

Halo's own smile tips up her lips. "We really did."

Fyve takes her hand, stepping back even though he doesn't want to. "Let's tell the others and decide what we should do next."

She nods. "We can see who else likes these weird-tasting straps."

Fyve scans the bracelet over the sensor and the door slides open. Justice jumps out in front of them, holding her wooden crutch high like a bat. She relaxes when she registers it's not the enemy. "Thank Terra. We were getting worried."

Fyve shuffles Halo through, then enters the ballroom. "We made sure there are no cameras left."

Halo holds up the jar of black straps. "And we found some food."

Justice grabs it along with the crutch they'd borrowed, her face lighting up. "You two are amazing, you know that?"

She spins around and rushes over to the teens as an excited murmur ripples through them.

The door closes behind Fyve with a click.

"I know that sound," Halo says with a frown. "I heard it after I used Nole's bracelet. It stopped working after that."

Fyve's gut clenches. He waves the bracelet over the sensor. Then the door. Then the sensor again.

The door remains shut.

He washes away the frown that folds over his brow. "We'll find another way out. And the Echelons won't know we've escaped."

Halo nods, although her face holds the knowledge Fyve's ignoring—they don't know another way out.

Fyve squeezes her hand. They're not going to let this get them down. Or what Nole said about the low fuel or the fact that Tomorrow Land is nothing more than myth. Not when they've come this far. "They have no hold over us, anymore. We'll figure something out."

Halo nods again, this time more firmly. "We're the ones who are going to call the shots."

Iva appears, holding one of the black straps, although she hasn't taken a bite. "Did you see the others?"

Halo's eyes widen as she looks around frantically. "We thought they'd been returned!"

A baby's thin wail carries over the teens' discussion of the strange food they're eating, making Fyve's throat tighten. Jiro said Cloud had been allowed to come back. Miracle and Marvel will starve without their mother.

The cry is quickly cut off, and Halo takes a step forward, only to stop. The crowd shifts and reveals Cloud sitting on the floor, nursing one of the babies.

"Cloud's here," Iva says, pulling on the black strap with agitation. "But no one else."

Fyve scans the group, even though he has no doubt Iva's telling the truth. Ajax isn't here. Neither is Sica. The other Treasures, he thinks bitterly of that awful name, aren't here.

Halo's hands clench by her sides. "Then the first thing we do when we get out of here is find them."

"Agreed," Fyve says, his voice hard. The Echelons might try and use them against them, especially considering they still have their chip embedded in their temples.

Justice returns, her teeth covered in a black sheen as she chews. "This stuff is freaking delicious!"

"It's called licorice," says Abe, stepping forward. Fyve had almost forgotten he was here. "Usually it's an acquired taste."

Justice grins. "I think I've acquired it already. I have so much energy, I could swim back to Treasure Island."

"Good," Fyve responds. "We're going to need it."

She grins, exposing more black-covered teeth. "So, what's the plan?"

Fyve scans the walls, the ceiling, the doorway to the bathroom. There has to be another way out of here. Just because it's not obvious at first glance, doesn't mean a way to escape doesn't exist. "Can you think of anything in that mind map of yours?" he asks Halo.

She chews her lip as she stares at the floor, deep in thought.

"If my calculations are correct, the floor above is a kitchen. The one below is cabins."

Fyve glances down, thudding his heel onto the parquetry. "You're thinking we bust our way through?"

"My crutches have certainly been versatile, but I don't think they can work as shovels," Justice says dubiously.

Halo looks up at Fyve, her eyes full of everything he's feeling. Hope that they can pull this off. Uncertainty as to whether it's even possible. And the heavy knowledge that either way, they can't stay here. The jar of black straps won't last, and their burst of energy will soon wear off.

"Where do the walls connect to?" he asks, suddenly gripped by an idea. It would be easier to try to smash through those than the ceiling or floor.

Halo's face clears as she realizes what he's thinking. She does a slow turn. "Well, obviously that wall goes to the corridor."

Where the Echelons will no doubt post guards once they discover the remaining cameras have been smashed.

"That side wall is parallel to the east side of the ship, and the opposite wall goes to a kitchen, I'd say." She frowns as she stares at the back wall. "The back wall…"

Fyve moves a little closer, wondering why it's taking her longer to answer. Maybe she doesn't remember? "Yeah? The back wall?"

"Shouldn't be there." The moment she says the words, Halo shakes her head, probably conscious they don't make sense. "I mean, it's there, but I would've thought it was further back. The ballroom should be bigger, according to the map I memorized."

Justice shrugs. "You can't remember it all perfectly. Maybe a few walls are in slightly different places in your mind."

Halo frowns more deeply. "Maybe."

"Either way, we won't go busting through that one if we don't know what's on the other side," Fyve says, wanting to focus on what they do know. "Have you got any idea, Abe?"

The old man runs a hand through his hair as he studies the wall. "No clue. Ravens aren't allowed to wander the ship as we please."

Fyve nods. "Let's put it to everyone and see what the consensus is."

"Good idea," Halo says, also seeming to shake off the fact she remembered the layout wrong. "The sooner we get out of here, the better."

They're about to join the others when another voice rings through the ballroom. A voice none of them want to hear.

"Hello, Treasures," Nole says through the speakers. "We know you took our food."

Almost everyone freezes. A few teens glance down at the licorice straps they're holding, no longer enjoying the unique flavor.

"And destroying the remaining cameras was...disappointing."

"Leave us alone!" Fyve shouts, uncaring that Nole can't hear him. "We don't care what you think!"

"But you've also shown us we underestimated you. You're stronger and smarter than even we, the ones who picked you, expected."

"You underestimated us even more than you think," Halo snaps.

"Which is why we'd like to discuss a truce."

A few startled gasps puncture the silence that follows. A truce?

"It's a trap," Justice snarls. "We can't trust them."

"We know you don't trust us," Nole continues, as if he heard her. "But we want to prove that you can. We need to work together, not against each other."

"He's lying," says Abe. "Don't listen to him."

Fyve's frowning so hard it hurts. An uneasy feeling is unfurling in his gut like a serpent getting ready to strike.

"We want to talk to you," Nole says, his voice calm and soothing. "Nothing more. Let us in so we can discuss peace on The Oasis."

Justice crosses her arms. "It's definitely a trap."

Fyve agrees, already shaking his head. "There's no way we're letting those scumbags in here."

"As proof of our commitment, not only will I come alone, but we'll return the others to you," continues Nole. "We don't want to hold anyone against their will."

"We need Ajax back!" Viney wails.

"And the others," adds Halo.

Iva shifts on her feet. "We can't just leave them with the Echelons."

"Dammit," Fyve growls. Seems the Echelons have something over them, after all.

Halo presses a hand to his arm. "They can't hurt us. We outnumber them and we're stronger than them. And we don't have our chips."

Iva nods in agreement. "And like Sica said, they can't use the flamethrowers in here. Not without burning the whole ship down."

Nole's purring tones filter through the speaker before Fyve can answer. "If you agree, knock three times on the door."

Fyve can hear his breathing in the silence that ensues. It's fast, a little raspy, as he struggles with the choice they've just been given.

Let the enemy in. So they can get the others back.

Including Halo's brother.

Cloud appears, cradling one of her babies. "I would still be out there if Jiro hadn't returned me," she points out softly. "And if they die, my children will lose their father."

Fyve doesn't point out that won't be much of a loss considering Ajax turned his back on the twins, but he remains silent.

The core of what Cloud's saying is true. They can't leave anyone behind.

He scans the somber faces of the teens. "This is a decision we'll make together," he tells them.

Halo takes a step forward. "Do we let Nole enter, giving him a chance to be a man of his word and return the others? Or do we focus on escaping, hoping we can free them?"

The teens shuffle and mutter amongst themselves, the licorice looking limp in their hands.

Justice grips her crutches until her knuckles turn white. "Not happening," she mutters. Fyve's not surprised. She's never trusted easily.

"I agree with her," says Abe, pointing at Justice. "I only just got away from Nole. He's up to something."

Fyve draws in a breath. "Raise your hand if you vote that we allow Nole in."

Cloud is the first, quickly followed by Iva. Halo's jaw tightens as she follows. Fyve watches as more hands slowly join the air laden with tension. What's more, he finds his joins them.

Within seconds, it's clear what the consensus is.

"Majority has decided," he says.

"I don't like this," mutters Abe.

Turning, Fyve strides to the door, deciding he won't give himself time to think.

Rap. Rap. Rap.

He jolts backward when he hears scuffling feet on the other side. This time, he jogs back to Halo and the others, his heartbeat feeling as loud as the knocks.

"Here we go," Justice says under her breath.

The door slides open, revealing Nole's rounded body. Although he obscures most of the doorway, Fyve can see movement behind him. His hands turn to hot fists at his side.

Nole steps through and Fyve tenses, ready for this to be

what Justice and Abe predicted—a trap. The moment Nole's in, he steps to the side, and Justice raises her crutch.

But it's Ajax who steps through. Then Sica. Then the others.

They break into a run, a mixture of bewilderment and relief on their faces, quickly falling into the waiting arms of their peers. Fyve's not surprised when Ajax barely glances at Halo as he strides past her.

But he is surprised when he heads straight to Cloud and engulfs her in a hug. "I'm so glad you're okay." He pulls back, tenderly brushing a strand of hair from her face. "And our babies?"

"They're fine," Cloud whispers, looking accepting but skeptical.

Behind them, Viney claps a hand to her mouth, tears glistening in her eyes. She's possibly the only one not happy with how this has turned out.

Seems Ajax's capture has shown him the error of his ways.

Fyve focuses back on Nole and the door, every muscle coiled. There's more movement on the other side, and he thinks he sees Jiro's rounded face. The other Echelons are there.

Waiting to attack.

Yet the door slides shut, leaving Nole with the teens. Alone.

He smiles like a gracious guest. "I'm so glad you agreed to talk."

The teens don't answer. In fact, a handful cross their arms.

Nole takes a few steps forward, holding his arms out wide, but Fyve calls out before he can speak.

"Stay right there," he states flatly, resisting the urge to take him captive. They need to hear what he has to say first. "You're not welcome in here."

Nole's smile deepens in his fleshy face. "Of course. I come here in peace." His gaze slides to Halo, and something about the hungry way he looks at her makes Fyve's skin crawl.

"What do you want?" she says, lifting her chin. Fyve hopes

Nole can't see how pale she is. Not when he's so proud of how brave she's being.

"I told you," Nole purrs. "We want peace. That was always our plan."

"You want to control and manipulate us!" someone shouts from the crowd.

Nole looks at her with almost paternal pride. "You're all so strong. We love that about you." He scans the other teens. "We love every one of you and want to work together. Why don't you let the others in so we can talk?"

"No!" Justice shouts, and no one objects to that. "If you open that door again, we'll kill you with our bare hands."

"Say what you have to say and we'll consider your offer," Fyve says, his voice as hard as every muscle in his body.

Something flickers over Nole's face, but he quickly pulls up a smile. "I speak the truth. We want peace. And for you to understand the price of rejecting it."

Fyve almost growls under his breath. He doesn't like the sound of that. It feels like a veiled threat.

Yet Nole is alone. And the teens are ready to do what it takes.

Fyve certainly is.

Nole reaches into his pocket, his gaze hardening.

"Put your hands where we can see them!" Fyve shouts.

But Nole ignores him. He delves deep, then pulls his hand out fast.

Fyve moves his center of gravity as he balances on the balls of his feet. Halo does the same. Justice already has her crutches ready. Abe has his fists raised.

Whatever the Echelon leader is about to pull out, it won't be good.

HALO

*H*alo's heart races as she studies what Nole's pulled from his pocket. It's black and rectangular, about the size of her hand.

"It's not a weapon," she says to Fyve. She's seen many of these things washed up on Treasure Island and knows it's an electronic device, but she's never seen one in working order. She hates how interested she is to see what it can do.

Nole holds it over his head, along with his other hand. "It's just a cell phone. I'm not going to hurt you. I told you, I come in peace."

"There are no cell towers left," says Halo, having a basic understanding of how phones used to work.

"I'm not going to call anyone." Nole gives her a wolfish smile. "My clever Treasure."

Fyve lurches forward but Halo grabs the back of his shirt.

"Wait," she says. "See what he has to show us first."

Nole slowly lowers his hands and presses something on the phone that lights up the screen.

"It's your home," he says, holding it up to the group of teens who all crane their necks for a better view. "Your families."

An image of Treasure Island fills the screen and Halo sees the people she grew up beside. Her heart aches with their familiarity. They're gathered on the beach, their dirt-stained faces turned to the burned orange sky as the sun sets.

"It's Gratitude," says Justice. "They're still giving thanks to Terra."

"Fools," grumbles Sica, cracking her knuckles.

"I see my father!" one of the teens says, tears rolling down her face.

"That's my sister!" says another.

"Where's that camera positioned?" Fyve asks, narrowing his gaze.

"The tires" says Halo, clearly remembering the wall of tires stacked on the beach to hold back the tide. "It must be hidden amongst them."

"Who put it there?" Fyve asks.

Nole snickers. "Same person who put all the cameras on the island. Your mother."

A gasp rolls across the teens like one of the crimson waves of the ocean. Fyve looks aghast.

"Traitor," one of them hisses.

Halo holds up a hand. "There's a lot we don't understand right now. Hold your judgment, everyone. She must have had a good reason."

"Halo's right," says Justice. "Just watch the screen."

"I can't see it," complains someone from the back.

"Neither can I," says someone else. "It's too small."

"Fine, then." Nole turns the screen back to face him and runs his fingertip over the device, tapping and sliding until a bright light shines from the narrow end. He points it at the wall Halo's convinced shouldn't be in the ballroom. She's certain there should be something behind it.

The blank wall fills with the image of Treasure Island at Gratitude. The people being captured by the camera are as large as anyone in the room. Jaws drop open as the teens try to process what they're seeing. A few reach out their hands as if they can touch their loved ones and a new pang of homesickness invades every one of Halo's cells. She'd give anything to be home, chasing rats with Fyve and Sevin. Life had felt complicated back then, but it was so much simpler. If only she'd known it at the time.

There's no sound in the recording that Nole's projecting, but it's not difficult to make out what the people are saying. The movement of their lips is so familiar.

"Praise Terra," they call as they lift their faces to the sky. "Terra is good."

"There's Sevin," says Fyve, slipping his hand into Halo's. "She looks happy, doesn't she?"

Halo nods. "She does."

Sevin is standing with her aunt Cee and her three young cousins, and Halo is sure she's thinking of Fyve as she looks out at the ocean. Most likely she's curious about what became of her beloved brother. Perhaps she's wondering if Halo has told him she saw her waving as the ship had pulled away. Or maybe she's imagining Fyve standing in a forest with birds swooping and deer wandering beneath a thick canopy that's hanging with fruit. Whatever it is, Halo knows his sister is happy for him. She's just glad Sevin doesn't know the truth. She'd be devastated to know Fyve has had to fight for his life every day since he stepped on The Oasis. And Tomorrow Land is turning out to be just as big a myth as Terra.

"Why are you showing us this?" Justice asks, leaning on her crutches even though she no longer needs them for support. "You didn't negotiate your way in here just for this."

"Don't you want to watch your father at Gratitude?" asks Nole, even though he must be aware of how complicated Justice's relationship with her father is. He seems to know everything about every one of them.

Justice shakes her head. "I don't have a father."

"And you don't have a brother either," says Nole. "Well, not since you killed him."

Justice pales. "I don't even know why you let him stay, let alone made him your spokesperson."

"Just for fun," laughs Nole. "He was very entertaining. But we were never going to allow him to live."

Halo's brows shoot up. Zake was no more than a pawn in their sick games.

"Unless you died, of course," Nole says to Justice. "Then we might have reconsidered his fate. Siblings don't work well for a diverse gene pool, and you were the far better choice."

Halo glances over at Ajax, realizing they're the only siblings left on the ship. Unless you count Nole and Jiro, of course. Or Miracle and Marvel.

"You two were an exception," says Nole, noticing Halo's gaze. "Elijah insisted we bring you both, as much as I strenuously argued against it."

Halo can't help but feel deep disappointment. She'd honestly believed she'd competed fairly in the first set of Trials, just like everyone else.

Viney pulls back her shoulders, glaring at Nole. "That's why you took my sisters, isn't it? Are they dead, too?"

"Now *that* was a pity," says Nole, nodding. "I just love the color of their hair. We still have you, though. You showed the most promise of the three of you. So keen to start breeding. We'll have babies with hair the color of the sunset all over Tomorrow Land the way you're behaving."

"Enough!" snaps Justice. "This is going nowhere. I thought this was supposed to be a negotiation for peace."

"She's right, Nole," says Abe. "You're taunting them."

"At least I'm not hitting them over the skull with a spanner," says Nole, putting a hand to his head and eyeing Abe. "I've come in peace, just as I promised."

Fyve clenches his fists at his side. "What's stopping us from killing you right now? We'll take your bracelet and storm the ship. Your men will never see it coming."

"No, you won't." Nole shakes his head, not seeming the least bit afraid.

"You hold nothing over us," says Halo. "You returned our friends. That's all we wanted. We don't have to listen to another word you say."

"Yes, you do actually." Nole rolls his eyes and points at the image of Treasure Island.

"We've seen enough," says Justice. "You can't use the promise of images of home to force us into doing what you say."

Nole nods, thoughtfully. "In that case, I'm going to give you all one last chance to be good little Treasures. Please raise your hand if you'd like to resume the peaceful existence we've enjoyed together so far."

Nobody moves. All hands remain firmly by their sides. If he thinks their journey on The Oasis has been peaceful, he's insane.

"Maybe you should listen to him," says Abe, his voice filled with concern. He knows Nole better than anyone else here, and that sets Halo on edge. "I think maybe you should raise your hands like he asks."

Justice lifts the sharpened end of her wooden crutch and points it at Nole. "I think he should raise his hand if he'd like to live."

Nole taps something on his phone and glares at Justice. "This is your fault."

Halo tilts her head, not understanding. Not trusting. Not moving an inch.

It's Fyve who leaps forward and grabs Nole's phone. The image of Treasure Island jolts from the wall and dances around on the ceiling as Fyve waves his hand.

67

Sica steps forward and roughly grabs Nole by the wrists, forcing them behind his back.

"Nothing is Justice's fault," growls Fyve. "This is your fault. All of it."

Halo moves to stand beside Justice, feeling the sudden need to protect her. Although, from what she's not sure.

Nole shakes his head, not fighting the hold Sica has on him. It looks strangely like he's enjoying himself. "Put the image back on the wall and you'll see what is Justice's fault. She made me do it. She gave me no choice."

"Do it," Justice tells Fyve. "This spineless rat can't hurt me."

Fyve points the phone at the wall. The image is upside down at first and he turns the phone over to correct it. Abe turns away, not seeming to want to watch.

Instead of seeing their people praising Terra with their faces pointed to the sky, Halo gasps as she sees a commotion on the beach. Hands are being thrown in the air and mouths are open with silent screams pouring out like lava. To one side of the screen, only just in view, is Justice's father. He's on his knees with his hands gripping each side of his head in a way that Halo's seen far too many times.

He's being claimed.

Blood pours from his nose and eyes and Halo quickly wraps an arm around Justice, trying to turn her away. But Justice doesn't want to be spared, and she holds steadfast, her eyes glued to the horrific scene of her father's death. He falls to the sand and jolts violently before becoming limp, then finally, completely still.

"Your fault, Justice," says Nole. "I offered you peace and you didn't accept."

"I'm glad he's dead," says Justice firmly, although given the way she's shaking, Halo isn't sure that's entirely true. Her father had been a brutal man, but that doesn't mean she didn't love him in some small way.

Nole turns his attention to Sica. "Your family will be next if you don't let me go."

Sica's eyes flare but she continues to hold on tight.

"Don't let go," says Fyve, letting his hand fall, along with the awful image on the wall. "He can't claim anyone if he doesn't have his phone."

"Let go," warns Abe, shaking his head. "That's not his only phone."

"Listen to my wise but very disloyal Raven," Nole sneers. "My men have instructions to claim one person on Treasure Island every hour that I'm in here. Which means you might want to get your filthy hands off me!"

Sica lets go immediately and takes two steps back.

"I'm sorry," she says to Fyve, holding up her hands. "I have a family to think about."

"Well, I don't!" Justice surges forward.

Halo grabs hold of her arm just in time. Still unsteady on her newly healed leg, Justice topples over and sprawls on the floor.

"What did you do that for?" She glares up at Halo. "You don't have family there, either."

"But everyone else here does," says Halo, gently. This isn't like Justice. She must be in shock having just witnessed her father die. She's not thinking clearly.

Nole snatches his phone from Fyve's hand and strides toward the door. Nobody makes a move to stop him. Not even Fyve. Not when Sevin's life is at stake.

They thought the Echelons had nothing to hold over them, when...

They have everything.

Or rather, they have everyone. Every last person left behind on Treasure Island is in danger. And there's not a single thing they can do about it.

FYVE

*S*evin was the first person Fyve picked out in the image projected on the wall. The jolt of joy he always feels when he sees his sister was there. It was quickly followed by the knowledge that he'll see her again in person.

Soon, Sevin, his mind had whispered.

Except the Echelons still have all the power. They can kill Sevin as easily as they just killed Justice's father.

The thought makes Fyve sick. And furious.

Nole scans the silent teens, triumph tugging at his top lip. He knows he's won. "Are you coming, Abe?" he asks, as he presses his wrist to the panel beside the door.

All eyes turn to the old man as they wait for his response. Fyve finds he's holding his breath as Abe looks from Nole to Halo and back to Nole again.

"I'm fine here, thanks," he says.

It's a small win, but a win, nonetheless. And the way Nole's face hardens is proof.

"You'll regret that." He leaves the ballroom without a backward glance.

The door slides closed, and Fyve holds Halo's hand tighter.

70

He doesn't know what he would've done if Nole insisted she go with him. He would've had to choose between Halo and Sevin, and that's not something he ever wants to do.

Fyve looks around. Everyone is frozen as they try to process what just happened. Some have tears rolling down their cheeks. Others are holding hands and shaking.

"What are we going to do now?" wails Viney. "They killed my sisters! I don't want to do what they say."

"Nobody does," snaps Cloud. "But what choice do we have?"

Miracle and Marvel begin to cry, picking up on their mother's distress. Ajax rocks Marvel awkwardly in his arms, which only seems to make his son cry louder. Fyve doubts the infant recognizes his father's touch at all.

"You're lucky he didn't kill any of you," grunts Abe.

"But he did," says Fyve. "He killed Justice's father. No matter what her relationship with him was like, he was still one of us."

Silence is his only response. It hangs heavily in the air, as stifling as the oppression they're living under. They have two choices.

Give in to the Echelons.

Or fight, sacrificing who-knows-how-many friends and family back on Treasure Island.

"We need to sleep," says Halo, gently squeezing Fyve's hand.

He glances around again, noticing the dark circles underneath the wide eyes around them. He has no idea what time it is, but if the sun has set back home then it's getting late. Everyone is exhausted. They're not going to be able to make any sensible decisions while they're tired and in shock.

"She's right." Fyve nods. "We can decide what to do in the morning."

Ajax struts forward, seeming to want to take charge. "Lie down everyone. We'll decide what to do when we're better rested."

Halo sighs while Fyve has to suppress an eye roll. Ajax has

always been determined to follow in his father's footsteps as leader and is willing to use his sister's brains to do it. Although, at this stage he has a follower of one...

"Good idea, Ajax," says Viney, right on cue. "Come and lie next to me."

"Can't you see I'm busy?" Ajax huffs as he jiggles Marvel, returning to Cloud and Miracle.

Abe grunts and takes himself to a corner. The teens spread out over the ballroom, feet shuffling and hands wrapped around their middle. Heads are bowed and shoulders are drooped as they lower themselves to the hard floor, overwhelmed and disheartened.

Just like Nole wants them to be.

"Come on," says Fyve, sitting down and reaching for Halo.

She collapses beside him, and he tucks her into his side as they lie down. Fyve pulls her in close, registering that she clings to him with just as much desperation.

Their world is falling apart.

Having each other is the only sure thing they can depend on right now.

"I love you," he murmurs, pressing a soft kiss to her forehead.

Halo angles up, her body grazing his as she brings her lips level with his. "I love you, too."

A breath shudders through him and his arms instinctively tighten. Halo buries her face in his neck, feeling as if she wants to curl right into him. Fyve holds her for long moments, wishing there was something to say to make this all better.

But there's not.

How can they continue fighting? The price is too high.

Minutes pass. Then hours. Fyve isn't sure whether he sleeps, but the passage of time blurs. Throughout it all, he doesn't loosen his hold on Halo. Nor does she ease her grip on him. Underscoring the soft sounds of snoring surrounding them are the occasional whimper or sniff. Everyone is coming to terms with the fact the Echelons are using their families against them. The decisions they make no longer impact only themselves.

Fyve and Halo must doze because they both jerk awake at the sound of Ajax's voice.

"It's morning," her brother says, clapping his hands. "Time to get up, my people."

"His people?" whispers Fyve.

Halo blinks, now noting that Ajax has his arms outstretched, looking more like their father than ever before. The image makes Fyve uneasy. They don't need another Elijah.

"I'm not your person," grumbles Antic as he sits up. "I belong to nobody."

"Exactly," says Ajax, undeterred. "We're the rulers of this ship. I think I should go back to Rhina to negotiate a peace deal. A real one this time."

The teens who had been already coming to a stand, freeze. Fyve, on the other hand, leaps to his feet. Peace? Didn't Ajax see what Nole's idea of an olive branch was?

"The Echelons don't negotiate," says Abe from his corner of the room. "Haven't you learned that?"

Halo's also standing now. "He's right, Ajax. They'll just try to manipulate us again."

Ajax frowns, glancing around at the teens who are watching this unfold. "You heard them. They're realizing they need to work with us. We can use that to our advantage."

Fyve shakes his head. "We can't work with the Echelons. We won't. They've done nothing but use us, and that's what they'll continue to do."

"What we need to do is survive," Ajax snaps. He points to Cloud, the only one still sitting as she nurses her twins. "I have two children to think of."

Viney was about to speak up, but at the mention of Ajax's children, she clamps her mouth shut.

Halo takes a step toward her brother. "Ajax," she says, sounding like she's talking to a child. "We need to think this through."

"What's the alternative?" he challenges. "What fabulous plan have you two come up with?"

Fyve grits his teeth. "We don't have one yet."

"You don't have one, period," Ajax shoots back. He spins on his heel. "I'm going to talk to Rhina."

Fyve draws in a deep breath, wondering if Halo will object to him driving her foolish brother into the floor. The guy is going to jeopardize them all.

"Let's vote." Halo calls out as she scans the pale faces around them. "Those in favor of Ajax negotiating with the Echelons, stand at the door. Those in favor of taking some more time to plan, stand over at that wall."

"This sounds like another Trial," says Sica, groaning.

Halo winces as she and Fyve move to the wall. Sica's right. "This time nobody's getting killed," Halo says resolutely. "We're sticking together."

Justice limps to the wall. "No freaking way do I want to negotiate with those bastards."

Iva joins her, followed by several teens.

"Come with me, my people," says Ajax, heading for the door with Viney close behind him. "Cloud?"

"Sorry, Ajax." Cloud picks up the babies' basket and stands in front of the wall. "I've had enough of talking. They're not interested in peace."

"Agreed," says Abe, making his choice, along with Sica.

The rest of the teens get to their feet and move toward the wall and within a minute only Ajax and Viney are at the door.

Red climbs up Ajax's cheeks as he sets his jaw. Then he spins around, shouting at the door. "Rhina! Let me out. It's Ajax! Your Treasure! I want to talk!"

"Ajax!" Halo shouts. "We agreed to vote. You were outvoted."

"You agreed to vote," says Ajax. "You can sit here and do nothing. I'm going to talk to Rhina. She'll listen to me. I know it."

Ajax lifts his fist to knock on the door, but Fyve was expecting that and he's already moving. All it takes are a few sprinted steps and he pushes his way between Ajax and the door, shoving him back. "This isn't how we do this. We work together."

Ajax's red cheeks are now several shades brighter. He points wildly at Cloud as she holds their children. "I'm trying to make sure we survive!"

Fyve wonders at the sudden change of heart. What happened with Rhina that Ajax is now so desperate to be a father? Especially if he thinks going back to the female Echelon is the answer...

Halo slips in beside Fyve. "You can't go yet, Ajax. You still have your chip. It's how they claim us. And talk to us. We all have a chip inserted just here." She points to the side of her head where a small scar is forming.

Ajax's hand flies to his temple as shock slides over his features. Pride fills Fyve's chest as he acknowledges that Halo just found a way to not only diffuse the situation, but to keep moving forward, even in some small way. They can remove the chips of the Treasures.

Ajax frowns as his hand falls away. "You're not cutting open my head."

Fyve has to suppress a frustrated sigh. Of course, her brother isn't going to make this easy.

Halo smiles reassuringly. "Most of us have done it. It hardly even hurts."

"No," Ajax says, his voice hardening. "I won't do it."

Fyve shakes his head. "If you don't, they could claim you whenever they want."

"They won't do that," Ajax scoffs. "We're their Treasures.

75

They picked each one of us out years ago. They have no intention of killing us."

The handful of gasps from the teens behind them are soft, but unmistakable. Ajax's words are a reminder of exactly how orchestrated each of the Trials were. Every teen who died was little more than collateral damage.

It's also a reminder that the Treasures are special.

Fyve's gut clenches. Who else will pay the price of the Echelons' greed?

Halo takes a step back. "So, you're refusing to take your chip out?"

"I want mine out," Sica calls loudly.

"Me, too," adds Cloud.

Ajax glares at his sister as if he's angry that she's putting him on the spot, rather than showing any self-awareness that he started this whole showdown. "Why won't you listen to me? Rhina is different. She can help us."

Fyve finds himself shaking his head before he can stop himself. Ajax has been told what he wants to hear. That he's special. That he could save them all.

What a fool.

Ajax raises his gaze, pinning Fyve with a hard stare. "Or we could do nothing, and hope the Echelons don't get impatient, and start killing our friends and family back on Treasure Island."

Every cell in Fyve's body goes still, one word holding him in suspended animation.

Sevin.

Halo's warm hand grips his arm. "We'll find another way. There has to be another way."

It's Ajax who makes the next move. He shakes his head, looking disappointed. "I can't believe you're making me do this."

He spins around and raps on the door, but unlike the three times that Nole outlined, he knocks twice.

Fyve has no idea what that means.

Suddenly, a loud siren pierces the air, causing everyone to freeze. A soft, grinding noise fills the silence. Fyve turns slowly, his attention drawn to its origin.

The back wall.

The wall Halo was so sure is not where it's supposed to be.

The wall shudders, half of it moving forward and then sliding back on itself like a giant door.

The teens step back, mouths popping open and hands fluttering to their chests.

"Get ready to fight!" calls Sica, raising her fists and proving she doesn't know the definition of the word fear.

Fyve tries to tuck Halo behind him.

"Not this time," she says, squaring up beside him.

The wall slides back to reveal the Echelons standing in a line, their flamethrowers held firmly at their chests.

Halo and Fyve look at each other.

"Are you okay?" he asks.

She nods. "Never better."

In unison, they surge forward.

HALO

*H*alo's heart hammers as she marches directly toward Nole. She can't be sure he won't roast her with his flamethrower but if any of these revolting Echelons will spare her, she's certain it will be him. He didn't bring her this far, then claim her as his Treasure, to smother her in flames.

Sica rips one of Justice's crutches from her hands and waves it wildly.

"Don't you come any closer," she snarls.

Justice holds out the point of her remaining crutch. "You saw what I did to my brother. Who's next?"

"Stand back!" Nole shouts. "All of you."

"We're leaving." Halo attempts to shove past, the wide open space behind him calling to her. She knew this ballroom was only half the size it was supposed to be. If a few of them can make it past this line of fire-breathing assholes, then it will divert their attention and she can come back to help Cloud get the twins to safety.

"I said all of you!" Nole shoves the tip of his flamethrower painfully into her chest. "Even you, Treasure. Stand back!"

"Get that thing away from her," shouts Fyve, pushing the tip of the weapon away.

There's a roaring sound, then a scream and Halo spins to see Antic on his knees a few feet away. His tunic is alight, hungry orange flames spreading quickly as they attempt to devour him.

Nole lifts his weapon in the air and laughs. "I warned you!"

Fyve pushes past Halo and dives, rolling Antic to the floor. His own tunic catches fire and Halo throws herself to the pile, ignoring the stench of burning hair and flesh as they desperately work to beat out the last of the flames.

"Get him to the bathroom!" cries Iva. "He needs cool running water. Fast!"

Two other teens come forward, and under Iva's instructions they carry Antic away. His tunic has been devoured and his skin is streaked with black and deep pink. He's groaning loudly. Halo can't see any human surviving that kind of injury.

"What the hell were you thinking?" Fyve screams at the smug line of Echelons.

"Stand back!" Nole shouts, ignoring the question. "Or we'll set you all on fire."

"You won't kill us all," says Fyve.

Nole scoffs. "We'll tell your families you made it safely to Tomorrow Land and we've come back for them. They'll happily take your place on this ship."

Halo gasps, not sure what's worse—claiming their unsuspecting families on the island or tricking them onto this ship of death. Maybe they have more fuel than they said they have? Nole seems to think so.

"You'll burn the ship down if you set us all on fire," says Fyve, still not willing to believe Nole's threats. His tunic is badly charred and he takes it off and throws it at Nole's feet. "Besides, it's not our families you want to take to Tomorrow Land. You chose us."

He jams his hands on his hips and Nole looks him up and

down, taking in the lines of muscle on his lean frame. Fyve is undeniably the perfect specimen of a young male, exactly who these creeps would want to mix their genes with. Even if the only female Echelon seems to prefer Ajax over Fyve... Perhaps problems with eyesight extend beyond the shores of Treasure Island.

"Step forward if you're a Treasure," barks Nole, tearing his eyes from Fyve's naked torso in disgust as he tries to gain control of the situation. "The rest of you move back."

Nobody budges. The smell of charred flesh has glued their feet to the ancient floorboards. They all know that they won't win, no matter what choice they make.

"For each minute this takes, we'll claim one of your family members back home," says Nole.

"Don't listen to him," Halo cries out, desperation threading through her veins. "He can't threaten to kill us all and rescue our families, and then threaten to kill them and save us. He has no plan."

"She's right," Fyve agrees. "The only true way for us to keep our families safe is if we have control. And it's time to take it."

A murmur of agreement bubbles from the crowd like a hot bowl of rat soup.

"Charge!" cries Sica, running forward and thumping one of the Echelons over the head with the end of the crutch. He cries out and tries to return the blow with the butt of his flamethrower, only to miss and swipe at the air. Sica hits him again, sending him crashing to the floor.

"They don't know how to fight!" shouts Justice, jamming the sharp end of her makeshift spear into Rhina's shoulder and swiftly pulling it out again.

Blood pools on the front of Rhina's tunic and Ajax is beside her in a matter of moments, tearing off his own shirt so he can press the cloth onto her wound to stem the bleeding. Halo doesn't have time right now to question him, but she's certain those two sharp knocks he made on the door were a prearranged signal with Rhina. He hasn't changed one bit, no matter how much he might have pretended to care about his babies.

Justice raises her weapon again and takes aim at Jiro, who leaps out of the way just in time. She surges forward, only to be pushed out of the way by another Echelon. She tumbles to the floor and Sica takes over, hitting the Echelon sharply on the arm with the crutch and filling the ballroom with the sickening sound of breaking bone.

Chaos erupts as teens scatter, some brave enough to push their way through the line of Echelons and others finding gaps and darting through to safety—although Halo's not convinced there's anywhere safe on this hulking hell ship. But anywhere other than here seems like a better option right now.

Sica and Justice unleash their fury, taking further swings at the Echelons, who frantically look around, trying to decide what to do. Fyve darts over toward Jiro, and Halo loses sight of him as she rushes to Cloud, determined to protect the babies.

Abe is already beside Cloud, holding the basket between them as they shield the twins from harm.

"We need to get them out," says Halo, aware that most of the teens have escaped, while several Echelons are sprawled on the floor holding their heads after being knocked down by Sica and Justice.

"You distract them while I get through with the babies," says Abe. "It's the Treasures they want. They won't be watching me."

"You hit Nole over the head with a spanner," Halo reminds him. "I think he's going to keep an eye on you."

"Not as closely as you two," he says, taking the basket from Cloud. "I'll get the babies out of here and wait for you."

Cloud looks at Halo, her face filling with anguish as she tries to decide what's safest for her children.

"We can trust him," says Halo, desperately hoping she's right. "He's on our side."

"I won't be separated from them again," Cloud wails, ripping the basket away from Abe and running toward a gap in the line of Echelons.

Fyve is shielding Jiro from Justice, shouting something Halo can't make out, and Cloud runs past them. Jiro leaps out from behind Fyve and grabs Cloud by the wrist. She jerks back violently, and Fyve's forced to fling himself at the basket to catch it when it flies from Cloud's grip. But as fast as Fyve is, he's not fast enough and Nole pounces, plucking Miracle from the basket and holding her at an awkward angle against his chest with one hand, brandishing his flamethrower with the other.

Halo rushes forward, her heart pumping so hard it causes a pain in her throat. Justice is beside her with her crutches raised, panting heavily. Almost everyone else has already found their way out of this room. Some of the Echelons have followed. But it's clear that Nole doesn't intend to leave just yet.

"Give the baby back," says Fyve, clutching Marvel in the basket with white knuckles while Cloud struggles to get away from Jiro. "She needs her mother."

"And I need my Treasure," says Nole, leering at Halo. "How about we do a swap?"

"How about you just give her back?" says Justice, waving her spear. "And I won't kill you."

"You're getting annoying," Nole sneers at Justice. "Maybe we should have kept your brother."

He squeezes the trigger of his weapon but struggles to control it with only one hand and the flame shoots above Justice's head. Halo and Justice drop to the floor and Abe appears, shielding them with his own body. If only Cloud had trusted him, he could have had the babies to safety by now!

"Get out of the way," Nole shouts, extinguishing the flame

before any part of the ship catches fire. "Roast raven sounds like a nice breakfast to me. Move!"

"It's okay," Halo says, pushing on Abe's back to move him out of the way. "I've got this. He won't hurt me."

Tucking Justice behind her, Halo stands tall. Abe moves out of the way and she locks eyes with Nole.

"Give me the baby," she says. "I know you're a good man. You don't want to hurt anyone. And you don't have to. Just hand her to me."

"I don't think so." Miracle is slipping out of Nole's grasp and she lets out a cry. If they don't get her back soon, he's going to drop her.

"Give her to me!" Cloud struggles to get free of Jiro, who's still holding her firmly in his grasp. "You're hurting her."

"You really should have let me kill him," Justice says to Fyve, pointing the tip of her crutch at Jiro.

"Murder isn't the answer." Fyve shakes his head, clearly still unable to decide if Jiro is friend or foe. "That makes us as bad as them."

"I'm okay with that," says Justice, her voice full of malice that wasn't a feature of her personality before these Trials began.

Miracle's wails intensify and Halo remembers the rush of love she'd felt when she was born. She'd known at that moment that she'd give her life for this small child. It looks like now's the time the universe is calling on her to come good on that promise.

"Fine," she calls to Nole, stepping forward. "Take me. Give the baby back to Cloud and let them both leave. I'll go with you without complaint. I swear it."

"Halo, no," pleads Fyve.

She looks into the pools of his dark eyes, wanting nothing more than to turn back the hands of time and sink into his arms.

"I'll be okay," she tells him, despite not being able to make any such claim. "Look after Cloud and the babies."

"Raven!" Nole barks. "Come here."

Abe's eyes flare in anger. "My name is Abe. I'm not your Raven."

"Take this child to her mother," says Nole.

"I'll do it," says Fyve. "Put her in the basket."

Nole glares at Fyve. "I'm going to count to three and if you're still standing there with that basket, I'll set it on fire."

"No!" Cloud cries out.

"One," calls Nole, his gaze fixed on Fyve while Miracle squirms at his chest. "Two."

"Go, Fyve," begs Halo. "I've got this."

Fyve nods, his eyes filled with pain and uncertainty, and he leaves the ballroom with Marvel, his feet seeming to be made from lead. She knows he won't go far. Not until he has her back safely by his side.

"Get over here," Nole says to Halo. "Now."

She scurries to him, followed by Abe who reaches out to take Miracle. Nole eyes Halo cautiously, then allows Abe to take the screaming baby. As soon as his hands are free, he clutches Halo by the arm, his fingers feeling like they're digging straight into her bones.

"Let Cloud go," Nole instructs Jiro. "Maybe if she feeds that brat, it will stop crying."

"But she's my Treasure," Jiro complains. "I have as much right to my Treasure as you have to yours."

Nole chuckles. "We all know that's not true. Let her go."

Jiro releases Cloud who dives forward and takes her daughter from Abe.

"Come on," says Abe, trying to lead her away from Nole.

"Halo." Cloud's eyes fill with tears as she turns to her. "Thank you."

Halo straightens her spine, doing her best to look brave as

she nods. She agreed to go with Nole without complaint, but she never agreed to stay with him. This was merely a move to buy them time. As far as she's concerned, she's already fulfilled her part of the deal and owes this scumbag nothing.

Abe and Cloud leave the ballroom and Jiro storms off to help one of his compatriots who's moaning in a corner of the room. Sica's injured an impressive number of Echelons. Some may even be worse than injured. Ajax is still fussing over Rhina, while Viney hovers anxiously nearby. Had he not even noticed that his babies had been in danger?

"Leave us," Halo says to Justice. She needs Nole to relax if she's going to take him by surprise and turn the tables on him. And that's not going to happen while he has a blood-stained spear pointed at him. "Go help Sica."

"She's fine," says Justice. A loud groan erupts behind them as Sica lands another well-aimed blow. "I'm not leaving you."

"Leave me," Halo insists, pleading with Justice with her eyes. "I'm okay."

"No," says Justice, firmly.

Nole points his flamethrower at Justice. "Last chance."

"Please, Justice!" Halo begs. "Go."

"Fine!" she huffs, then sneers at Nole. "But I'm not done with him."

Nole drags Halo toward the door. Not the one in the secret wall that had rolled back, but the one they've always known as the door to the ballroom. She'd been hoping to leave through the same door where she's certain Fyve will be waiting for her.

"Alone at last," Nole says as he swipes his bracelet on the sensor.

The door slides open and he retrieves a white cloth from his pocket.

"I know you don't trust me," he says, flashing his yellowing teeth. "But I have a secret to tell you."

Halo leans in as they step through the door, and it slides

closed behind them. She smiles, trying to convince him she's no threat. "What is it?"

He pulls her close. The movement is fast and rough, taking her by surprise. He drops his flamethrower so it's hanging on the leather strap around his neck and uses his free hand to clamp the white cloth over her face.

"I don't trust you either," he sneers.

Halo's vision clouds with spots as she struggles to make sense of what's happening. Her legs turn weak and she buckles, the only thing keeping her on her feet is the tight clamp Nole has on her arm.

She collapses against him as the black spots grow and merge until her entire world turns dark.

FYVE

*F*yve glances at the corridor that the Echelons would've come down as they snuck up on them. Bastards.

Marvel releases a soft mewl and Fyve's arms tighten around the basket protectively. The baby's asleep, but he doubts that's going to last long. The moment he rouses enough, he'll discover there's something deeply wrong. His sister isn't beside him.

Just like Halo isn't with Fyve.

He grips the handle again, his hand flexing around it as the same battle that's been waging since he was ordered out here pulses through his muscles.

The need to keep Halo safe.

The knowledge that Marvel's life depends on him staying out here.

Hatred for Nole, for all the Echelons, blazes through Fyve. They always have one up on them. Some way to tie their hands.

To keep them prisoner.

Suddenly, the door opens, revealing Justice. "They're gone," she pants. "The cowards ran and took their injured with them."

Fyve rushes past her and into the ballroom, his heart clattering against his ribs. "Halo!"

"She's also gone," Justice says, now more subdued. "He took her."

"Marvel!" Cloud cries, rushing toward Fyve as she clutches Miracle. "My baby!"

Fyve passes the infant and Cloud hiccups a little as she places Miracle in the basket. Although the twins are asleep, they curl into each other. Their little hands lock, tiny fingers winding together. Marvel lets out a sigh while Miracle's soft lips twitch with the ghost of a smile.

Fyve's gut tightens as the twins' world is made right again now they're reunited.

His own world won't be made right until he's holding Halo again.

He turns to Justice, noting there's only Sica and Abe left in the ballroom. "Take them and find the others."

She nods sharply. "We'll need somewhere to hide."

That has Fyve hesitating. There's nowhere safe on this ship.

Abe steps forward. "We need to get to the wheelhouse."

"Which is?" Fyve asks, glad that Abe's shown he's trustworthy. Otherwise, sending him to find the remaining teens would be not only dangerous, but disastrous.

"It's where you steer the ship," says Abe. "My guess is the Echelons must have a Raven at the wheel."

"Then that's where we need to go," says Fyve, seeing the wisdom in the old man's words. "We'll take control of the wheelhut."

"Wheelhouse," Abe corrects.

"Whatever." Fyve waves a hand as he strides toward the door Nole would've dragged Halo through. "It's the only way we can even the playing field."

Iva appears from the bathroom, her face somber. "Antic didn't make it. He was too badly burned."

Justice curses. "Another death at the hands of the Echelons."

There's so much fury coursing through Fyve, it's burning him from the inside out. He looks from Justice to Abe. "Find the others and take them to the wheelhouse. Don't let anyone else in."

He's taken two steps when Abe reaches out to grab his arm. "Where are you going?"

"To get Halo," Fyve grinds out.

Abe's hand tightens, digging his fingers in. "That's not a good idea."

"It's not an idea," Fyve snaps. "It's what's happening next."

Iva frowns. "You don't even know where they are."

"I'll search the whole damn ship if I have to." Starting with the dining room Jiro led him to. Then maybe the secret wall where he'd seen Terra. He won't stop until he's found Halo.

Abe's lips thin. "They'll head to the engine room," he says, glancing toward the door.

"How do you know?" Justice asks, crossing her arms.

"That's where they moved the cans of food a few days ago. It's always been their plan to retreat there if they needed to."

Fyve nods. The Echelons have chosen the hub that drives this ship as their fort. He's about to step around Abe when Justice speaks.

Her arms tighten. So does her jaw. "He might be lying."

Cloud frowns. "Abe's shown he can be trusted more than once."

Justice lifts her chin. "Yet you didn't give him your babies."

"That's different," Cloud says, drawing the twins closer to her chest. "I couldn't leave them. Not again."

Justice steps closer to Fyve. "If he sends you into a trap, then we no longer have you or Halo," she says, her voice tight. Something flashes in her gaze that Fyve hasn't seen before.

Vulnerability.

He hesitates. When did he and Halo become the leaders of this group of teens? Of this rebellion?

Possibly the first moment they met.

One of their first kisses was followed by Halo's admission. *"I...I'm not sure Terra is even real some days."*

Fyve grips Justice's upper arms. "We've got this far because Halo and I found something worth fighting for. Because we learned we're stronger together."

Justice chews her lip, suddenly looking like a young girl who's been trapped on a ship, fighting for her life, knowing everyone in her family is dead.

But then she straightens. Her face hardens. "Get her back," she says, once more picking up the mantle of warrior woman and wearing it like it fits. "Then meet us at the wheelhut."

"Wheelhouse," Abe interjects.

She throws him a glare. "That's what I said."

Abe grunts and looks away, obviously deciding this isn't a battle he wants to engage in.

"Then we can turn this ship around." With a quick squeeze of Justice's shoulders, Fyve breaks into a run. "Find as many of the others as you can," he calls over his shoulder.

Out in the corridor, he sprints for the stairs, his feet rapping out a staccato almost as fast as his pulse. He goes down a level, then another. Three words ricochet through his head.

I'm coming, Halo.

The sound of the engines grow steadily louder as Fyve descends. What's more, he sees the odd splatter of blood along the way, telling him he's on the right track. Injured Echelons have been this way.

Then Fyve hears murmurs. The odd grunt. Then a distinct voice.

"Hurry up! We need to close the door!"

"No," Fyve breathes.

He injects more speed into his steps, his heart rate also leaping. He vaults down the last few steps that lead to the level of the engine room, landing on the balls of his feet and powering forward. There's a turn ahead, the roaring of the engines almost drowned out by the roaring in Fyve's ears.

He rounds the corner, this time shouting the denial. "No!"

Nole has Halo slung over his shoulder, the pink staining his puffy face apparent even at a distance. He's standing on the other side of the door, inside the engine room, his panting breath cut short when he registers Fyve at the other end of the corridor.

"Close it!" he screams.

The Echelons behind him jolt into action. Two raise their flamethrowers and point them at Fyve. Another lurches forward, blood trickling down his temple as he grabs the door and shoves.

"No!" Fyve screams again. "Halo!"

But her still form doesn't twitch, hanging over Nole's shoulder like a limp sack. The sight is progressively cut off as the door is shut.

Fyve runs as fast as he can, even as he knows he won't get there in time. The *thud* of the door slamming shut is like a blow to his chest. He reaches it a few seconds later.

Too many seconds too late.

A *clang*, then a low grating noise echoes from the other side, telling him a massive lock has been engaged. Fyve grips the large handle and pulls, pushes, then shoulders the door.

Not only does it not move, the thick mass absorbs every attack as if it never happened. Fyve may as well be pushing against a cliff face.

Desperate, he pulls out the bracelet and waves it over the door and every inch around it. He growls in frustration when nothing happens, even though he's not surprised. This isn't a door opened by the bracelets. It's a thick piece of metal designed to keep intruders out.

TAMAR SLOAN & HEIDI CATHERINE

That doesn't stop Fyve from trying.

He thuds his fist on the gray surface, trying to make each blow louder than the last. They explode through the small space, bruising the air and echoing deep in his chest. They give voice to his frustration and helplessness. To each heartbeat that calls out to Halo.

But the door doesn't budge. There's no sound from the other side. Even the roar of the engines is muted.

The Echelons have shut themselves off from the rest of the ship. Fyve rests his forehead on the cold steel, breathing hard. They have weapons. According to Abe, they have food.

And they have Halo.

Along with the ability to kill anyone on Treasure Island if everyone else doesn't bow to their whims.

Fyve's hands spread out, the palms absorbing the cool, indifferent surface, his fingers twitching with agitation. They rebelled, but all it got them was another death and Halo captured by a man obsessed with her.

Their hands are still tied.

Pushing back, Fyve scowls. He refuses to give up.

There has to be a way.

If only...

He spins around, breath catching on an idea. On a way to solve this. On a way to end the Echelons' control, once and for all.

A quick glance over his shoulder is all Fyve allows himself before breaking into a run. As much as it feels like something's tearing inside at the prospect of leaving Halo, he acknowledges this is the only way.

If Justice and the others find the wheelhouse and take it over, they control where this ship goes.

If Fyve can pull this off, then the Echelons won't be able to stop them.

He vaults up the stairs two at a time, then up three more

flights. Once he's on the right floor, he sprints to the room that's always held all the answers. That holds the connection to Treasure Island.

Fyve bursts into the room full of screens, skidding to a stop when he discovers he's not alone. Jiro yanks his fingers back from the screen he was touching. Almost caressing. He curls his hand into a fist and tucks it into his side as he slowly rises from the seat. "I suspected you'd come here."

Fyve's chest pumps in and out, and it's not just from the run. Anger and confusion are crowding his lungs as they fight for dominance. Jiro helped him. Saved his life. And yet, he's one of *them.*

"What are you doing here, Jiro?"

He straightens, his gaze holding Fyve's. "I wanted to say thank you. For saving me back in the ballroom."

Fyve doesn't answer straight away. He was surprised he did that himself. "You saved me, so I owed you," he says, his own gaze sliding away. He refuses to have a connection with this man.

Jiro nods, his shoulders drooping as if the weight of his rounded body is taking its toll. "Thank you, no matter the reason."

Fyve closes the door, even though he's not sure why he bothers. The Echelons are holed up in the engine room. "Shouldn't you be with your brother?" he asks, sneering the last word.

Jiro winces. "You don't understand why we're doing this, Fyve. Why we *have* to do this."

"No, I really don't," Fyve spits. "And I never will." He walks further into the room, noting all the screens are black apart from the ones projecting Treasure Island.

And that the one Jiro was just touching has Sevin on it.

Fyve's legs go weak as he moves closer, even as his stomach tightens. He brushes past Jiro, pretending to ignore him as he focuses on the grainy image of his sister. "How could you?" he asks through a tight throat. "How can you take their lives so easily?"

Jiro collapses back into the chair. "It's never been easy." He sighs. "Well, not for me, anyway."

Fyve ignores the heaviness in Jiro's words. He refuses to feel empathy for the Echelon. He's made his choices.

Sevin's standing on the beach, her back to the water as she tucks a strand of wild hair behind her ear. She's gazing at Treasure Island.

Even though she's not smiling, Fyve can sense she's happy. At peace.

That is, until she draws in her bottom lip and glances over her shoulder. All she'd see is endless red sea, yet her gaze still searches for long seconds. Fyve steps closer, finding his hand rising to touch the screen in the same way Jiro was moments ago. He makes a fist, his nails digging into his palm. "I want to talk to her."

Jiro draws in a sharp breath. "What?"

"You heard me. I want to tell her the truth." The anger returns at the injustice of this all. "If they remove their chips, you can't blackmail us anymore."

The idea that propelled Fyve here, that felt like the answer to all this, doesn't seem to surprise Jiro.

He shakes his head as he returns to his feet. "The moment Nole realizes what you're doing, he'll kill as many as he can."

"You've thought of this yourself," Fyve says, stunned.

Jiro's gaze returns to the screen where Sevin's standing, the edges of his mouth tight. "That doesn't matter. All that does is that it won't work."

Sevin's looking back at Treasure Island, and Fyve almost lets out a choked groan when a tear trickles down her cheek, catching on the edge of the faint smile playing along her lips. She's happy, but she's living with the lie she told her last remaining sibling—that she's dead.

Even as she has no idea she could be killed at any second. Claimed by an omnipresent Terra that doesn't even exist.

Even the young girl who they used to portray Terra is another pawn in their sick plans. A girl who's Jiro's daughter.

Fyve spins to face the Echelon. "What if that were...." He hesitates, realizing he doesn't even know the girl's name. "What if Sevin were your daughter? Would you just stand by and let this happen to her?"

That has Jiro reeling back so hard he stumbles. His mouth works soundlessly, his jowls wobbling with the effort.

Realizing he's hit a nerve, Fyve advances on him. "There has to be a way to end Nole's control over Treasure Island. We can stop the senseless killing."

Jiro shakes his head vigorously. "No, there's not."

"There has to be," Fyve maintains, backing Jiro against the wall. He refuses to consider any other option.

That means Sevin could be taken at any moment, as punishment for Fyve rebelling.

It means Nole will always have control of them all.

And Fyve will lose Halo.

"There's...there's not," Jiro says, his voice climbing then jerking to a halt when he comes against a bank of screens.

Fyve slams his hand against one beside Jiro's head, cracking the glass. "There has to be!"

Jiro jolts, a flash of anger flaring in his eyes, only for it to quickly extinguish. He sags, seeming to use the wall for support. "There is a way," he whispers.

Fyve knew it. "Tell me," he grinds out.

"We..." Jiro swallows, then looks up, a battle clearly waging in the depths of his gaze. "We'd need to cut all contact with Treasure Island."

It's Fyve's turn to stagger back. "What?"

"It's the only way." Jiro wipes his hand down his face. "If

there's no connection to Treasure Island, they can't be claimed. But we also can't contact them. Or see them."

Fyve's gaze pivots to the screens. Sevin's still standing there, the breeze playing with her hair.

He knew what a gift it was to not only know she's still alive but be able to see her. To watch her build a life of her own.

Now, the only way to keep her alive is to lose that link.

He walks slowly toward her, drawn to the connection they've always had. The one he'll have to sever to save not only her, but every teen on the ship.

Including Halo.

How can he make this choice?

Fyve's body sags in the same way Jiro's did, yet he doesn't have a wall to support him. He crumples to his knees. Yet it's not the weight of indecision that he can't bear.

It's the overwhelming burden of the decision he's already made.

"Do it," he says, the words coming out as a hoarse whisper. "Do it!" This time, the words are a sharp shout, one that's still rough with pain.

Jiro's shuffling footsteps come closer. "Didn't you hear me? You'll never see her again."

"And she'll get to live without the Echelons' interference!" Fyve says, surging to his feet. No one's life will be taken before it's supposed to. "So will every soul on Treasure Island. And every teen on this ship."

Jiro studies his face for long seconds, then nods slowly. "You always had your mother's strength."

Fyve has no idea what that means, but he's not going to ask. He's working hard enough not to shatter as it is. "Do it, Jiro."

The Echelon moves slowly, as if it's painful, opening the secret compartment behind a section of screens that he'd used to help Fyve escape. Inside are a series of switches Fyve hadn't noticed last time. Jiro looks back at him, a question in his agonized eyes.

Fyve isn't sure whether he's asking him to take it back.

Or to finally make this happen.

Jiro seems to answer it himself because he returns his attention to the switches. One finger hovers over the first. Fyve devours the image of Sevin, committing it to memory. The tear still clinging to the edge of her ghost-smile is a bittersweet image, but one he's determined to cherish. Sevin will be free of the lies Terra is built on.

That has to count for something.

Except Jiro hesitates. He looks back at Fyve. "Did you want to say something to her?"

"I can do that?" Fyve's heart constricts at the thought.

Jiro smiles. "Yes. Just a few words. Before…"

Before the connection is severed forever.

Jiro points to a small black stick with a round ball on the end. "Push the button down beside it and talk into the microphone."

Fyve moves toward it on autopilot, bringing the chair with him. This is the device the Echelons have used to control and manipulate the people of Treasure Island for generations.

And now it's his opportunity to say the goodbye they were robbed of by the Trials.

Fyve leans in and presses the button. "I love you, Sevin."

At first he doesn't think she heard him, but her head suddenly snaps up. She mouths one word. "Fyve."

He swallows, not wanting the pain lodged in his throat like a boulder to obstruct his next words. "I'm so proud of you."

The smile that blooms across her face is beautiful. Full of joy, brimming with peace. Fyve presses two fingers to the image, his own tears tracking down his cheeks.

The screen goes black and he almost cries out with pain. The severing is a physical one just as much as a mental one. Fyve's fingers slide away as a shuddering breath racks his body.

"Goodbye, Sevin."

A crash has him turning around, finding Jiro slamming another thing he called a microphone into the control panel holding the switches. His face is twisted with pain as he beats it over and over again. A spark arcs from the panel, crackles, and goes silent again.

It's done.

Fyve's breath is shallow in his tight chest. That hurt as much as he thought it would. He just didn't expect that it would look like Jiro was just sliced open, too.

Jiro drops the microphone like it's burned him. His barrel chest inflates and deflates with exertion. Or pain. He just helped Fyve and the teens again.

Yet he turns and walks to the door, not looking at the damage he just wrought.

"You're going back, aren't you?" Fyve's not sure why, but that hurts.

Jiro stops. "He has my daughter."

Terra, or whatever her name is.

Seems Nole still has a few bargaining chips. Including Halo.

Fyve strides past him and out of the screen room, deciding to never return. "What are you going to do now?" Jiro calls from behind him.

Fyve doesn't answer, even though he knows exactly what he's doing next. It's time to show Nole who's in control.

They're turning this ship around.

HALO

*H*alo resists the urge to open her eyes. Partly because her eyelids feel too heavy, but mostly because she doesn't want Nole to know she's awake. She needs a chance to work out where she is. And more importantly, if she can get away.

She's tied to a chair by her wrists and ankles. Another rope is fastened around her waist. Thankfully, her mouth hasn't been gagged and she can't feel a blindfold. Mentally sweeping down her body, she assesses herself for injuries. Apart from a few aches, a fuzzy head, and a gaping feeling in her empty stomach, she doesn't feel too bad. Whatever Nole drugged her with is wearing off.

She thinks back to the scene in the ballroom and all the confusion that had come with it. It's hard to know how long she's been unconscious. Fyve must be out of his mind with worry.

"You're awake, my Treasure," purrs Nole.

Her eyes snap open, wondering how he knew.

"I've been watching you," he says, in answer to the question she didn't ask. "Your breathing became lighter. Sometimes I think I know you better than you know yourself."

Nole is sitting on the other side of a table. There are several candles burning in jars, and artificial flowers floating in vases. It would be romantic if it were Fyve smiling at her, instead of a creep with a revolting leer plastered to his face. And the fact she's tied to a chair.

They're in a small room with a desk off to one side and a metal cabinet positioned behind Nole. The loud humming and clanking noises tell her they're near the engine room. Possibly in an office connected to it. She can't see a door, which means it must be behind her. Her escape route once she works out how to get out of this chair.

"My clever Treasure," Nole says, noticing her eyes roaming. "Always assessing your next move."

"Untie me." Her voice is so croaky she barely recognizes it.

Nole tips back his head and laughs. "That's not happening."

"Why not?" She glares at him, wondering if she'd get further by pretending to actually like this bloated monster.

"Halo." Nole leans forward, resting his elbows on the table as he steeples his chubby fingers. "My dear Halo."

She decides she prefers him calling her his Treasure. The sound of her name on his moist lips is too much to bear.

"Untie me," she repeats.

"I'm very fond of you," he says. "But I don't trust you. Not yet. In time, you'll learn to trust me and maybe then we can develop an understanding. However, I'm afraid that for now I need to take some precautions."

She tugs at the ties that are binding her wrists to the arms of the chair.

"I won't run away," she says. "I was true to my word in the ballroom. I went with you when I promised. Just untie me."

He taps his fingertips together. "But would you have run

away if I hadn't taken a little extra precaution by giving you that restful sleep?"

She shakes her head. "I always keep my word. And I'm telling you that if you untie me, I won't run away."

She doesn't mean it. Not for a moment. He doesn't deserve her truth. But if he's as enamored with her as he seems to be, then maybe he'll believe her.

"Let's eat." He pushes back his chair and walks behind her, knocking twice on what she assumes is the door. "I'm starving."

Taking his seat again, he smiles at her over the double chin that indicates he's anything but starving.

"I'll need my hands to eat," she tells him, eyeing one of the vases. It would make the perfect weapon if she could get her hands on it.

Nole shakes his head, his watery eyes laughing at her in a way that makes her skin crawl. "I'll feed you, Treasure. Don't worry. You won't go hungry."

"I need to empty my bladder," she says, trying a different approach.

This seems to amuse Nole even more. "Oh, I can help you with that, too. Happily."

Halo blanches, deciding not to push that point further.

The familiar sound of a door sliding open comes from behind her, and the Raven she believes to be Dargo appears, wheeling a small trolley that he parks beside the table. Still wearing his Raven mask, he sets down two plates of steaming food and cutlery for Nole. The band of white skin on his wrist is exposed when his sleeve pulls up. Halo tries to catch his eye, but he avoids looking directly at her.

"Iva misses you so much," she says quietly as Dargo takes a wine glass from the trolley.

The glass shakes, and red liquid spills over Dargo's hand and sloshes onto the floor. His dark eyes, visible in the cut-outs of his mask, turn to her and she sees them fill with tears, confirming that he's exactly who she believes him to be.

Remembering himself, he removes a towel from the pile on the bottom shelf of the trolley and cleans up the mess.

"She found your leather bracelet," Halo says, trying to recapture his attention. "She never takes it off. And she's never given up believing that you—"

"Enough!" Nole slams his palm on the table, no longer seeming so amused with the situation.

Dargo visibly jumps, then shrinks back from Nole. It's as if he expects to be struck, which Halo suspects is exactly what Nole normally does. Quickly setting down the two wine glasses on the table, Dargo pushes the trolley out of the room.

"He isn't who you think he is," says Nole. "You're mistaken. We brought that Raven over from the Outlands."

"I don't know what the Outlands are," says Halo. "But I know exactly who that is. And he grew up on Treasure Island."

Nole leans back in his chair and his smug smile returns like nothing happened. "I forget how uneducated you are."

Halo rolls her eyes. The people on Treasure Island aren't as stupid as Nole may believe them to be. "I know how to read and write."

Nole nods as he cuts up a piece of meat on his plate into small pieces. "But you know nothing about the world."

He stabs the meat with his fork and leans over the table, waving it in front of Halo's mouth.

"I'm not hungry." She turns her head away.

"Yes, you are." He pokes the salty meat at her lips. "It'll give you strength. That's what you want, don't you? So, you can run away from me the first chance you get."

She snaps her head forward at those words and opens her mouth to take the food on offer.

"That's exactly what I want," she says while chewing.

Nole chuckles as he feeds her another piece. "See why I like you? You're honest. Not like that brother of yours who's doing an excellent job of fooling Rhina into thinking he likes her. I mean…have you seen her?"

He splutters into laughter and takes a large sip of wine to clear his throat, completely oblivious as to how unattractive he is. Halo would rather be wooed by Rhina than the likes of him.

Chewing loudly, Halo opens her mouth for more food. She's starving and if he's offering sustenance so that she can gain strength to escape him, then more fool him.

He feeds her the remainder of his plate, piece by piece, then holds the wine glass to her mouth so she can drink. She knows it could be poisoned, but she doubts it. Nole's had plenty of opportunities to kill her. It's clear that what he wants with her, requires her to be alive.

"Have you had enough?" he asks.

She nods, trying to raise her hand to wipe her mouth and realizing the action is useless.

Nole switches his empty plate for her full one and settles into feeding himself, making revolting slurping sounds as he chews.

"This is nice, isn't it?" His eyes mist over. "I've waited a long time for this."

"How long have you been spying on me?" She narrows her eyes.

He waves his fork in the air, almost losing his piece of soggy carrot. "Your whole life. I knew you were going to be beautiful the moment you were born. But that may have been because of how attractive your mother was."

Halo had only been young when her mother had died. She hates that this creep remembers what she looked like more clearly than she can.

"Did you kill her?" she asks, for the first time questioning the pains in her mother's stomach that had led to her death.

"Halo, I'm no monster," Nole says, indignant. "Her

appendix burst. Or at least that was our best guess at the time. Had she been in the Outlands, we may have been able to save her."

Fury burns in Halo's gut. These Echelons have treated them like rats in a cage. They've studied them. They've killed them. They've experimented on them with their sick games. And her mother paid the ultimate price. When Halo gets her hands on that vase in front of her, she might even enjoy cracking it over Nole's head.

She tries to lean forward. "If these Outlands are so amazing, why are we on a ship searching for a place that you don't even know exists?"

Nole swallows his food and takes a long sip of wine.

"They're not so amazing," he eventually says. "How much do you know about the world, Treasure? Outside your island, I mean."

She shrugs. She read every legible word of every book and resource that beat the odds and washed up on Treasure Island, trying to piece together the mysteries of the world. Her knowledge is basic at best.

"I know there used to be forests," she says. "I had pictures stuck on the wall beside my bed. But you already know that."

He smiles. "That calendar was a gift from me. See, I do care about you, Treasure."

She frowns. If he's expecting a thank you, he's going to be waiting a long time.

"I had Dee leave it on the beach where you'd find it," he says. "And many of the books you found, including those instructions for the motor you were determined to build. You didn't really think they'd survive the ocean on their own, did you? We sent you lots of gifts."

Halo feels a slight burn sting her cheeks. She *had* thought that. What else was she supposed to think?

"We even sent you fireworks," he says, smiling. "Remember

the night we filled the sky with lights to prove to you that Terra exists? You loved that gift the most, I think."

Halo winces. She remembers that night only too well. It was the first time Fyve had kissed her. Except now that memory is tinged. What else can this evil creep take from her that he hasn't already?

"The world is bigger than you can ever imagine," says Nole. "All the distance we've covered in The Oasis so far is only a drop in the ocean, so to speak."

Halo doesn't join him to laugh at his pathetic play on words.

"Our planet was once a paradise," he says. "A thriving haven for people and nature alike. But then humans decided they had other ideas. Population exploded across the globe and the fight for resources became fierce. Wars broke out. Disease spread. Forests were destroyed. Governments collapsed. Hunger and violence became the norm. And the planet began to heat up. Ice-caps melted, oceans turned to acid, storms annihilated and fires ravaged the land."

With eyes wide, Halo realizes she's hanging on Nole's every word. To live on a planet and not understand its history is like spending your life never knowing your name.

"The Echelons were the cream that rose to the top of that stinking bowl of crap soup." Nole's chest puffs out. "We were the richest humans left on the planet and we realized that coming together was the only way we stood a chance. So, while humanity destroyed itself, we bunkered down. We built an entire world underground, digging containers into the earth and forming tunnels deep in a cliff where nobody would find us. We filled our new home with everything we'd need. Food, weapons, technology. You name it, we brought it with us. While others starved, we thrived."

"That would take years," says Halo, not sure if she believes a man of less than half a century would be capable of witnessing all that. "Decades."

Nole nods. "It did. I was a very young boy. The son of the richest Echelon of all. I owe everything to my father. That's why it's so important to ensure his genes are passed on. It would be a waste for our family line to end here."

"What are we doing here, then?" Halo tries unsuccessfully again to sit forward. The bindings on her wrists are starting to sting. "If you were thriving, why didn't you stay there?"

Nole taps the side of his head with his index finger. "Always thinking, aren't you, Treasure?"

Halo makes no effort to hide the rolling of her eyes at his condescending tone.

"Our resources were plentiful," he explains. "But they were finite. We needed to think about the next generation, just like our parents had thought about ours. And one day, while I was roaming the clifftop in search of answers, I saw a raven with a small branch in its beak."

Halo's brow crinkles as she tries to piece together the relevance.

"I saw more ravens after that," says Nole, running his finger over his empty plate and sticking it in his mouth. "Many with branches to build their nests. Not straggly branches like those that cling to the trees in the Outlands, but ones covered in lush leaves, the richness of the color like nothing you've ever seen. And the birds always came from the same direction." He points to the bow of The Oasis. "That's how we know it's out there. Tomorrow Land exists, Treasure. And we're going to find it. We're going to populate it. And with careful selection of our gene pool, we can ensure that we care for the land for all the tomorrows of generations to come."

The door that Halo can't see slides open and she hears Dargo's trolley wheeling back in. He parks it beside the table and loads the empty plates onto it, while Nole huffs impatiently. From the corner of Halo's eye, she sees a subtle movement on the lower shelf of the trolley where the towels are stored.

Resisting the urge to take a closer look, Halo keeps her eyes on Nole. Something is going on and she's not sure what. All she knows is that whatever it is, it has to be better than being tied to a chair across the table from Nole. Which means she has to keep him talking.

"If your genes are so superior, why do you need us?" she asks, certain that something has just crawled from the trolley to underneath her chair.

Nole glares at Dargo. "Raven, are you quite finished?"

Dargo quickly refills the two wine glasses and wheels the trolley away, leaving Halo alone with Nole and whoever is currently hiding underneath her chair.

"We had a small issue," says Nole, fixing his gaze back on Halo as he takes a large gulp of wine. "You see, the pioneering Echelons were mostly male and for reasons I can't quite explain they seemed to produce mainly sons. We went on searches for more females to bring into our sanctuary, but unfortunately, they proved to be uncouth. We couldn't possibly consider mixing our genes with them."

"Perhaps they were uncouth because you were keeping them captive?" Halo suggests, feeling strongly that there are parts to this story that are being left out.

"And then we met Dee," Nole gulps the rest of his wine. "Her raft washed up right on our shores like a gift from the gods. She was only a young girl of about your age, but we saw her potential right away. Much like your own mother, she was quite the beauty."

Halo pictures the weathered skin and hardened eyes of Fyve's mother, imagining the beautiful young girl hidden underneath years of hard work and poverty.

There's a tug on her left ankle as the cord binding her to the chair comes free. Someone is helping her! Someone small. Halo suppresses a smile as she thinks she's worked out who it is.

Oblivious to what's happening right in front of him, Nole

continues. "How an island made of nothing more than a pile of trash could produce such a fine specimen as Dee was beyond our wildest imaginings. We knew we had to capitalize on it. And we did. We had Dee install the cameras, we procured this ship, and devised a way to bring all our worlds together. Sacrifices had to be made. But it was all for the greater good. You can see that now, can't you?"

Halo thinks of all the deaths she's witnessed and shakes her head defiantly as she feels the cord released from her right ankle. "Nothing can justify what you did."

"We couldn't bring everyone," says Nole, his voice slurring slightly, either from too much wine or possibly something Dargo may have slipped into it. "Tomorrow Land would follow the fate of the Outlands if we let just anyone come. We had to be selective."

The cord around Halo's waist loosens, now hanging freely across her lap. The only thing left binding her to the chair is her wrists. Those cords are going to be impossible to remove without Nole noticing. She fixes her gaze on the cabinet behind Nole and furrows her brows as if something has caught her attention.

Nole notices, and spins around. Halo looks down to see Terra staring up at her with wide eyes. Halo nods and Terra's nimble fingers quickly free her right hand. Leaving the cord across her wrist, Halo waits for the next opportunity. Nole's unlikely to fall for the same trick twice.

"What did you see?" Nole snaps, looking back to her then behind him again.

Halo pretends to look annoyed. "There's someone in the cabinet, isn't there? I saw the door slide open then closed again. You have someone spying on us, don't you?"

"I do not!" he roars, leaping up and going to the cabinet, stumbling as he moves.

Terra frees Halo's right hand, and she wastes no time in rising from her chair and picking up one of the vases. Except in her haste, she grabs one of the jars with the candle inside and the heat singes her hand. But there's no way she's letting go. It can burn her to the bone. She's not putting down the only weapon she has.

Nole turns to see her and his face lights with fury. "Don't even think about it."

Terra emerges from under her chair and slams her wrist against the sensor beside the door. "Quick Halo!"

Nole lunges forward, grabbing Halo roughly by her free hand and she wastes no time in swinging the jar into the air. Hot wax flies out and lands on Nole's face, followed by the crash of the jar against his skull.

"I can't see!" he screams, letting go of her instantly to press the balls of his palms to his eyes as he collapses to his knees.

"Quickly!" Terra cries again.

Halo runs to her and together they emerge into the engine room, just as Halo had suspected. Terra slips her hand into Halo's, and they dart between generators and control panels, weaving in and out in a maze-like pattern that Halo can only assume is to avoid being seen.

"Wait," Terra hisses, pulling her to a stop.

Getting control of her breathing, Halo studies her tiny savior. Dressed in black trousers and a tunic instead of her former robes, Terra looks more human than ever before. Her hair has grown back in dark stubble and her eyes are shining with hope. It's a sight that makes her miss Sevin with an acute pain in her heart.

"Nole's injured!" a deep voice booms. "His Treasure's escaped!"

"Now!" Terra pulls Halo forward and they run across an area of open space to get to the door. Dargo is beside it, holding it open for them.

"Over there!" one of the Echelons calls and now all Halo can hear is the pounding of footsteps behind her.

They reach the door and run straight through it. Dargo follows, but just as he's crossing the threshold, he's pulled back into the room and the door slams shut.

"No!" screams Halo. She can't leave Dargo alone with those monsters.

"Come on!" says Terra. "He can't hold them back for long."

Feeling torn, but realizing Terra's safety is also at stake, Halo follows her down the corridor and up the stairs. The ship lurches and Halo grabs at the stair rail wondering if her wine had been spiked.

"Did you feel that?" Terra asks when they get to the top landing and are thrown against the wall.

Halo nods, hardly daring to believe what she thinks it means.

"The ship is turning," says Terra. "Your friends have made it to the wheelhouse. You're going home."

FYVE

"Fyve. Please, you need to listen."

Jiro's voice chases after Fyve as he strides down the corridor, and he ducks his head as if he can dodge it. He needs to get back to the others. Not only will they then turn this ship around, but they can work together on freeing Halo.

"Fyve!"

A few more steps and he'll be at the stairs, and once he's there, the two of them will be back to being on opposite sides of this war. He's saved Jiro's life, so they're even. The slate's been wiped clean.

Nothing Jiro can say will change that.

"Fyve! Stop!"

This time, Jiro barks the words. They don't chase Fyve, they shoot down the corridor and slam between his shoulder blades. They're a demand. No, a command.

As if Jiro has some authority or power. Fyve ignores the words like he has all the others, but the flare of anger has his gait stiffening. It takes a second longer for his foot to lift off the floor, ready to take the final step onto the stairs.

That second is all that's needed for Jiro's next words to register.

"Your mother wouldn't have wanted this."

Fyve spins around, anger morphing to fury. Then exploding into rage. He breaks into a run, his sights on the man standing in the doorway at the opposite end of the corridor. "Enough!" he screams.

Jiro's eyes widen as Fyve powers toward him, no doubt registering that something's snapped. That he's pushed Fyve over the edge.

Yet he doesn't run. He doesn't struggle when Fyve grabs him by the shirt and slams him back into the wall. He only winces when Fyve shakes him, pulls him forward, and shoves him again because the first time didn't yield a large enough thud.

"Why do you keep mentioning my mother?" Fyve screams in Jiro's face. "Why?"

Jiro's body is almost limp as his gaze connects with Fyve's, calm in the face of his storm of fury. "I knew her. She..." He stops, then sighs. "I knew Dee."

Fyve slams him into the wall again. "That's not possible!"

"She knew about us," Jiro says, almost a rag doll in Fyve's hands. "She visited the Echelons in the Outlands."

His mother's endless search for Tomorrow Land. The months of absences. Surely not...

Fyve shakes his head. "You're lying."

"I'm not. The Echelons have been hiding in the Outlands for generations. Dee found us, realizing we're all searching for the same thing."

Tomorrow Land.

Fyve releases Jiro as if he was just burned. He steps back, gut churning. "She..."

"She helped us, Fyve. She's the one who brought the chips back to Treasure Island. She's the one who helped Elijah. She knew everything."

That the entire existence of Terra was a lie.

That the Trials were a lie.

That everything was a lie.

"No," Fyve chokes. "She wouldn't..."

All those years when he was so angry at her for leaving, he believed she was driven by some sort of madness. A compulsion to escape their sorry life. That she didn't actually *choose* to leave. Knowing that somehow made it easier.

But not only did she do this willingly, she was part of the system. A system that killed innocent lives. Including Coal's.

Jiro holds Fyve's gaze, his own steady and unwavering. "She did. Because she believed in what we're trying to do. She knew this was the only way to give her children a life beyond poverty and starvation."

Another step backward and Fyve slams into the wall himself. He stops, knowing no amount of distance is going to make this easier. That he can't escape the truth.

In fact, Jiro takes a step forward. "She did it for you. And Sevin. So you wouldn't be a victim to the same fate inflicted on every other child she lost and mourned."

Fyve's body wants to sag against the wall. Possibly slide down and crumple under the weight of what he's hearing. But he doesn't let it. He locks his knees in the same way he locks his gaze on Jiro. He needs to know it all.

"She returned with the chips?" he asks.

Jiro nods. "Elijah inserted them when they visited each newborn on the island. And in anyone who was injured or sick."

"Did she..." Fyve clears his throat. "And the claimings?"

"That was Nole," Jiro says, his gaze shuttering. "He was the one who spoke to Elijah. We needed to make sure people were staying true to Terra."

We.

Jiro isn't hiding from the fact he's also a part of this.

That they killed in the name of founding an entire belief

system that would allow them to pick and choose their Treasures.

"Why?" Fyve whispers. "What makes this all worth it?"

Jiro's lips hover on the curve of a smile. "Dee asked the same question in the beginning. It killed her to leave you all behind. To realize what needed to be done."

"Why?" Fyve snaps, no longer wanting to hear that he has anything in common with his mother. That she cared for him.

He's nothing like her.

And in the end, her professed love for him wasn't enough.

She was part of the suffering the Echelons inflicted on Treasure Island and now The Oasis.

Jiro takes another small step forward, a pleading edge tightening his voice. "For humankind," he says. "To not only ensure our survival, but that we could thrive. That we'd be smart enough to learn from our mistakes, and strong enough to do what needs to be done."

"To do what needs to be done," Fyve echoes hollowly. "Even if it means losing the part that actually counts?"

Fyve's hands are hot fists by his side as he glares at Jiro, wondering if he'll actually hear this.

"Even if it means losing your humanity."

Jiro looks like he's about to close the gap between them again, except he pauses. Freezes. "I didn't say it was easy. Sacrifices were always going to be inevitable."

"Is that what Nole says?" Fyve demands. "Is that what you really believe?"

Jiro clamps his mouth shut.

Fyve pushes away from the wall but doesn't move any closer. "When is the price too high, Jiro? When is the cost too much?"

Jiro blinks. Doesn't move.

Seems struck speechless.

When Fyve's shoulder bumps into the wall, he wonders if the shock, no doubt the exhaustion, is finally catching up with him. But he quickly realizes it's not tiredness. The change isn't within him.

It's his surroundings.

A grin bursts across Fyve's face. "They did it."

"What?" Jiro asks, looking panicked. "What have they done?"

"The other teens. The ones you manipulated and used. They're turning the ship around. We're going back to Treasure Island."

"No!" Jiro half-shouts. "We can't!"

"Tomorrow Land doesn't exist," Fyve spits. "The reason you justified all this is nothing more than myth."

Jiro shakes his head so hard, his jowls wobble. "No, you don't understand. We don't have enough fuel to get back. We'll be stranded."

Jiro's panic grips Fyve for a second, but he quickly shakes it off. "Then we'll get as far as we can, then let the ocean do the rest of the work for us. Everything washes up on Treasure Island eventually."

"No, no, no," Jiro moans. "That means this all would've been for nothing. Everything I've had to sacrifice."

"Everything *you've* had to sacrifice?" Fyve hisses, the fury blazing once more.

"Fyve?"

The voice that carries down the corridor has him spinning around, his heart stuttering and soaring all at once.

"Halo?" he asks, not quite believing what he's seeing as she runs toward him.

But the smile blooming across her face is like sunshine. The joy coursing through his veins is like a song.

And the sensation of clasping her to him is the sweet joy of coming home.

They hold each other tight for several long seconds, breathing deeply as their heartbeats slow. Then meld. Aligning and merging in the same way their souls are.

Fyve's the first to pull back. "How…how did you escape?"

Halo turns to look over her shoulder at the stairs. "Terra helped me. I wouldn't be here if it weren't for her."

The little girl is walking down the corridor, her hands tightly clasped. Her gaze darts around, then quickly spots Jiro. "Daddy!" she cries, now breaking into a run herself.

Jiro drops to his knees, a smile so soft it's almost beautiful spreading across his face as he opens his arms. Terra leaps into them, echoing the way Halo just ran to Fyve, and wraps her thin arms around Jiro's fleshy neck.

"I thought you were back in the lockdown room."

Jiro presses his lips to her forehead. "I needed to do something first."

Terra turns, remaining in her father's embrace. "You wanted to talk to him?"

Fyve stiffens, feeling Halo wrap her arms more protectively around his waist. "You've said enough." He looks down at Halo. "He told me everything. That my mother visited them. About why the Echelons are doing all this."

She nods. "Nole told me, too." She frowns at Jiro. "I've never heard anything so heartless."

Jiro's brows flicker and he opens his mouth to speak, but Fyve looks away.

"Justice and the others have turned the ship," he says to Halo.

"I noticed." She beams up at him. "We did it, Fyve."

His heart swells. "We're going home."

That awful goodbye to Sevin will have been all for nothing. Maybe they'll even laugh about it one day.

The sweet happiness blooming around Fyve and Halo is punctured by Jiro's next words.

"You've just declared war on the Echelons."

Halo turns to glare at him. "Their price for peace was too high," she says sharply.

Pride inflates Fyve's chest. Halo just reiterated what he just said only a few minutes ago.

"Fyve—" Jiro says.

"No," he snaps. "I've heard enough. Nothing you say will change my mind."

"But—"

"Nothing!" Fyve shouts, injecting all the disgust and anger at everything the Echelons stand for into that one word.

Jiro's face tightens, but Fyve can't tell why. He's disappointed? Angry? Preparing to wage this war just like Nole is?

He pushes to his feet and takes his daughter's hand, stalking toward them as he keeps his gaze solidly on the stairs. Fyve and Halo step back, allowing him to pass. Jiro walks past, his gait stiff and his face pale and hard. Despite its round curves, it looks like it's been carved from stone.

As they pass, Terra glances up at Fyve, then Halo. Tears are glistening in her eyes.

Halo frowns, but before she can do anything, Terra halts, dragging Jiro to a stop only a few feet away.

"I don't want to go back, Daddy."

Jiro tugs on her hand. "We have to. You know that."

Yet Terra doesn't move. Her lower lip trembles. "Don't let them hurt me anymore."

Fyve draws in a sharp breath. "You let them hurt her?" he asks incredulously. The need to draw Terra to his side is overwhelming.

Jiro allowed Nole and the other Echelons to use his daughter. But he also stood by while they *hurt* her?

Jiro's eyes close for long seconds as his chest expands on a slow, deliberate breath. When he's done, he kneels before Terra, taking her shoulders. "This will all be over soon, I promise."

"Your job is to protect her," Fyve spits. "No matter what."

Jiro slips his arm around his daughter, acting the part of protective parent, even though he's never been that. He cared for her as much as Fyve's mother cared for him. "I didn't have a choice. Nole could've taken so much more from me." He holds Fyve's gaze. "He not only threatened her life. I had to think of Sevin. And you, Fyve."

Each thread that's made this intricate web of lies they're trapped in is suddenly obvious. The reason Jiro reached out to him from the beginning. Helped him. Saved his life more than once.

The truth that his mother visited the Echelons and the Outlands regularly.

And Jiro knew her. He knew her well.

Fyve almost moans. No.

It can't be true.

His body is so still, he can't breathe. Can't speak. Can't even try to fathom what this will mean.

It's Halo who moves. She squats down, coming to eye level with the trembling girl. Fyve instinctively knows she's about to ask the question that matters, like she always has. That's going to slice straight to the core of the truth.

"What's your name, Terra?" Halo asks softly. "Your real name?"

The little girl beams, looking relieved. Proud. Even as if she's looking forward to sharing this.

Her small shoulders pull back as she pushes out her skinny chest. "My name is Tenn."

HALO

*H*alo looks up at Fyve to see his reaction to those explosive words.

Terra's name is Tenn.

But for once, Fyve isn't looking at Halo. His eyes are glued to the girl who is undoubtedly his younger sister. Which means…

Fyve's confused gaze shifts from Tenn to Jiro.

Jiro nods, his eyes filling with both love and tears as he holds his hands at his chest. "You're my son. Sevin is my daughter. And your mother was the love of my life."

"No." Fyve stumbles back, reaching for the wall to steady himself. "No. I had a father. On Treasure Island. He raised me."

Jiro nods. "And for that I'm grateful. But he was also infertile. Not that he knew that, although, surely, he must have made the connection between Dee returning to Treasure Island and her belly swollen with child so soon afterward. I always thought that maybe he didn't want to know. That maybe he was grateful to me."

"No." Fyve repeats. "No."

Halo hears a whimper and looks at Tenn to see her trembling. This news seems to be just as surprising to her as it is to

Fyve. Remaining squatting beside the small girl, Halo pulls her in close and wraps an arm around her.

Fyve's hands clench at his sides. "If you loved my mother, why did you allow her to be killed?"

Jiro's mouth drops open as the tears slide from his eyes. "I didn't. I would never have. That was Nole. I loved Dee. I still do. She's the only woman I'll ever love."

Halo's head snaps up at these words. "Yet you were only too happy to choose Cloud as your Treasure."

"Why do you think I chose her?" Jiro asks. "Cloud's the only one I can get away with not touching. She's just given birth. Her body will take time until it's ready to breed again."

These words have Fyve barreling forward until he's standing only inches from the man who's claiming to be his father. It's only now that Halo can see the resemblance hidden beneath the years of excess that have made their mark on Jiro's face. They have the same nose. The same color eyes. The same shape to their hands.

"Breed?" sneers Fyve. "You continue to use that offensive word. We're not your livestock. Your rats in a cage. We're just as human as any of you."

"I know that." Jiro touches Fyve on the arm, then seems to think better of it and lets his hand fall. "I do know that. I'm sorry."

"What about Sevin?" Halo stands, keeping hold of Tenn's hand. "Why would you leave your own daughter behind like that?"

Jiro shakes his head. "You don't understand. She'd never have been allowed to compete in the Trials if I hadn't insisted on it. Dee helped, too, by lying about her age. But then Sevin's eyesight became an obvious issue and Nole wasn't happy. He said it was a fault in Dee's genetic line. He wanted to claim all my children. Fyve. Sevin. And Tenn."

Halo pulls Tenn a little closer, trying to soothe the pain these words must be causing. Her own uncle wanted her dead.

Jiro wipes his eyes. "The best I could manage was for Nole to spare my children in exchange for Sevin failing the final Trial. He didn't want her on the ship, and he didn't want you either, Fyve. He thought that if Sevin stayed behind, then so would you. But it seems my daughter is smarter than any of us gave her credit for. Just like her mother."

"Is mommy dead?" Tenn's voice rings out clearly and breaks Halo's heart in two.

All the anger seems to drain out of Fyve as he goes to Tenn, kneeling down in front of her.

"She's gone, Tenn," he says. "But I'm here. And Halo. We're your family now. And we'll look after you. I swear it. We won't let anybody hurt you ever again. Do you understand?"

Tenn nods, letting go of Halo's hand to reach out to her big brother. Without hesitation he embraces her, lifting her small frame from the floor as he stands, holding her tightly against his chest. Halo knows how it feels to be locked in Fyve's arms. Right now, Tenn would feel like nothing and nobody in the world can touch her. It's a feeling she deserves to have always.

"Why?" Fyve asks Jiro as he sets Tenn back on the floor, keeping one arm around her. "Why did you separate Tenn from us? Why didn't you let her grow up on Treasure Island?"

"Because I wanted to keep just one," says Jiro, his voice breaking with pain. "It wasn't fair. Each time Dee left the Outlands pregnant with my child, I felt a desperate sense of loss. It wasn't right. The Echelons are known for producing male heirs. I wanted more. And I wanted everyone to know I was capable of more."

"You kept her as a trophy," Fyve growls. "Nothing more than a means to impress your brother. You allowed her to be hurt. To be used. For her head to be shaved and propped up in front of a group of people to fear her as some kind of god, when all she is, is a child."

Halo looks at Fyve, pride swelling in her chest. She couldn't have said it better.

"I love her," says Jiro. "I love all my children."

"Well, your children don't love you." Fyve takes a step away. "Go back into hiding with your beloved brother. Tell him to stay there or his nephew will kill him."

"You can't take my daughter." Jiro reaches out his hands. "Tenn stays with me."

Tenn presses herself into Fyve's side. "No, Daddy, I'm not going. I'm staying with Fyve."

Halo stands on Tenn's other side, wanting her to feel cocooned in love.

Real love.

"You took everything from me," says Fyve. "You took my cousin—my best friend. You took my mother. You took my sister. You took my home. You're not taking Tenn. Not when I've only just found her."

"Then come with me," says Jiro. "We have plenty of food in the engine room. I can have both my children with me."

Halo knows that will never happen. She can't believe Jiro's desperate enough to even suggest it.

"Don't forget to give *Uncle Nole* my message," says Fyve, leading Terra and Halo away. "We'll see you on Treasure Island."

"I told you we don't have enough fuel," Jiro calls after them. "And you won't have enough food."

"We'll figure something out," Fyve mutters.

"We always do," Halo adds for Tenn's benefit. "We have each other and that's all that matters."

"Knock two times if you change your mind," Jiro shouts after them.

"I'll knock you over the head," grumbles Fyve.

"Fyve." Halo tilts her head at Tenn, reminding him she's there.

"I won't really knock him on the head," says Fyve. "I just feel like it."

Tenn nods. "Me, too."

"Me, three," says Halo, which makes Tenn giggle even though it must be one of the oldest jokes on the planet. She imagines there are a lot of things Tenn's never heard.

"Where's this wheelhut?" asks Fyve as they turn a corner, leaving his father behind.

Halo doesn't correct him on the name of the room. Instead, she points up and leads the way to the stairwell.

"Do I look like her?" Tenn asks as they take the stairs. "Sevin, I mean. Do we look alike?"

"You actually do," says Halo, realizing she'd thought of Sevin when she'd imagined Tenn with hair. The clues had been there all this time. She just had never thought to put them together.

Tenn seems to like this answer and falls deep into thought as they continue to climb the stairs.

"Was Mommy a bad person?" Tenn asks Fyve when they get to the top. "Like me."

Fyve makes a strangled sound. "Why do you think you're a bad person?"

"Because Mommy stopped visiting me," she says, plainly. "She said she'd see me soon, and then she never came back. I hardly ever saw her. She was always with you. I must have been bad."

Fyve stops still on the landing and turns to his sister. "Growing up, I always felt the same. Mom would be gone for weeks at a time, sometimes months, and I thought it was because I'd done something bad. I thought she didn't love her children enough. I had no idea how wrong I was. She left us because she loved her children—*all* her children. She was torn between us. Never happy when she was with us because she

123

missed you. And never happy when she was with you because she missed us."

"Your mom was a kind person," says Halo, even though she's no longer sure what to think about Dee. "I was sick once after being made to run for a very long time and she gave me water. She looked after me when she didn't have to. She wasn't a bad person, and neither are you."

Tenn nods and casts her eyes down, looking so much like the strange, bald girl she'd seen when they'd first arrived on The Oasis.

"Come on," says Halo, trying to inject some enthusiasm into her voice. "I want you to meet my family. Properly, I mean. Miracle and Marvel are getting so big already. They need someone to look up to. You'll be like a big cousin to them."

Tenn smiles at this. "I've never had a cousin. I'd like that."

"You have plenty of cousins back home," says Fyve as they step into the corridor. "There's Rubee and Jett and Bloo. They're about the same age as you. When we get back to Treasure Island, you can meet them all."

A heavy feeling settles in Halo's chest at these words. She wants to go home. They're heading in the right direction at last. But…can they really make it? Not wanting to voice her concerns in front of Tenn, she smiles along. They have to make it! There's no other choice. Like Fyve said, everything washes up on Treasure Island eventually. They will, too.

"This way," she says, taking them down the corridor. According to the map she's been carrying in her head, the wheelhouse isn't far away now. They're almost at the bow of the ship.

They reach the door at the end of the corridor and knock on it.

"It's us!" Fyve calls out. "Fyve and Halo! Let us in!"

"How do we know it's not a trick?" comes Justice's voice from the other side.

"Because it's not a trick." Fyve rolls his eyes.

"What's the secret password?" Justice asks.

Halo and Fyve look at each other.

"Nole's an asshole," says Fyve.

"That will do," says Justice and the door slides back. It had been propped closed with one of Justice's crutches and Halo remembers that none of these teens would be in possession of a working chip.

"What's she doing with you?" Justice asks, tilting her chin at Tenn.

"Everyone, I'd like you to meet Tenn," says Fyve, stepping into the room. "My sister. You can trust her."

There are several surprised glances, but after what they've experienced lately, nobody questions this strange revelation.

Halo follows Fyve into the room and her jaw drops as she takes in the enormous windows that span the front wall, providing a breathtaking view of the crimson ocean. The nose of the ship is cutting through the water with ease, and it makes her dizzy to realize they're traveling at a greater speed than she'd imagined was possible. There's a large wheel in the middle of the room that's set into a panel filled with buttons and controls. Abe is sitting proudly at the wheel, surrounded by the remaining teens.

"Is Ajax with you?" asks Viney, stepping forward.

Halo hadn't even realized Ajax was missing. He must still be tending to Rhina with her injured shoulder. Or he's in the engine room feasting with the Echelons. Maybe both.

"I haven't seen him," Halo tells Viney. "But I'm sure he'll show up. He always does."

"He'd better," says Viney. "I need to tell him something."

Halo narrows her eyes, hoping Viney's announcement has nothing to do with the way she's standing with her hand resting on her belly. Two babies are more than enough to look out for right now.

TAMAR SLOAN & HEIDI CATHERINE

"We're going home," says Cloud, appearing by Halo's side and giving her a quick hug. "Did you feel the ship turn around?"

Halo nods, far preferring her brother's original choice of partner.

"Can I please meet your babies?" Tenn asks Cloud quietly. "They're very cute."

Cloud gives Tenn a warm smile and puts out her hand. "Of course. They're asleep right now but why don't we go and have a look at them?"

Tenn glances up at Fyve as if asking permission and he nods. Cloud leads Tenn away, and a warm feeling fills Halo's heart. But as she watches, a new and far more disturbing feeling chases the warmth away. As Tenn walks past Abe, her back stiffens. It's as if every one of the short hairs on Tenn's head stands up at once and she presses herself to Cloud's side.

Fyve sees it too and he raises his brows at Halo.

"We'll ask her later," Halo whispers, still sure they can trust the old man. "It was probably just unexpected for her to see him here."

Fyve nods. "Maybe."

"I need to talk to Iva," says Halo, spotting her familiar blonde braid in the group of teens. She has to tell her what she saw in the engine room. And who had helped her escape.

But before she can get to Iva, there's another knock at the door and Viney runs to it, trying to shove Justice out of the way and almost sending her toppling.

"It's Ajax!" she shouts. "It has to be. He's the only one missing."

Justice regains her balance and blocks the door once more. "We don't know that."

"Open it," pleads Viney. "I have to tell him something."

Halo and Fyve rush to the door and Fyve assists Justice to keep it closed.

"Who's out there?" Halo calls through the paneling.

There's no response. Just another weak knock.

"Ajax, I'm late!" Viney shouts. "I'm pregnant. Tell them who you are so they let you in."

Halo searches the room for Cloud until she meets her eye. Cloud nods, letting Halo know she's fine with this latest revelation. Was even expecting it, perhaps. It seems any love she had in her heart for her twins' father had long ago sunk into the depths of the ocean.

"It's me," says a deep voice from the other side of the door. "It's…"

There's a thump like whoever it is has collapsed against the door.

"That wasn't Ajax," wails Viney. "Don't open it."

Halo pushes forward, trying to open the door. "I know who that is. Open it, Justice."

Fyve seems confused by this but trusting her implicitly, he moves Justice out of the way and the door slides back.

Dargo is crumpled on the floor outside, blood trickling from his nose and the side of his head.

"Iva!" Halo shouts. "Hurry!"

There's a commotion behind her as Iva dashes forward and throws herself to the floor beside Dargo. She rolls him onto his back and immediately starts assessing his injuries, all the time making a harsh sobbing sound as she comes to grips with the fact she may have just been reunited with her love, only to lose him once more.

"Dargo," Iva says. "Can you hear me? It's Iva. Dargo!"

"Let's get him inside." Fyve crouches beside Iva. "It's not safe out here."

Iva nods and Fyve lifts Dargo and carries him across the threshold while Justice secures the door again.

"They tried to claim me," Dargo says, his voice so soft it's barely audible. "I ripped out my chip before they could finish."

Halo gasps to realize the damage on the side of Dargo's head was self-inflicted. A far messier and more dangerous procedure than when they'd carefully removed their own chips. But it had saved his life.

Hopefully.

He really isn't in a good way, but Iva seems to know what to do, and she gets to work tearing strips from her tunic and stemming the bleeding as she motions for everyone to stand back and give her some space.

Viney slumps against a wall and sobs. "Where's Ajax? What's taking him so long?"

One of the other teens goes to comfort her and Halo is ashamed to admit she's relieved it doesn't have to be her. Viney may be carrying her future niece or nephew but she's not sure she'll ever warm to her in the same way she warmed to Cloud.

There's a lurching motion and the wheelhouse falls silent. Everyone looks around at each other, wondering what's changed. Something feels different.

"It's the engines," says Abe, his eyes glued to the ocean ahead. "I can't hear the humming. We're slowing down to a drift."

In the window beyond, the movement of the watery landscape ceases to pass so quickly.

"But we can't have run out of fuel already," says Sica.

Abe shakes his head. "We haven't. The Echelons have cut the motors. It's the only bargaining chip they have left."

Halo goes to Fyve and wraps her arms around his waist. He pulls her close and she buries her head in his chest, trying to recreate the feeling of protection that Tenn had felt earlier when he'd promised to keep her safe.

She's not sure how much more of this she can take. They thought they had all the power. They thought they were going home.

But once again, the Echelons have shown them who's really in charge of this ship.

FYVE

"There's nothing," Justice says sourly, her hands on her hips as she surveys the dining hall. "They've taken every last crumb."

Fyve's teeth are jammed so hard into each other, he's not sure how they haven't cracked. "Of course, they have."

Sica appears from the kitchen, huffing a strand of hair out of her face in frustration. "Nothing."

Halo enters through the main doors, the group of teens who went with her to search the other areas of The Oasis all holding their shoulders at various levels of dejection. "They've cleaned the place out," she says, her gaze heavy as she returns to Fyve's side.

He slips an arm around her shoulder, needing the comfort as much as he wants to give it. The Echelons holed themselves up in the engine room two days ago, taking all the food and weapons with them.

Now, they're drifting at sea, not getting any closer to Treasure Island, with no way to feed themselves. With no way to fuel their fight for freedom.

And they have a nursing mother with infant twins. Viney's

pregnant. Along with an injured Dargo who Iva's determined to save through sheer force of will.

A small hand tugs Fyve's shirt on the other side. "What are we going to do?" Tenn asks.

And a sister Fyve didn't know existed.

He releases Halo to squat beside Tenn. The protectiveness that's wound through his DNA contracts around his heart. "There's a solution. There always is," he promises her.

Tenn nods, her eyes wide and trusting. Even in the two days that have passed, the stubble on her scalp has grown a little more, framing her face in a dark halo. Now that he knows who she is, he can't believe he didn't see it before. The likeness to Sevin, even his mother, is there. Undeniably connecting her to him.

He reaches out to squeeze her shoulder. "I'm going to look after you." He has no idea how, but that's not going to stop him.

To his surprise, Tenn unleashes a bright smile. "I'd rather be hungry than with Nole, anyway."

Fyve straightens, hiding the frown that was triggered. He finds himself jamming a hand into his pocket and gripping the vial of poison he's carried since the Trials. He had no idea what he was saving it for, and now it's abundantly clear.

Nole will pay for everything he's done.

With a taste of his own medicine.

"Let's get back to the wheelhouse," Halo suggests.

The teens nod, one or two most certainly frowning. Fyve wonders whether it's because hunger has once more sunk its claws into their stomachs. Or whether it's because the wheelhouse is a hollow victory now that The Oasis is no longer moving. There's no triumph in controlling a ship that's dead in the water.

Fyve squats down, trying to banish the sense of hopelessness that's hovering at the edges of their existence. "Come on, Tenn. Climb on."

Her eyes light up with such excitement, it's as if Fyve just offered her Tomorrow Land. She squeals, leaps, and clamps on with all the strength in her skinny arms and legs.

Fyve stands, something else clamping around his chest. Then his heart. The one thing he thought he'd lost has been found. Family.

Jolting forward before thoughts of Jiro try to invade this moment—the father he didn't know existed—Fyve pretends to stagger. "Whoa, what have you been eating? Canned elephant?"

Tenn giggles, bouncing a little. "It's delicious. You should try it!"

This time it's Halo who laughs, her eyes warm as she takes in the two of them. She angles her head. "Can I climb on, too? I promise I haven't had any canned elephant."

"Yes!" Tenn squeals. "There's plenty of room!"

Fyve chuckles, making a show of staggering again. "No way! I think you've turned into a baby elephant."

Tenn giggles again in the way all children do—with her body. She wriggles as the laughter ripples through her, in just the same way it did with all his other siblings. She even buries her head between his shoulder blades, capturing the sound between the two of them.

Halo's eyes soften. "Come on. It's getting close to sleep time."

Not meal time.

Not play time, because no one can afford to waste that much energy.

Fyve's flash of playfulness quickly dies. They need to find a way to get to the engine room. He doesn't know which he wants to do first—start the engines or finish the Echelons.

The teens make their way down the corridor and to the stairs, silent and subdued. A few glance at Halo and Fyve, obviously looking for some guidance on how to feel about this. That there's some plan on what to do next.

He straightens, holding each one of their gazes. "Sleep is just what we need. We need to be ready."

He just has no idea for what.

"Looking forward to it," Justice growls, spinning on her heel and stalking up the stairs.

The others follow, a mixture of her determination echoing on their faces.

It has Fyve letting out a slow breath. They have hope.

For now.

He and Halo follow as everyone makes their way through the bowels of The Oasis. Silence reigns, with only the muffled sounds of their footsteps interrupting it. Even Tenn goes quiet, tucking herself into Fyve's back. Although the Echelons have locked themselves away, hostages to their greed and thirst for power, everyone still feels they're the ones who are prisoners.

In so many ways, they still are.

There's only one more floor to the wheelhouse when Fyve pauses. The deck isn't far away, and the need to be out of the confines of their floating jail is strong. Halo turns, always seeming to be sensitive to his every movement. He glances at the door that will take him to fresh air and open space, his sense of responsibility tying him to the spot.

"Ooh, can we go outside?" Tenn asks, her head popping up over his shoulder.

Fyve hesitates. "Do you want to come?" he asks Halo.

Halo's face softens into a smile. "You go," she says. "Spend some time with your sister," she says warmly.

He's about to object when he realizes Halo's giving him an opportunity to connect with Tenn. That she's giving him an opportunity to honor finding a sister, when he thought he'd never have family again.

Fyve decides to make the most of it. He grins, placing a quick kiss on her cheek. "We won't be long," he promises.

She swats his arm playfully. "I probably won't even notice you're gone."

He grins even wider. "If that's the case," he jostles Tenn a little higher up his back. "I'll need to find a reason for you to miss me."

He turns and jogs up the stairs, his sister giggling on his back, before Halo can answer, his own smile hovering on his lips. Maybe just a few minutes outside will recharge him.

As Fyve steps out onto the deck into a world of purple twilight, he realizes that's exactly what it's going to do. He draws the briny, sulfurous scent of the sea deep into his lungs. All it needs is a tinge of garbage and it would smell like Treasure Island. Like home.

Tenn wriggles and he releases her so she can slide down. She darts away the moment her feet hit the deck, clearly relishing the freedom to move. Fyve watches her run through the twilight, her feet slapping faintly as her tunic flutters. He pulls in another lungful of air, glad he did this. It's hard to escape exactly how desperate their situation is when the walls are constantly crowding around you. When you're breathing the same air that's as trapped as they are.

Tenn gasps, stops, then runs ahead.

Alarm shoots through Fyve. "Tenn!" he calls. "Be careful!"

She covers a few more feet then falls to her knees. "Fyve!"

He's by her side in a blink, heart pounding, ready to do whatever it takes to save her. She smiles up at him. "Look," she says, wonder softening her voice.

He glances at where she's pointing, realizing it's the pool. And that in the twilight, the pods within it are a moving constellation of light. Fyve sinks to his knees, the same sense of wonder on his sister's face blooming through him. "Wow."

Tenn flattens out to lie on her stomach. "They're so beautiful."

Fyve finds himself doing the same as he lies beside her. "They really are."

He gently pushes away a floating island of green so they can see better. Only a few feet below, the ethereal-looking creatures flap their see-through wings, mesmerizing in their fragile beauty. Their glowing centers pulse delicately, creating constantly shifting patterns in the night-colored water.

"Our cousin, Coal, was the one to find these," Fyve says as he watches unblinkingly.

"He did?" Tenn asks, shuffling a little closer to him.

Fyve chuckles. "And the first thing he did was eat it."

"Ew!" Tenn's face scrunches up. "They look really...gooey."

"They're actually really good for you. Like a burst of energy that lasts for days and days."

Fyve reaches down to scoop one up, but the moment his hand breaks the surface, the pods shoot away in alarm. He chases one, except the second its strange, clear wing brushes his hand, it slips through.

Tenn spears her hand down and catches it. She holds it up with pride. "I got it!"

Fyve beams right back. "Now you need to eat it."

The same expression of disgust screws up Tenn's face. "Really? I gotta eat it?"

"It's good for you," he encourages. "And I want you to stay strong and healthy."

Tenn looks at the flapping, glowing pod in her palm. "Okay..."

She slides it into her mouth, her face twisting even further as she chews. Fyve laughs, remembering the burst of bitterness when he ate one himself.

Tenn pokes her tongue out at him, lies back down, and in a lightning quick movement catches another pod. "Your turn."

Fyve's about to protest when she sets her jaw at a familiar tilt. Sevin used to look at him like that when she was being stubborn about something. "I want you to stay strong and healthy, too, Fyve."

Any objection dissolves under the sweet earnestness in Tenn's voice. She's saying he's just as important to her as she is to him. He takes the pod, swallowing it without chewing. Although the feeling of the wriggling, gelatinous blob slipping down his throat isn't pleasant, he'd prefer not to taste the thing.

Despite knowing the burst of energy he's feeling would only be in his mind, like he once tried to convince Coal, Fyve suddenly feels stronger. In one swallow, their obstacles don't seem so insurmountable. He focuses on the fact that they now have a food source.

Even if it might be short-lived. They can ration the pods, but once they're all gone...

Tenn grins. "Daddy told me I had brothers and sisters and that one day I'd meet them. I would pray to Terra that he was telling me the truth."

Fyve blinks, unsure what to say to that. He's just as glad to find out he has a sibling, although he certainly doesn't want to talk about Jiro. And he's shocked that Tenn still believes in Terra. What does that even mean?

She saves him from answering as she returns her focus to the pool. She kneels down, pointing. "Look, there are baby ones!"

Tenn's right. Fyve peers closer, registering the tightly knit groups of smaller pods flitting closely together. "They're breeding," he breathes.

Tenn nods vigorously. "Just like Ajax is with Cloud and Viney!" Her brow furrows as she focuses. "And they're closer to the surface here."

Fyve realizes she's right again. The group of tiny pods are all congregated above the larger ones. Not only that, they're all on this side of the pool.

He looks over his shoulder, trying to understand what

Tenn's bright mind has pointed out. "They're staying in the warmer water!" he cries out.

Tenn frowns as she pokes her finger, making the school of pods contract. "How do you know? Feels the same to me."

"The difference would be small, but the water's warmer closer to the surface," Fyve explains, excitement climbing up his spine. "And this part of the pool gets the afternoon sun." He points to the west, where the sun is now long gone. In fact, it's almost dark.

Tenn nods sagely. "Cloud said that babies like to stay warm."

Fyve blinks slowly, an idea forming in his mind. He encouraged Sevin to breed rats. The first thing she did was try to give them all the conditions they needed to do that.

Could he do the same with the pods?

Could they keep feeding the teens and outlast the Echelons in this war of attrition they've found themselves in?

He leaps to his feet and scoops Tenn up, swinging her around. "You're a genius, just like our sister and Halo!"

Tenn throws her arms out, giggling as she enjoys the impromptu ride. Fyve finds himself chuckling as he slows, suddenly wanting to see Halo and tell her the good news. This moment will be complete when he shares it with her, too.

"If I'd known there would be dancing…"

Fyve spins around, wondering if he just wished Halo into existence. She walks toward them, her pale tunic almost glowing in the growing dark. He watches her, his breath caught in his throat.

"Halo!" Tenn squeals. She runs toward her, stops, then darts back to the pool, squatting down to catch a pod. "Have one! They're gross!"

Halo's face lights up, making it even harder for Fyve to breathe. "We forgot about the pods!"

She slips the wriggling creature into her mouth, chews, and grimaces. "You're right, Tenn. They're gross."

Tenn giggles. "But they make you strong and healthy."

Halo beams. "I'm feeling better already." Yet, it's Fyve she looks at as she says the words, as if he's the true reason.

He clears his throat, wondering if pods make you emotional as well as strong. "Let's collect some for the others."

All they find is one of the jugs that were used in the Trial out on the deck, but they make short work of collecting enough pods for the teens to have two each. Fyve glances at the pool when they're done, wondering how many times they'll be able to do this before numbers get too low.

Just like on Treasure Island, how soon before they're going to have to choose being hungry now so they can eat later? And how many teens are going to be willing to do that...

Tenn looks down into the jug and the swirling mass of light inside. "The others are going to be so excited."

"Why don't you take it to them?" Fyve suggests.

Halo nods. "We need to be quick so the pods are fresh."

Tenn glances between them, straightens her shoulders as if she's just been given a quest, then spins and walks away, her hand over the top of the jug. The dark swallows her before she's reached the door, but the sound of her feet skipping down the stairs is unmistakable.

Fyve turns back to Halo, his breath catching all over again. Although they're surrounded by deep indigo, her pale tunic and blonde hair are like a beacon. A lighthouse in dark times.

One he doesn't fight the draw to.

She moves toward him in the same way he does, looking up as they stop with inches between them. "It was harder to stay away than I thought."

Fyve grins, enjoying the sweet happiness dancing through his veins. "I missed you, too."

He hadn't realized exactly how intertwined Halo is with the one emotion that's keeping him going.

Hope.

It's the fact they're together that has made it possible.

Then he realizes something else. They're most certainly together. And they're alone.

Every hour is spent with someone else. Cloud and her babies. Tenn. Iva and Dargo. Even Viney and her whining.

Yet they're here, on the deck, the night sky their only companion.

Fyve's grin fades away, a new emotion flushing through him.

Desire.

HALO

*H*alo feels the change in Fyve more than she sees it. It's like a fuse has sparked deep inside him as he closes the gap between them and presses his lips to hers.

Letting out a small groan, Halo returns his kiss, wanting this as much as he does. Maybe even more. He rakes his fingers through her hair, cupping her face with his other hand and she knows this is the moment she's been waiting for since they first met. It was like some part of her had known this was always going to happen.

"Fyve," she whispers, pulling back.

Confusion crosses his face under the dying light of the day. "I thought—"

"Shh." She presses a finger to his lips. "You thought right. I want to show you something, that's all."

He tilts his head and Halo's heart expands with everything she's feeling for this guy. He's been her best friend, her protector, her partner. But never her lover. Life had other plans for them, forcing them to fight for their survival over everything else. Until now...

Taking Fyve's hand, Halo leads him to the stern of the deck

where there's a curtain made from dozens of strings of delicate white flowers hanging from a beam. While searching the ship for food, Halo had found boxes of plastic flowers, just like the ones on the table in the engine room. The flowers that she'd thought would be romantic, if she were with the only guy she'll ever love.

Fyve pulls back the flowers and steps through the curtain, letting out a gasp as he takes in what Halo had set up.

Still holding his hand, she follows, smiling at the explosion of color that surrounds the mattress she'd hauled up here. She doesn't know the names of all the flowers, but there are large red ones on long green stems, tiny bursts of purple wrapped in tight bunches, and sprays of yellow blooms with bright orange centers. They remind her of her tree back on Treasure Island. A homage to mother nature. Not Terra, who most certainly doesn't exist, but whatever or whoever created such precious treasures of the Earth.

"You did this?" Fyve asks, trying to take in the scale of what she created. "When?"

"When you were sleeping last night," she says, feeling suddenly shy. "Do you like it?"

He shakes his head. "I love it, Halo. It's the nicest thing anyone has ever done for me."

Tears sting her eyes as she wishes that wasn't true. Fyve should have wonderful things done for him every day of his life. He gives so much and never asks for a single thing in return.

"And you still let me come up here with Tenn?" He gives her a smile. "If I'd known..."

"Your time with her is important," says Halo. "Besides, it gave me time to organize for Cloud to keep her distracted."

"Halo!" Fyve laughs, although he doesn't seem at all displeased. Nor had Cloud, who'd looked confused when Halo had first asked for what she needed from her. Then she'd given

140

Halo a knowing smile, perhaps remembering how Ajax had made her feel in a time long ago.

The ship is rocked by a wave and Halo wobbles.

Fyve immediately pulls her down to the mattress. She giggles as they fall and he lies beside her, his chest pressed firmly against her side.

"Sorry, that was just a precaution." He runs a finger down her cheek. "I didn't want you to get hurt."

She nods, glad there's still just enough light in the sky for her to look into the depth of his eyes. "We can't be too careful."

The movement of his hand freezes and they stare at each other for long moments, the anticipation of what's to come hovering between them.

"I love you, Halo," he says. "Sometimes, I feel like I loved you before I was even born."

A smile lights her face and he bites his lip.

"Too cheesy?" he asks.

"Not cheesy enough," she says, closing the gap between them and showing him, rather than telling him, that she loves him, too. It's in the way she kisses him with so much more than just her lips. It's with every ounce of her being as her tongue darts forward, and he meets her with the same all-consuming passion that quickly evades all sense and reason.

Fyve slips his hand up Halo's tunic and now it's skin on skin. Her back arches as if it has a mind of its own as he slides the warmth of his palm across her bare stomach, sending warm shivers tingling down her spine.

Quickly undoing her tunic, she shrugs out of it, then slides out of the cropped singlet she wears for support. She knows she should feel exposed, yet somehow underneath the stars that are blinking into the night sky, it's like she's at home. All the feelings of missing Treasure Island vanish and she knows for certain it doesn't matter where she is in the world, just as long as she's with Fyve.

"You're so beautiful," he says, running his hand across her breasts, pausing at the racing of her heart.

The desire to feel more of him burns at her and she undoes his tunic. Helping her to remove it, he lies on top of her, supporting his weight with his elbows as he presses his bare chest against hers. She runs her fingertips across his back, reveling in the exquisite luxury of the moment.

Alone. At last. With Fyve.

His kisses become more desperate, his breathing more ragged, and she wraps her legs around him, wanting him closer. But there's still too much fabric between them and she groans in frustration.

"Are you sure you want this?" he asks, pulling back, the separation seeming to cause him pain.

"I want you," she replies, wriggling out of her trousers.

In a few frenzied motions, he's lying beside her again, stripped of his clothes, his entire soul bared to her. It feels so right that it almost feels wrong. That anyone could be this perfect. This pure. This…hot!

Feeling like a flame thrower has been set alight inside her, Halo gets to her knees and sits across Fyve. They make love with true abandon. Like two people who could die at any moment. Like two people who *have* almost died in many moments. But that moment isn't now. Right now, they're alive. Their hearts and minds are both completely free, yet totally consumed by each other as they move as one.

The Oasis is drawn by the current, and as it slices through the water, mounting the cresting waves, Halo feels tears rolling down her face.

Letting out a gasp of surprise when a current of a completely different kind rolls through her body, she leans forward to hold Fyve close, and he lets out a moan that she wants to hear every day for however long she can continue to pull air into her lungs.

They hold each other tight, their breathing coming in sharp

gasps as they try to regain their senses while savoring every one of these precious moments. That was undoubtedly one of the happiest moments of Halo's life and she wants to hold onto it as long as she can.

Life aboard this ship has been cruel. So much that she'd begun to think life wasn't fair. But that's no longer true.

Because she has Fyve and all the good things that come with being close to someone like him. He's shown her that there's true beauty left in this world. Not an imitation like the flowers they're surrounded by, but the real thing. Fyve is everything that's kindness, strength, loyalty and love. And somehow, she's the one he chose to share all that with, which makes her the luckiest person left in the world. If Tomorrow Land exists, she'll spend all her tomorrows caring for this most incredible of humans.

"What are you thinking?" he asks, resting his hands on her hips.

"That I love you, too," she says, needing him to hear it as well as feel it.

"Come and lie next to me," he says, taking her hand and bringing it to his lips. "I need to tell you something."

She nestles down beside him, feeling safe in the crook of his arm, no matter what it is he has to tell her. She trusts him more than she's ever trusted anyone. There's nothing he could say that would ever change that.

"What is it?" she asks.

"I want you to know that I'm glad you didn't tell me." His voice cracks with emotion. "About Sevin, I mean. I'm glad I got on this ship, even if it meant leaving her behind."

Halo's eyes open in the darkness and she rests a hand on his chest, waiting for him to continue.

"Sevin's going to be okay," he says. "She's already okay. I know that. I've seen it with my own eyes. She still loves me, but she doesn't need me anymore. Tenn does. I had to be on The

Oasis so I could look after her. And I can do that now because of you. What would have happened to her if I wasn't here?"

Halo lets out a long breath, feeling tension she hadn't known she was storing slide from her body. No more guilt. No more regret. Fyve doesn't just forgive her, he's *happy* about what she did.

"But it's more than that," says Fyve. "I needed to be here for Tenn, but if I'm honest, I needed to be here for me, too."

"You did?" Halo asks softly.

"I need you, Halo." He presses his lips to her forehead. "I need you like I need air. I'd have died without you back on Treasure Island. I'd only have ever been half the person that I am when I'm with you. Is that selfish of me to admit?"

"No." Halo reaches for his beautiful face and holds it. "No. Because I need you, too. Maybe that's part of the reason I couldn't tell you about Sevin. I don't want a life if it's without you."

Fyve kisses her, tenderly this time, the passion that was all-pervasive still present but muted for now. This is a kiss of nothing more than the purest form of love.

And she's here for it.

A sound has them jumping back from each other as their eyes open wide in the starlight. It hums and roars and a vibration in the deck picks up in response.

"It's the engines." Halo sits up. "The Echelons have started the engines."

"What does that mean?" asks Fyve.

Halo gets to her feet and reaches for her tunic. "I have absolutely no idea."

FYVE

*F*yve and Halo are dressed and running toward the door that will take them into The Oasis before he's even really processed what Halo just said.

The Echelons have started the engines.

Although the truth of that statement is undeniable in the faint hum he'd barely noticed until it was abruptly gone, it's the why that's deeply disturbing.

The Echelons haven't conceded defeat, Fyve can guarantee it. That leaves the reason The Oasis is moving once more a mystery.

And he's had enough of questions without answers. Of phenomena that have no explanation.

They're clattering down the first set of stairs when Justice almost careens into them. "There you are," she gasps in relief. "We're moving again!"

"We noticed," Fyve says. "Any idea why?"

Justice draws in deep breaths, suggesting she ran the whole way here from the wheelhouse. "We were hoping you'd be able to answer that."

Fyve and Halo glance at each other. It's odd to know that less than ten minutes ago they were in each other's arms. The moment was fated. A gift. Even if it was short-lived.

Because although nothing's changed, everything has. Halo's his. And he's hers. In every way possible.

Which means although so much is wrong right now...

There's a rightness inside of him he knows will be there as long as Halo is beside him, looking at him like that. Their hands gravitate toward each other, their fingers intertwining. They turn back to Justice.

"We don't know what's going on," Halo says.

"But we're going to find out," Fyve finishes.

Justice nods. "Tell me what needs to be done and I'll do it."

Fyve's tempted to hug the strong, determined girl pledging her unconditional support. "Once we find out what the Echelons are up to, we'll act."

They make their way back to the wheelhouse in silence. Fyve grips Halo's hand the whole way, trying to hold on to the last threads of their time up on the deck. Who knows when they'll be able to capture that magic again.

Inside the wheelhouse, Tenn quickly slips to his side. She doesn't say a word. Doesn't smile. It means even at her age, she knows this new development can't be celebrated. Not yet.

The others leap to their feet the moment they enter. They anxiously study Fyve and Halo's faces, trying to understand whether the ship slicing through the water once more is a good thing or not.

Fyve wishes he could give them an answer.

Abe points to the window, even though there's nothing but night beyond. "We're moving," he says, stating the obvious. "The Echelons have decided to give us what we want."

Fyve glances at Justice. She's the one coordinating the watch schedule keeping an eye on the door to the engine room. "Have they left?"

She shakes her head. "The door hasn't moved. No one's been in or out."

Halo frowns. "That doesn't make sense. They wouldn't do something for nothing."

Abe shrugs, but before he can speak, the ship tips sharply to the right. He moves back to the controls, sitting in the large chair before them. "Storm's coming," he grunts.

"But we were just up on the deck," says Fyve. "It was fine."

"They can come fast out at sea." Abe adjusts a lever, then presses a button. "Can be damned ferocious, too."

The Oasis rocks again and a few of the teens reach out to each other to steady themselves.

"Won't be nothing to worry about," Abe assures them. "Just Terra showin' us who's boss."

Fyve nods, opting to ignore the reference to Terra again. How could two people like Abe and Tenn, who know Terra was nothing but a lie, still talk about her like she exists? As if she's real?

As if to corroborate Abe's words, lightning slices through the sky, briefly illuminating an ocean now forged from angry hills and turbulent valleys. The thunder that follows is muted by the walls and windows of The Oasis, but the power behind it is undeniable. The energy waiting to be unleashed is coming.

"Can you think of why the Echelons are doing this, Abe?" Halo asks.

"The bastards never shared a thing with us Ravens." The old man shrugs again. "Maybe they know they're beat."

"You're kidding, right?" Justice demands. "They've been planning this for decades, and they're just gonna give up? I'll lose what little respect I have for them if they do."

Fyve walks to the corner of the room where Iva is kneeling over an unconscious Dargo. "Has he said anything?" he asks softly. Dargo's the only other one who might have some idea of why the Echelons have done this.

She shakes her head. "No." Then lifts her chin. "But he will," she says, her voice hardening. "The pods are just what he needed."

Fyve squeezes her shoulder, admiring her tenaciousness. He'd be exactly the same with Halo.

Viney steps forward. "Surely this is a good thing? We're heading home!" Yet the fact her first statement is a question, and that she's wringing her hands, conveys that even the girl who only sees what she wants to see isn't so sure.

And yet, she has a point.

"Viney's right," says Fyve. "We don't know why, but we're heading in the right direction." He tightens his grip on Halo's hand and pulls Tenn a little closer. "We're heading home."

The teens look between one another, and Fyve can almost see the hope kindling in the spaces between them. A fragile, intangible emotion trying to gain life.

Halo nods firmly. "Every second, we're moving that little bit closer to Treasure Island."

A few people let out a breath, then smile. Iva leans over Dargo and presses a kiss to his bandaged forehead. "Did you hear that, Dargo? Home."

The door to the wheelhouse slides open, sending a ripple of alarm through the room. Fyve and Halo leap into action, Justice right behind them. In the excitement and birth of so many more questions, they forgot to stand guard.

But it's Ajax who saunters through the door, thumbs hooked into the band of his trousers. He jolts when he sees three bodies careening toward him, scrabbling to come to a stop. "Whoa, guys. I'm with you, remember?"

Justice takes a few steps back, crossing her arms. "Well, you haven't been for a few days now."

Whatever Ajax was going to say is cut off by Viney's squeal. She rushes past Justice and almost knocks over Halo as she catapults into Ajax. He lets out an "oomph," but quickly catches her.

"Ajax!" she cries, peppering his face with kisses. "I knew you'd come back."

He grins. "At least someone believes in me."

"I'm pregnant," Viney blurts. "We're going to have a baby!"

"Wow," he says, clearly shocked, even though he shouldn't be. He'd already impregnated Cloud by the time he moved onto Viney. He knew the consequences of his actions.

Fyve stills. He and Halo...just engaged in the same actions. He hadn't considered there could be...consequences.

Ajax clears his throat. "That's, ah, great news, Viney."

"I knew you'd be happy," she beams. "We're going to be a family."

The sound of someone clearing their throat has Fyve and the others turning. Cloud steps forward, cradling Marvel and Miracle in her arms. "Have you forgotten you already have a family, Ajax?"

Viney steps in front of him protectively. "He never loved you. Not in the way he loves me." She drops her chin, scowling. "You probably got pregnant so you could trap him."

Halo gasps in indignation. "Viney!"

Ajax steps around the second mother of his child, shaking his head good naturedly. "Viney," he chides. "There's no reason we can't all get along. Like one big happy family."

Fyve almost does a double take. Did Ajax just suggest what he thinks he did?

Cloud snorts. "You're a father to my children and nothing else." She looks to Viney. "He's all yours."

For the first time, Viney looks uncertain. She glances from Cloud to the babies she's cradling, to Ajax, and then to her stomach. She blinks, and Fyve wonders what she's thinking.

That Ajax is as reliable as the weather?

That he could leave her as quickly as he did Cloud, and then try to convince everyone they all just need to get along?

That maybe she, too, needs to put some boundaries in place or Ajax is going to walk all over her?

Viney wraps an arm around her flat belly, looks up at Ajax, and beams. "One big happy family."

Ajax chuckles, placing what's probably supposed to be a tender kiss on her forehead, but just looks condescending. "I always said you were smart."

Cloud snorts again and turns away. "Your only job is to be a good father."

She takes a step, only to stumble as the ship angles sharply. Two teens leap to steady her and she smiles at them gratefully. Cloud takes a few more steps, then sinks to the floor beside a stand of more buttons and levers, tucking the twins in close.

Tenn looks up at Fyve and he nods, knowing what she's asking. She darts over to Cloud, offering to take one of the babies, and Fyve's surprised when Cloud agrees. Tenn tucks in close to her as they each settle an infant in their lap. Seems Cloud's more comfortable trusting a child than some of the teens or adults on this ship.

Halo turns to her brother. "Where have you been, Ajax?"

He puffs out his chest. "Negotiating."

Fyve doesn't like the sound of that. "What do you mean, negotiating?"

"Exactly that," Ajax says, flicking a superior glance. "Rhina listens to me."

Justice scowls as she tightens her crossed arms. "She's one of them."

"But she cares," Ajax shoots back. "I told her what we want to do and why. That returning to Treasure Island is the best thing for all of us."

The moment the words are out Ajax's mouth, Fyve doubts

them, even though he's reached the same conclusion himself. Is it because he instinctively rejects anything Ajax says?

Or because returning to Treasure Island isn't the solution he's hoping it is...

Ajax looks around the room. "And the engines are working again. The Echelons listened. They're taking us back home."

A low murmur filters through the wheelhouse as Fyve shifts uneasily. There's no way it's that simple. Especially when the Echelons have remained hidden in the engine room.

Halo shakes her head. "Why?" She pins her brother with a glare. "Why did they agree to do this for us?"

Ajax rolls his eyes. "Why can't you just congratulate me? I got us what we want, didn't I?"

"Maybe. Maybe not." Halo steps closer, her eyes narrowing as she watches him closely. "But did you ask Rhina what's in it for them? Because the Echelons haven't done this out of the goodness of their hearts."

Ajax scowls at his sister. "Is this because you're threatened? Is that what this is? You and Fyve have been all, 'we'll save everyone,' and now that someone else is actually doing that, you don't like it."

Halo's hands clench into fists. "You know that's not it, Ajax."

Fyve steps beside her, not liking what her own brother is insinuating. "We agreed we wouldn't make any moves until we know what we're dealing with."

"You made that call," Ajax spits. "And while you sat around pretending to come up with a plan, I acted. And got results."

Fyve grits his teeth, understanding why Halo's hands are tight fists. The need to punch that haughty expression off Ajax's face is overwhelming.

Ajax must register the danger because he takes a step back. Once there's a little more distance, he lifts his chin. "I'm going to go see my babies."

Taking a wide berth, he makes his way to Cloud. Viney takes

a hesitant step toward him, but Ajax imperceptibly shakes his head. Her shoulders droop, but she does as she's asked.

He's only a few steps from Cloud when she sits up suddenly. The next instant, she's leaning away from Tenn and retching all over the floor. Ajax blanches, smoothly changing direction, indicating to Viney to come to him. She does so more than willingly, avoiding looking at Cloud as she passes her.

Fyve and Halo rush to the young mother, Fyve picking up one of the cloths they use for the babies along the way.

"Cloud," Halo asks, concerned. "What's wrong?"

Cloud blinks at the small puddle on the floor. The contents of her stomach aren't much. Two pods. But it means the nutrition they could've provided her has just been lost.

She sits up, wiping her hand across her mouth. "Sorry. It's all the rocking of the ship. One of the reasons Elijah hid me so easily in the beginning is that I was too sick to move." She smiles faintly. "He was so worried about the babies."

Fyve smiles reassuringly, even though he knows how Elijah felt. Cloud needed those pods.

Tenn rubs Cloud's back, her face earnest. "Does that help?"

Cloud's smile gains a little more life. "Yes, thank you," she says, her pale face suggesting otherwise.

The sound of gagging somewhere else in the wheelhouse jolts Fyve into action. He makes quick work of wiping up the vomit, conscious that if anyone's feeling the same way as Cloud, then this smell isn't going to help.

"I'll wash this out," he tells Halo. "I'll be back."

She nods, her face tight. "Maybe grab a few more sheets while you're there."

Cloud doubles over again, retching even though nothing comes up. Tenn moves with her, rubbing her back more vigorously as she murmurs encouragement. It's as if she grew up with far too many siblings and is used to this, just like Fyve did.

He wonders if she knows this could only be the beginning.

Fyve exchanges a look with Halo. They might have a long night ahead of them.

Striding quickly to the door, he leaves the wheelhouse, already thinking of the closest cabins that may have sheets in them. Otherwise, he'll go to the dining room and use some of the curtains. The thought gives him a small burst of pleasure.

Once he's finished washing out the cloth at a nearby basin, Fyve means to go as far as a cabin, but he finds himself drawn back to the deck. Maybe he wonders if he should scoop two more pods out for Cloud. Maybe he wouldn't mind a breath of fresh air before returning to the wheelhouse.

Maybe he's already missing the stolen moments with Halo.

The moment the door slides open, the storm hits him like a wall. Wind rips at his clothes while rain pelts at his skin. Fyve lifts his arm to protect his face, realizing he won't be collecting any pods. Or getting fresh air. As the ship tilts wildly, he steps back, preparing to return to safety.

Something slaps against his shoulder and Fyve realizes it's one of the flowers that Halo had arranged to create their beautiful escape. He narrows his eyes against the droplets that feel like needles, then draws in a sharp breath.

More flowers are now scattered across the deck, tumbling and tattered. As Fyve watches, a handful are lifted by a gust of wind and thrown overboard. Blown into the acidic sea, where their colors will dissolve, their petals will disintegrate.

He steps back and slams the door shut. Shaking off the water, Fyve tries to do the same with the cold that doesn't belong in his veins.

Mother Nature is telling them something.

It feels like a warning.

An ominous one.

HALO

*H*alo paces the wheelhouse, her eyes fixed on Miracle, who's sleeping in her arms. The lighting is dim, casting an eerie glow across the room. Tenn is sitting in a corner, cradling Marvel. They're trying to give Cloud a chance to rest after vomiting up the little food she had in her belly. She's stopped being sick now, but there's still the sound of retching punctuating the roar of the wind as someone else falls victim to the incessant movement of the angry sea.

Miracle's eyebrows contract as the ship lurches again, but her eyelids remain closed. Halo's no expert when it comes to infants but she's certain babies should start to become more curious about the world around them, not less. Lately, the twins wake and cry for milk, then fuss at Cloud's breast until they fall asleep again. Cloud has been making sure she stays hydrated—thankfully the Echelons haven't cut off their water supply—but the lack of food is starting to take its toll. The rest of them can survive for weeks, if necessary, but the babies will rapidly decline if Cloud's milk dries up.

"You have to be strong," Halo tells her niece, leaning forward to kiss her forehead. "You can do this."

Fyve is taking a long time to return with more towels and Halo suspects he's gone up to the deck to check on the welfare of their only remaining food source. She does her best not to worry, even though a hundred possible scenarios are running through her mind. Fyve being ambushed in a corridor by Nole. Fyve being thrown overboard by one of the giant waves that are sending the ship wildly swaying. Fyve accidentally breaking the vial of poison she knows he's still carrying and the liquid seeping into his skin. Fyve being blown over and knocking his head on the edge of the pool and drowning...

"I'm getting a message!" Ajax announces, leaping to his feet and pressing his index finger to his temple. He's the only teen who elected to keep his chip, insisting it might be useful. Halo suspects it makes him feel special. The son of the great Elijah, getting messages that nobody else can hear.

Halo watches a flush rise to Ajax's cheeks and suspects she knows exactly which Echelon is delivering the message.

"It's Rhina." Ajax puffs out his chest. "The Echelons want to know if we need any food. They have plenty to share."

"What's the catch?" Halo's stomach groans even though she's certain she won't be eating anytime soon.

"We're starving!" says one of the teens, rising to her feet. "Tell them I'll be their Treasure if they feed me."

"Caddie!" The girl beside her pulls her back down to the floor. "You don't mean that."

"I do," Caddie moans, holding her stomach. "I really do."

Ajax holds up his palm. "If we agree to comply with their wishes, they'll give us food."

"What are their wishes?" growls Sica, cracking her knuckles. "Because so far, the wishes I've heard from them aren't exactly appealing."

"They want their Treasures," says Ajax. "And the two Ravens. For each person who surrenders themselves, they'll give us twelve cans of food."

Halo glances to the door, wishing Fyve were here, but also glad he isn't. This request would make him furious. Especially because it's one she knows she has to consider. Twelve cans of food would be enough to restore Cloud to health. She looks down at Miracle. Twelve cans of food would be enough to save this precious child's life, along with her equally as precious brother.

"I'll do it," says Halo, hating what she's saying the moment the words leave her lips.

"You mean you don't want to have a vote this time?" Ajax arches a brow. "It's not like you to make a decision without asking everyone else first what they think."

"This decision is different." Halo glares at her brother. "It only impacts me. The other Treasures can decide something different if they prefer. And I have the potential to save the babies. Which is why I'll only do it if the food goes to Cloud."

"You can't do that!" Viney wails. "That's not fair. I have a baby to think of, too."

"Dargo also needs the sustenance," Iva says a little more quietly. Dargo is still sleeping with his head resting on her lap. "With a little food, I'm sure he'd improve."

For the first time, Halo's not too sure. Shouldn't Dargo have woken by now? In fact, he looks more pale and lifeless than when he arrived.

"Then Dargo can go back," says Caddie. "He'll get fed and we'll get twelve cans of food to share."

"He can't go back," snaps Iva. "Look at him. He's far too weak."

He looks more than weak to Halo...

"Why do you even trust them?" Justice steps forward and plants her hands on her hips as she glares at Halo. "I can't believe you think they'd actually keep their end of the deal and give us the food. Nobody's going back. Our power comes from our numbers. They're trying to divide us to weaken us."

"I'm so weak already," says Viney. "I'm supposed to be eating for two."

"Then Ajax should go back," says Halo. "He's a Treasure."

"They didn't mean me," Ajax says quickly. "I don't count."

"Why not?" Iva tilts her head at him.

Justice rolls her eyes. "Because Rhina knows her Treasure will go running back to her the minute she clicks her fingers. Or wiggles her hips."

"How dare you!" Viney marches to Justice and jams a finger into her chest. "Ajax has been negotiating with the Echelons at great personal danger to himself and that's the gratitude you give him?"

Justice steps back. "I had enough Gratitude back on Treasure Island. And Terra's concern for us was about as real as Ajax's is."

"They might be telling the truth," Halo says, knowing she has to take that chance if the babies are going to survive. "I'll take the deal, but the food goes to Cloud. The rest of us can survive a bit longer. The babies can't."

"Nobody is returning to the Echelons," says Sica, coming to stand beside Justice. "If they see that they can divide us over a few cans of food, we lose all power."

"Twelve is more than a few cans," Caddie points out. "Please, tell them yes, Ajax. Halo said she'd go."

"I can't tell them anything." Ajax crosses his arms. "Not since Fyve destroyed the cameras and speakers."

"We all agreed to do that," Halo reminds them. "And my twelve cans go to Cloud or it's no deal."

"They won't give you food," says Sica. "Justice is right."

"We don't know that." Halo looks down to see Tenn standing beside her. Marvel is held carefully to her chest and she has tears welling in her eyes.

"Nole will hurt you, Halo," she says. "I don't want you to go."

"Nor do I. But Cloud needs food," says Halo, not wanting to go. "For the babies."

"You should talk to Fyve," says Tenn. "He'll know what to do."

"Okay." Halo sighs. "I'll hold my decision until I've talked to Fyve." She already knows what he'll say. Which is likely exactly why Tenn is suggesting she talks to him. And as much as she doesn't want to tell him what she knows she must do, she has to. Especially after everything that passed between them the night before. She can't leave him without saying goodbye. If she can find the right words, surely he'll understand. He loves those babies, too.

"I'll go back," says Abe, standing from the ship's wheel.

"No!" several of them say at once, as the ship bucks up over a wave.

"We need you to steer us home," says Halo. "You're the only one who knows how to do that."

Abe sinks back into his chair and looks ahead at the dark ocean that stretches before them. "The offer's there if you want it. You people sure do look hungry. Twelve cans of food would go some way between you."

"You think we should send back the Treasures?" Ajax asks.

Abe continues to look ahead. "Don't matter what I think. It's just that soon you won't have any Treasures left to send back. I didn't bust my way out of there, only to starve to death."

Caddie and Viney wail in unison.

"How long until we get back?" Halo asks.

Abe shrugs. "Longer than we'll survive without food."

"We have the pods," says Tenn, scowling at Abe. "They're breeding. Fyve and I saw them. You're just trying to scare us."

Halo frowns, deciding she really needs to ask Tenn about her odd reaction to Abe.

Marvel lets out a cry in Tenn's arms and Cloud sits up and rubs at her eyes. "My babies."

"They're fine," says Halo, hurrying to her.

Cloud reaches out her arms and Tenn hands her Marvel while Halo settles Miracle in her basket.

"Nobody makes any final decisions until we're all here," Halo says to the rest of the room. "That includes me. Understood?"

There's a round of reluctant nods and the ship lurches to one side, sending them all wobbling.

"Tenn and I will find Fyve," Halo says. "We need the food. The Echelons need to divide us. We can come up with a way to outsmart them.

Dargo lets out a groan and struggles against Iva to sit up. Halo notices he's wearing his leather bracelet again.

"Shh," hushes Iva. "Don't try to move. You're injured."

But Dargo manages to sit up and scans the room as he tries to get his bearings. His gaze falls on one person, then his eyes widen.

Abe.

"Him!" Dargo gasps.

"You're safe," says Abe soothingly, even smiling. "You got away."

Iva wraps a protective arm around Dargo, frowning.

"He thinks he's still being held prisoner when he sees me," says Abe, his face full of pity. He turns back to the wheel and steers the ship over another giant wave before pressing a few buttons on the controls.

"You're safe, Dargo," says Iva. "Abe's helping us. You're back with me."

Dargo looks around, bewildered.

"Hold onto something!" calls Abe. "This will be a big one."

The ship rears up and the wheelhouse plunges into darkness. Tenn's arms wrap tightly around Halo's waist and she braces herself, feeling the rush of people moving around her as everyone scrambles for something to hold. The Oasis crashes back down with teeth-jarring intensity.

"I don't like the dark," Tenn sobs.

TAMAR SLOAN & HEIDI CATHERINE

"We're okay," says Halo, putting one hand on her back and using the other to grip the wall. "It will be morning soon."

There's the sound of scuffling, a few cries of alarm, but they remain plunged in darkness. Long moments pass as Halo wonders what they should do now. She's about to go after Fyve when the dim glow of the lighting returns, and Halo blinks in her surroundings.

"There we go!" Abe turns the wheel with a satisfied smile. "Power's back on. Worst of the storm is passing now."

"Dargo!" Iva is stroking his cheek and trying to rouse him. "Dargo, wake up!"

But he's deeply asleep once more.

"Give him time, Iva," says Halo, hoping her next words aren't a hollow lie. "He'll be okay."

Iva nods, her eyes spilling over with tears.

"Let's find Fyve," says Tenn, edging away from Abe.

"Sure." Halo leads Tenn from the room, and they head straight up the stairwell that leads to the deck.

"He was getting towels," says Tenn, looking confused.

"He was," says Halo. "But there's a lot you have to learn about your big brother. I'm betting he got distracted by something else."

"Like the pods," says Tenn. "Do you think he's making sure they're safe?"

Halo nods. "That's right. He knows they're our only food source for now."

"Don't go back to Nole," says Tenn, avoiding Halo's eye. "He'll hurt you."

"Tenn, can I ask you something?" she says carefully.

The small girl nods.

"Why don't you like Abe?"

Tenn's eyes widen and she looks away, continuing to climb the stairs. "I don't trust the Ravens."

160

"But Dargo's a Raven," says Halo. "And I know for certain he's good."

Tenn shakes her head. "Not if he'd stayed a Raven. They all turn bad eventually."

"Abe saved me from Nole," says Halo. "And he turned the ship around. He even offered to go back to the Echelons so we could have a meal."

Tenn shrugs this evidence away.

"Has Abe hurt you, Tenn?" Halo turns the small girl to face her, pausing on the stairs. "I need to know if he's hurt you."

She shakes her head.

"Then what is it?" Halo implores.

"He didn't stop Nole," she whispers, looking down at her feet. "He saved you from Nole, but he never saved me."

"Maybe he couldn't." Halo pulls Tenn close to her. "But nobody will hurt you ever again."

Tenn breaks away and continues up the stairs. "Let's find Fyve."

With her heart breaking, Halo follows. She doesn't know what happened to Tenn. She may never know. But she does know she's going to keep her promise. Nobody will ever hurt that little girl again.

The door to the deck opens and a blast of cool air buffets them. Halo scans the deck, desperately searching for Fyve. The sky is an eerie violet as the sun begins to rise and it casts the deck in an ominous glow.

"Stay close to me," Halo calls over the sound of the dying wind as she takes Tenn's hand.

"There!" Tenn points ahead. "He put a net across the pool."

Halo shivers, remembering when she'd been caught in that same net during the Trials. By her own brother, no less.

Tenn lets go of Halo's hand and runs ahead. The ship has stopped lurching so wildly, but Halo runs after her anyway. She's just as keen to see Fyve as his little sister is.

Fyve looks up from where he's fastening a corner of the net. He doesn't look happy to see them. "What are you doing up here? It's dangerous."

Halo rolls her eyes. "Not too dangerous for you, I notice."

The ship rocks to one side and Halo and Tenn instinctively crouch down, holding onto the side of the net for balance.

"I had to save the pods," says Fyve. "The plankton was about to blow right out. Without their food source, they'd all have died."

"Abe says the worst of the storm is over," Halo tells him, as she fixes part of the net that was starting to pull away.

Fyve nods, seeming relieved. The water in the pool is already down to about halfway. "If he's right, we might just have saved these little guys."

Halo notices he uses the word *we* when it was clearly all him. She bites down on her lip, not looking forward to telling him about the Echelons' offer.

"Halo wants to go back to Nole," Tenn blurts out. "Tell her not to."

Fyve looks up in alarm, letting go of the net to shuffle closer to Halo until he's sitting right in front of her with his small accomplice beside him.

"What's she talking about?" He narrows his eyes.

Halo hesitates. The morning sun is rising faster now, bathing Fyve in soft light that's making his skin glow. She looks at his lips, wishing she could kiss him, rather than talk to him. Maybe she can tell Nole she's pregnant, which would mean he'd have no use for her at all. Maybe she *is* pregnant... That's not an altogether horrible idea. Although, right now she's having enough trouble keeping her niece and nephew alive, let alone a child of her own.

"Halo!" Fyve puts a hand on her arm. "What's Tenn talking about? Why does she think you're going back to Nole?"

162

"It's the babies," Halo says. "They're not doing well. Cloud's milk is running out. She needs food."

"And you think Nole's just going to give you some food if you ask him nicely?" Fyve lets out a loud huff.

"The Echelons offered us a deal," she says. "Twelve cans of food for each Treasure who surrenders. I offered to go, as long as Cloud gets the food."

"Nobody liked that idea very much," Tenn adds.

Halo shoots Tenn a stern look.

"What makes you think they'd even hand over the food?" Fyve asks.

"That's exactly what Justice said." Tenn nods.

"Enough of the special comments," says Halo through gritted teeth. "Please let me handle this."

"There's nothing to handle," says Fyve. "You're not going back to Nole. There has to be another way. If they've offered us a deal, it means they're getting desperate."

"They could just be bored," says Tenn. "They like to play games when they're bored."

Halo's jaw drops. "Is that what the Trials were about?"

Tenn shrugs. "Partly. They were making bets over who would win each Trial. Cheering when their favorites won. And also when people lost."

A bitter taste lodges in the back of Halo's throat to know that includes Coal.

"You think this deal is another game?" asks Halo. "That they're placing bets if we'll take it or not?"

Tenn nods solemnly.

Fyve tenses up. "They can't keep playing with us like this! Not if we refuse to play."

"Except..." Tears well in Halo's eyes. "Except, they don't care about the babies. We have to do something soon to bring back Cloud's milk. I can't think of anything else."

"We'll give her extra pods," says Fyve, looking down into the pool as the morning sun breaks through the clouds. "The storm's passing now. She'll keep her food down this time. She can have my share. I'm not even hun..."

Fyve's brow furrows and Halo follows his gaze to see what's distracted him.

"What is it?" she asks.

Fyve looks to the sky then back down at the pool again, like he can't quite believe what he's seeing.

"Tenn..." He looks to his sister. "Do you remember where the pods were swimming when we were watching them last night?"

Tenn bounces to her feet and points to the same place the pods are congregating now, as they bask in the morning sun. "They like this spot the best."

Fyve shakes his head. "They like the warmth. And this is the part of the pool that was getting the afternoon sun yesterday. So why—"

"Why is it getting the morning sun?" Halo finishes as she looks across at Fyve in alarm.

"We're not heading home," says Fyve, getting to his feet. "We're going the wrong way."

Halo lets out a small gasp as she realizes Tenn's reservations about the old Raven were for good reason.

In the distraction of the storm, the ship has been turned around.

FYVE

*F*ury throbs through Fyve, feeling like it starts somewhere deep in his marrow.

Abe has been working for the Echelons all along.

And they're using what little fuel they have to find something that doesn't exist.

"I feel like such a fool," Halo gasps. "I should never have trusted him."

Her words are what finally snap Fyve's fragile thread of self-control. Halo should never feel guilty for trusting. Or stupid for believing a slave to the Echelons would want to be saved.

"Enough," Fyve growls.

He spins on his heel and strides toward the door, a thin ray of light breaking through the clouds and hitting the deck from the opposite side it should be. The unfettered fury explodes into rage, fueled by this final betrayal.

The manipulation that never stopped.

The undermining of Halo.

The knowledge that they may never see Treasure Island again.

"Fyve!" Halo gasps, running to catch up with him. "What are you going to do?"

"Try not to kill him," he snarls over his shoulder.

He takes the stairs two at a time, the corridors a blur in the red haze that's clouding his vision.

"Fyve!" Halo calls, but he doesn't respond. Nor does she try again.

She either knows Abe needs to be held accountable.

Or that Fyve won't be stopped. That he meant what he said.

Enough.

He storms through the door the moment it slides enough for him to fit, finding Abe where he's been since they reached the wheelhouse—at the controls of this ship.

The Raven always intended on turning them around. Nole's probably been speaking to him the whole time.

Abe glances over his shoulder, his eyebrows flutter, then his face clears. If Fyve wasn't so full of rage, if the truth wasn't so blinding in its pain, he would've missed the fleeting hesitation.

But he didn't.

Because now he knows.

"Why have you turned the ship around?" he shouts.

Every teen in the wheelhouse stills. A few draw in sharp breaths. One of the babies lets out a weak cry.

Abe shakes his head. "I would never do that."

Fyve points out the window, his arm trembling with the blazing emotion that's taken over his body. "Then why are we heading north? Treasure Island is south."

Gazes dart to the windows. Eyes widen as the teens register he's telling the truth.

"No," Ajax gasps. "Rhina promised me they were taking us back."

Fyve ignores him. Resisting the urge to form his hands into fists, he takes a step closer. "Why, Abe?" he demands.

From the corner of his eye, he sees Tenn cross her arms.

She's the only one who doesn't look surprised. She scowls as she waits for this to unfold. Possibly looking forward to it.

Abe slides off the seat he's barely left. "Because I owe everything to the Echelons."

The words are so unexpected that Fyve's fury abates for a second. He'd assumed Abe was doing this under duress. That his life was under threat.

The old man lifts his chin proudly. "Nole took me in. Fed me. Gifted me the honor of being the one to care for his every need. Without him, I'd be dead, like the rest of my foolish family."

"He's serious," Halo says, clearly just as shocked.

"Of course, you wouldn't understand," Abe growls. "You haven't seen the Outlands. Treasure Island is the land of plenty compared to what we have there."

"All the more reason to go back," Fyve snaps. He jabs a finger at the control. "Turn us around."

Abe takes a step away from the controls, his hard, cold gaze scanning the teens. "You ungrateful, selfish children."

"Is that what Nole told you?" Halo demands, and Fyve finds she's beside him. "No doubt enough times for you to believe it."

Abe curls his lip. "I can't believe I hurt the man who's cared for me all these years, just so I could convince you to trust me." His lip climbs high enough to flash yellowed teeth. "When you're stupid enough to have trusted me, anyway."

Halo's flinch is like a switch. It breaks the flimsy dam that was containing Fyve's anger. He leaps forward, hands finally forming the fists they've been thirsting to. Abe has no intention of turning them around.

The old man's eyes flare when he registers the intent on Fyve's face, his wiry body launching to meet his opponent. He swipes a calloused fist the moment Fyve is within reach, but he was expecting that. He won't be underestimating Abe like he did Zake.

If Abe grew up in the Outlands, his early years may have been just as violent.

Fyve ducks and a whoosh of air slices above him. The moment it's passed, he powers back up, slamming his fist into Abe's gut. The old man grunts as he curves from the impact, but it doesn't stop his momentum.

It barely even slows it.

He brings his arms down, slamming the hard bones of his forearms onto Fyve's shoulders, the blow bringing him to his knees. They've just touched the floor when Abe's knee smashes in Fyve's face, exploding agony through his skull.

"Fyve!" Halo cries out.

He staggers to his feet, the pain growing exponentially, but so does his fury. Abe's not doing anything the Echelons haven't done from the beginning.

Trying to beat him down.

Batter his spirit.

Get him to break.

He runs at the Raven, the blood streaming down his face dotting the air as he bellows a roar. Abe's eyes widen, suggesting he hadn't expected Fyve to come back for more. It's all the opening he needs.

He slams into Abe, propelling him backward until he crashes into the chair he commandeered with a groan. The chair where he sat as he undid everything Fyve and Halo have been fighting for.

It cracks, leans to the side, but Fyve grabs Abe before he can slam into the controls. There could still be a chance to undo his treachery.

Fyve spins and shoves Abe back, making a few wide-eyed teens step quickly out of the way as the old man stumbles before righting himself.

"After everything the Echelons have done for you, this is

how you thank them?" Abe shouts, digging his feet in and propelling forward again. "You don't deserve them!"

He's taken two steps when a much smaller foot darts out, neatly pushing his rising foot behind the other. Abe's mouth opens in shock as he finds himself suddenly propelled toward the floor. His arms shoot out to catch himself, only to find he's too late. One shove by an extra set of hands and he's driven into the floor.

Fyve glances at his helpers as he runs toward the Raven.

Tenn tripped Abe.

Halo hastened his inevitable crash.

Abe grunts as he lands, his teeth clicking as his chin connects with the floor, then quickly scrabbles to all fours. This time, a kick comes flying from the right and slams into his torso. He falls to the side with a groan, clutching his stomach.

Justice wrinkles her nose at Fyve. "Didn't want to miss out on the fun."

He's not sure whether he should grin or scowl. All he knows is that the knowledge he's part of something bigger than him has the fire of fury cooling.

Abe flops onto his back and Fyve's standing above him before he can make his next move. He grabs the Raven by the tunic, bringing his face close. "Turn us around," he grinds out, giving the old man one last chance to make this right.

"I'll die seeking Tomorrow Land," Abe spits, zealousness alive in his eyes.

"Plenty of us already have," says Fyve.

"They deserved it," Abe spits out. "I haven't come this far to give up now. The Echelons will always have my—"

One punch is all it takes to knock him out, which is almost disappointing. But when pain explodes through Fyve's knuckles, then straight up his arm, he's glad for the reprieve. Without the anger to fuel him, he admits he's not a fighter. He never has been. He just does what he needs to protect.

He drops Abe, disgust churning low in the pit of his stomach as the old man flops like a lifeless doll. The Raven was just another victim of the Echelons and their deluded plans.

Tenn appears, peering down at Abe. "Ooh, is he dead?" He pulls in a faint, raspy breath and her shoulders sag with disappointment. "Nope, still alive."

Fyve steps back, wiping the blood from his face as he tries to get his breathing under control. Halo rushes to his side, wrapping a gentle arm around him. "Are you okay?"

He nudges Abe with his toe, but the lifeless body barely moves. "A bit better now, to be honest."

She shakes her head as a smile dances along her lips. "It did feel good, didn't it?"

"I kinda want to do it again," Justice says with a grin.

This time, it's Fyve who shakes his head. Justice is most definitely a fighter.

She squats down beside Abe and Fyve almost jumps forward. Being a fighter still doesn't make it okay to hit an unconscious man.

But Justice quickly and efficiently rifles through Abe's pockets. "Maybe he has something we can use."

"Nole's probably been talking to him this whole time," Halo says sourly, echoing Fyve's earlier thoughts.

Justice tips Abe's head to the side, brushing aside the wiry hair at his temple. "Yep, there's the chip," she says, poking at the rectangle just below the skin.

She checks his last pocket and her eyes pop open. "I found something!" She yanks out a cloth, then glares at it in disappointment. "Urgh, it smells."

She flicks it away and it lands near Halo's feet. Halo stiffens, leans closer, then reels back. "I know that smell!" She kicks away the crumpled material. "That's what Nole used to knock me out."

Fyve frowns. "Why would he have that with him?" Was Abe waiting for the right moment to kidnap Halo?

Iva gasps, rushing back to Dargo and wrapping herself protectively around his unconscious form. "Dargo almost died trying to escape, and then Abe was trying to finish him off!"

Fyve straightens as he realizes she's right. "Dargo recognized him. That's why he freaked out when he woke up."

"Yes," Halo says. "And the lights went out right after that."

Iva's hand flies to her throat. "And then Dargo slipped back into unconsciousness."

Their eyes fall to the cloth on the floor. Abe's been keeping Dargo silent. In fact, he probably would've killed him if Iva wasn't so glued to his side.

And the Echelons would've ordered it.

Iva's face hardens. "No deal."

Justice nods resolutely. "No freaking way. They can take their cans and shove them up their—"

Sica steps forward. "No deal."

"No deal," echoes Caddie.

Fyve glances at Halo, who's looking at Cloud as she clutches Marvel and Miracle. He knows why Halo wanted to agree to the trade of Treasures for food. There's nothing she wouldn't do for those innocent babies.

Halo looks up at him. "We can't trust them," she says, her voice hardening. She turns to the other teens. "No deal."

"No deal!" Tenn shouts, punching her fist into the air.

Fyve finds himself smiling. "No deal!"

The two-word echo that is thrown back at him is projected by every teen in the room. Even Ajax. They're said as a challenge. A battle cry.

Fyve nudges Abe's body again with his toe. "And I know exactly how we can let them know."

He leans down to grab Abe by the shoulders when Halo

ducks away. "Here," she says, grabbing one of the sheets he'd brought during the storm. "We'll roll him on this."

The teens make short work of loading Abe on the makeshift sled and dragging him out of the wheelhouse. Gripping a corner each, Fyve and Halo hold their ends up high enough that Abe's head doesn't hit the stairs as they descend through the levels to the engine room. They may not like him, but that doesn't mean they want to hurt him anymore than they already have.

Each step hardens Fyve's determination. He doesn't know what rejecting this offer is going to mean. Somehow, they're going to have to turn the ship around again.

And survive on the pods long enough to reach Treasure Island.

All he does know is that rejecting the Echelons and everything they stand for is the right thing to do.

The growl of the engines grows the closer they move. The hum beneath their feet becomes a vibration. It would be a welcome sound and feeling if they weren't heading toward the wrong horizon.

They've just dumped Abe's body by the door to the engine room when there's a break in the steady throb they're surrounded by. Like The Oasis just hiccupped. Then another. This one longer and more pronounced. Like a cough.

"Let's get out of here," Sica mutters.

Fyve's about to agree when the lights flicker. The hum stops. And silence reigns.

Fyve's gaze falls on Halo, noting the same dread growing in his gut blooming across her face.

The engines just shuddered to a stop, but not like they did the first time.

"It's like the ship just died." Halo presses a hand to her mouth.

Fyve swallows. "I think we just ran out of fuel."

HALO

"*C*ome on," says Sica. "We need to get out of here."

Halo nods. She's right. If this ship really has run out of fuel, the Echelons will be desperate. And desperate people do desperate things. They don't want to be standing here for that.

"Let's get back to the wheelhouse," says Fyve. "We have to stick together."

"The wheelhouse is useless now." Halo climbs the stairs beside him. "It's not like we can steer the ship when the engines aren't running."

Fyve nods. "Then we're better off taking everyone to the deck. Then we can guard the pods."

"Good thinking," says Sica. "They're not getting their filthy hands on our pods."

With each step they take, the ship slows a little more until it feels like they're bobbing in the ocean. The eerie silence that seeps into the stairwell screams of hopelessness. It was one thing to be held captive at the mercy of the Echelons. Now they're held captive by the sea. And Halo isn't sure which is worse.

As they pass the landing for the deck, Sica pauses.

"You two go on," she says. "I want to make sure the deck's safe before we bring everyone out there. Besides, we shouldn't leave the pods unattended."

"No," says Halo, knowing it's far more dangerous to head to the deck alone than the safety of the wheelhouse where numbers are on their side. "We'll do it."

"Fine." Sica cracks her knuckles and takes a few more stairs. "But be careful. I don't trust those bastards."

Fyve opens the door to the deck, and they step out. Halo surveys the open space, thinking about everything that's happened out here. It was the place they first met the girl they were told was Terra. The place where they first saw the Echelons. The place where they gathered for their Trials. The place where her father died. And it was also the place she gave herself to Fyve in body as well as soul.

Sensing the vulnerability that's crawling up her spine, Fyve puts an arm around her and pulls her close, pressing a kiss to the top of her head. They both know the ship running out of fuel signified an ending. They're just not sure what chapter comes next.

"No matter what happens, I'm glad I got on this ship," Fyve says. "If I could go back, I'd do it all again."

"No, you wouldn't." Halo looks up at him and smiles. "You'd drag both me and Tenn off this ship and we'd all grow old together on Treasure Island."

He returns her smile. "Now, there's an idea. If only I hadn't misplaced my time machine."

Fyve wraps his other arm around Halo. She tucks her face into his neck, trying to take in this moment with him. It won't last forever, but maybe if she preserves it in her mind, she can return to it when she needs to.

"I love you, Fyve," she says. "Always."

"I love you, too, Angel." He tilts up her face and presses his lips to hers.

It's a kiss that's filled with tenderness. Heartbreak. Fear. But most of all, it's filled with restrained passion. One that they know has the power to spark into a burning flame if only the situation were different.

"It's going to be okay," Fyve tells her as he breaks away.

She nods. "It is."

They walk to the pod pool, both knowing that of all the paths their future may take, *okay* isn't very likely.

"Should we remove the net?" Halo asks. "The storm has passed."

Fyve nods, seeming glad to have something to do to keep himself busy. He crouches at the edge of the pool just as the door to the deck bursts open.

Halo turns and smiles, pleased that Sica hadn't taken too long.

But it's not Sica. Or Cloud. Or Tenn. Or Justice. Or any of their friends...

It's the Echelons.

Halo rushes to Fyve, who's already standing. They're outnumbered. By a lot. But somehow with him by her side, she feels safer.

Nole is at the front of the pack with Rhina and Jiro. The rest of the Echelons are close behind them, their flamethrowers gripped at their chests.

Halo and Fyve put their hands in the air, her mind whirling fast as she tries to figure out a way out of this.

"Sica won't be far away," Fyve says under his breath.

Halo nods. As much as she doesn't want to have to be rescued, she can't see any other way. For any of them. If the Echelons kill them now, the others will be in an even worse position.

"Don't look so afraid!" Nole laughs as he walks forward, his empty hands extended. He's the only unarmed Echelon. "We come in peace."

"I'm not sure you know the meaning of the word," says Fyve.

"Now, now." Nole smiles as if he's the kindest man in the world. "Put your hands down. We just want to talk."

Halo studies Nole carefully, not trusting him one bit. She sees a hint of something in his face she can't quite place. He swallows and wipes his palms on his trousers as his eyes dart from Fyve to Halo, taking in their defensive body language.

Uncertainty.

That's what it is. Nole is nervous about the outcome of this interaction.

But why?

"Where's Ajax?" snaps Rhina, looking around. Her shoulder is bandaged but other than that she seems in good health.

"He's coming," says Halo. "Everyone is. So, I wouldn't do anything stupid right now."

"We outnumber you," says Fyve. "If you lay one finger on us, we'll kill you all, just like we killed your puppet, Zake."

"You're unarmed," growls the Echelon who Halo recognizes as the one who claimed Sica as his Treasure.

"How do you know that?" Fyve pats his pocket. "Are you sure you took all the knives from the kitchen?"

"There's no need for that," Nole says. "We've come in peace. We want to call a truce."

"Prove it." Halo jams her hands on her hips. "Throw your weapons overboard."

"Let's not do anything too rash." Nole smiles, revealing his yellowed teeth. "We might need these weapons. In case of…pirates."

This makes Halo laugh so unexpectedly that she splutters.

"What's a pirate?" asks Fyve.

"Someone who attacks ships at sea," Halo replies. "And robs

them of everything they have. Pretty sure we're already full up on pirates on The Oasis."

"We've taken nothing from you!" Nole seems genuinely outraged.

"You took our freedom," says Halo. "You took our safety. For some of us, you took our lives."

"You took our future," Fyve adds. "There's no such place as Tomorrow Land."

"But there is!" Nole protests. "We just haven't found it yet. If we hadn't wasted fuel going in that ridiculous circle maybe we'd have found it before it was too late."

"You admit it's too late?" Halo cocks a brow.

Nole nods slowly. "We have no fuel. Our food supplies are getting low. We were hoping..."

Halo follows Nole's gaze to the pool.

"Get your greedy eyes off our pods!" Fyve bellows. "Just because you've eaten all your supplies, now you want the only food we have. Food that we've been rationing. Not that you'd know the meaning of the concept."

"We know how to ration." Nole looks aghast, although the rounded bellies of the Echelons compared to the lean frames of the teens on this ship say otherwise. Only one group of people has been starving here. "We have plenty of food left."

"Meanwhile Cloud barely has enough milk to feed her babies," says Halo, shaking her head.

"We asked for our Treasures back," says Jiro from the front line of the Echelons. "So we could share our food with them. I wanted to make sure Cloud had enough to eat. She chose not to come."

"Saint Jiro at it again." Halo rolls her eyes, then remembers this is Fyve's father she's talking to. "We couldn't trust your offer."

"Yet you expect us to trust you after what you did to our

Raven," sneers Nole, seeming to forget he's trying to be friendly here.

"His name is Abe," says Fyve. "And he deserved everything he got."

The door to the deck opens and Justice and Sica step out, each holding one of Justice's crutches. Their eyes widen to see the Echelons, but they don't back out.

"Get out of here!" Justice shouts at Nole. "And take your filthy men with you."

The teens pour out onto the deck, proving that their numbers are strong. Numbers that would have been even stronger had the Echelons not forced them to walk the plank. Cloud goes directly to Halo's side and Fyve instinctively places himself in front of the basket with the babies. Tenn sits beside it and rubs Marvel's back as he threatens to wake. Iva and Dargo are hand in hand. Dargo still looks a little groggy but at least he's on his feet again. Ajax hovers on the edge of the group, his focus on Rhina, despite Viney clinging to his side.

Each and every one of them is sneering at the Echelons, their faces filled with hatred.

"We come in peace," Nole shouts over Sica's cursing.

This causes more teens to join Sica in her leers.

"You're not capable of peace," Iva calls out.

"We are," says Jiro, stepping forward. "And we'll prove it to you."

Jiro nods at Nole, whose eyes flare. They hold each other's gaze in a silent conversation between brothers. Eventually, Nole nods in response.

"We're all equals here," says Nole. "Humans stuck on a ship with no fuel and limited food. We mean you no harm. And we're going to prove that to you by throwing our weapons overboard."

Halo gasps. When she'd suggested that, there was no way she'd expected it to happen. Once again, she finds herself wondering whose side Jiro is actually on. Is it possible that it's both?

"Our weapons are only weighing us down," Nole says to the Echelons, who are still clutching their flamethrowers to their chests. "We don't need these. Let's prove to our Tre—friends that we come in peace."

"They won't do it," whispers Fyve, planting his feet, ready to launch forward and attack.

"Go on." Nole points to the railing. "Throw those useless things away."

Jiro is first. He marches to the edge of the deck and tosses his flamethrower over the railing. It flings high in the air, spinning dramatically before gravity pulls it out of sight.

Rhina takes a long look at Ajax with an expression that appears strangely like love. She passes Jiro on her way to the railing and uses her good arm to throw her weapon over. Giving Ajax a wide smile, she stands beside him instead of returning to the Echelons.

"He's mine," Viney hisses at Rhina. "I saw him first."

"Pretty sure that was Cloud," murmurs Justice.

"I heard that, Justice," snaps Viney. "But I'm carrying his child, so that gives me rights."

"Good to hear," says Rhina, pulling back her shoulders. "Because I did a test this morning and I'm pregnant."

Halo's hand flies to her mouth. This is somehow more shocking than Nole's agreement to dispose of their weapons.

Cloud rolls her eyes. "Doesn't feel nice, does it, Viney?"

Viney lunges at Rhina, scratching at her face. Ajax leaps between them, tearing Viney away as he tucks Rhina behind his back.

"Violence solves nothing," Ajax tells Viney.

"How could you do this to me?" Viney wails. "You said you loved me."

"I didn't have a choice," he says. "I was forced."

"Ajax!" Rhina gasps, wriggling out from behind him, red lines streaking down her face. "You were the one who wanted it. You said you'd never felt like anyone the way you feel about me."

"That's true," says Ajax, color rising to his cheeks. "I feel very differently about both of you. That doesn't mean I love either of you any less."

"You don't love her!" Viney dives past Ajax and gets her hands into Rhina's hair, pulling hard.

Rhina bends forward and squeals.

"Holy Terra!" Halo breathes. Her brother really has taken his philandering to the next level. Kind of ironic given that he really isn't very much of a prize.

Fyve lets out a loud sigh and goes to the commotion, helping Ajax prize the two women apart before one of them gets hurt.

"Is this what you call peaceful?" Iva shouts out, clearly still furious with the Echelons after what they did to Dargo.

"She attacked me!" Rhina says, clutching her bandaged shoulder.

"You provoked her," says Iva.

"I did not!" Rhina protests. "If telling Ajax he's the father of my child is provoking him then that's just…insane."

"Enough!" Nole's voice booms across the deck, bringing instant silence with it. "We need to work together, not tear each other apart."

If it weren't for who had spoken the words, Halo would wholeheartedly agree.

"Let's continue with the weapon disposal, shall we?" Nole raises his eyebrows at the remaining Echelons. After a few grumbles, they walk as a group to the railing and throw their flamethrowers overboard.

"Excellent," says Nole. "Now we're on even ground to negotiate the terms of our truce."

"Terms?" asks Halo, leaving Cloud to go to Fyve. "You're either calling a truce, or you're not. There are no terms."

"Great!" Nole claps his hands and rubs them together, his eyes darting toward the pods.

"Don't even think about it," says Sica, waving the crutch at him.

"Oh, so there *are* terms?" Nole's tone drips with sarcasm.

Halo is starting to see how this cunning creep became the leader of this pack of evil Echelons.

"You have plenty of food," says Fyve.

"They don't have plenty," says Dargo, who seems to have snapped out of his stupor. "They've been eating like pigs at a trough in the engine room. Once their food is gone, they'll starve. The pods are the only renewable source of food on this ship."

So, that's why Nole had been so nervous about this interaction. They have something that he not only wants. They have something he needs.

Nole holds up his hands and backs away from the pool. "How about you come with us to the engine room and we'll share with you all we have left? After that, we can talk about the pods."

"No deal!" shouts Justice. "We don't need your stinkin' food. I never liked that salty meat anyway."

Marvel chooses that moment to wake and let out a cry. Miracle is quick to join him. The babies are hungry. Which means Cloud needs food. She can't wait for the pods to breed enough to feed them all. She needs sustenance right now.

Halo slips her hand into Fyve's and he squeezes it tight.

Together, they step forward and draw in a deep breath.

"Deal."

FYVE

*F*yve doesn't like this one bit. The moment they
follow the Echelons into The Oasis, it feels like the
walls are closer than they've ever been. Their proximity mimics
the tightness in Fyve's chest as Nole glances over his shoulder,
smiling encouragingly at Halo.

They're willingly following these bastards to the engine
room.

They're trusting that these selfish, manipulative, greedy
people will stay true to their word.

Except, what choice do they have?

A thin wail pierces the narrow hallway, and Fyve recognizes
it as Miracle. Her cry has always been a little sharper, purely
because she's more determined to demand food. Plus, Marvel
stopped asking a day ago.

They have to accept this olive branch, no matter how flimsy
it is. Cloud needs food. The babies won't survive if she doesn't
get any.

Jiro glances back, his gaze dark and unreadable. Fyve still
struggles to understand exactly who the man is. His father. The

man who saved his life. Yet, an enemy. A brother to Nole. And one of *them*.

Beside Fyve, Tenn imperceptibly lifts a hand and wriggles her fingers, a fleeting smile gracing her lips. Jiro's eyes soften a second before he turns away. Tenn's shoulders sag as her arm drops back to her side. It's clear Jiro's torn, yet Fyve can't help but think that's not enough. Who would Jiro choose if it came to the ultimate test of loyalty? Fyve doesn't want to know the answer.

He clenches his jaw, once again hating that they're following the Echelons. None of this feels okay, let alone safe. And Halo and Tenn, along with every other teen, are right here with him.

If the Echelons hadn't given up their flamethrowers, there's no way he would have agreed to the unexpected truce.

They reach the door to the engine room and the Echelons step through, Rhina glancing back and seeking out Ajax so she can smile encouragingly. Her hair is still a mess and the red lines down her face haven't faded, making her look almost sinister. Ajax seems to think so, too, because although he smiles back, he moves a little closer to Viney.

Fyve pauses when they reach the door. He glances down at Halo, seeing the same trepidation in her eyes. Along with the same knowledge they have no other choice. He wishes he could take her and everyone else away from this. To never have to step into the lion's den, one where a pride of predators is now waiting for them.

All he allows himself is a squeeze of her hand, his heart constricting when she clenches his back. It reminds him they have something the Echelons never will. Something that will give them the advantage. Actually, more than just one thing.

Loyalty. Faith. A heart.

Fyve and Halo step through into the engine room together. The Echelons are spread out, the silent motors behind them.

They're smiling proudly and Fyve quickly sees why. A handful of gasps tell him the other teens have seen it, too.

A pyramid of cans is stacked up several feet away, looking just as proud as the silver glints softly. A table is before it, dozens more sitting on it.

Nole waves his hand expansively. "See? We told you we're willing to share."

Fyve glances over his shoulder, finding Cloud among the teens. She drags her gaze away from the stack of food, quickly wiping away the longing that had slackened her face. She straightens, telling Fyve everything he needs to know.

She's starving.

And strong in ways no one thought she could be.

Cloud won't eat the Echelons' offering if it means putting others at risk. Halo was right. They have to make this decision for her.

Fyve turns back to Nole. "No one's had anything to eat, yet," he points out.

Nole's lips tighten around the edges. "Let's remedy that, shall we?" He picks up a can and turns to Jiro. "One can per teen. Just like we agreed."

Jiro nods, looking relieved. "Yes, just like we agreed." He takes the can and holds it out Fyve. "It's yours."

Fyve doesn't hesitate. They didn't come this far to turn away from the whole reason they're here—to survive. He grabs the can from Jiro, finding it's open, even the tip of a spoon pointing up through the brown contents. The smell of the salted meat has his mouth watering and stomach contracting, yet he sits it between his feet. "I'll save it for later," he tells the others. "For Cloud."

When he turns back, Nole's already passing another, but this time it's directly to Halo. He takes far too long to withdraw his hand. "For my Treasure," he murmurs in that lecherous way of his.

Halo snatches it to her chest. "This one's also for Cloud," she says loudly.

Jiro picks up another can from the table and holds it out to Fyve, imperceptibly shaking his head. Fyve draws in a deep breath through his nose seeing as his jaw is clenched too tightly. Nole disgusts him. Repulses him. Has images of Fyve's fist powering through the Echelon's nose coursing through him.

Yet, as much as Fyve would love to defy his father's advice, he knows it's sound. Especially when more food is being offered. So, he takes the can and passes it to Tenn, then another to Justice, then Sica, and eventually every other teen. For each one, Nole passes it to Jiro, who gives it to Fyve, the Echelon leader clearly enjoying being the gracious host.

"Here, Cloud," Justice says quietly. "You can have mine, too."

Pride warms Fyve's chest. The teens are looking out for each other. He doubts the Echelons wanted that to happen. Not when they've done everything they could to establish a kill or be killed culture, starting right back at the Trials on Treasure Island.

"See?" Nole says, beaming so widely both rows of yellow teeth are visible. "I told you we've realized we need to work together." He looks directly at Fyve. "Now, eat."

Fyve's stomach gurgles in agreement, but he takes some measure of satisfaction in knowing he won't be following Nole's order. His can will be used to feed Cloud, maybe even Tenn and Halo. He can survive on pods for a little longer.

Ajax groans, and Fyve turns to see him shoveling another spoonful into his mouth. "This tastes amazing."

Yet Viney's looking a little pale. "I can't believe I'm so hungry yet feel so sick at the thought of eating."

Rhina rolls her eyes. "Only someone as weak and as selfish as you wouldn't be able to eat, despite your condition." She pats her fleshy stomach. "I'd do whatever it takes to ensure my child grows healthy and strong."

Viney frowns as she glances down at her can. She pulls out the spoon, the meat making a soft squelching sound. Her face takes on a pale shade of green.

Fyve looks away, knowing if she doesn't hurry up, Ajax will be finished and more than happy to have hers. Muted *clangs* and groans fill the engine room as many of the teens eat as quickly as they can.

Nole glares at Fyve smugly. "You keep up this self-sacrificing stupidity and she'll be mine far sooner than I'm hoping," he sneers, glancing hungrily at Halo.

Fyve takes a step forward, his blood heating, but Jiro appears in front of him. "Although he's trying to bait you, he has a point." He lowers his voice as his gaze flickers to Tenn. "You need your strength to protect them."

Behind Jiro, Nole's eyes flare with victory. A victory that doesn't make sense. Nole wouldn't want him to eat. Or is this just because Jiro agreed with him, essentially taking his side?

Fyve turns away, bitterness coating his tongue. Jiro's always ultimately taken Nole's side.

He thinks of the can resting between his feet. Of the sustenance it holds. Of the responsibility he has to Halo and Tenn and Cloud and Marvel and Miracle. And every other teen on this ship.

Should he have just a few mouthfuls?

The sound of a can clanging to the ground has Fyve spinning around, several teens doing the same. The rows of backs frame Caddie as she stands at the rear, her hands clamped around her throat.

"She's choking," someone gasps.

Fyve jolts into action, leaping between the teens as he sprints toward Caddie. He's almost there when she doubles over, red foam bubbling over her bottom lip and down her chin. She drops to her knees, eyes wide with terror.

And the undeniable truth.

More bloody froth spills from her mouth and she coughs. The teens surrounding her leap back as it sprays like one of the showerheads they've only just discovered. Caddie drops to her knees, then falls face forward with a dull, sticky thud.

Fyve skids to a stop, his heart thundering against his ribs. He's seen this before. The same crimson foam. The same quick ending of a life.

When they completed the Trial on the deck and were forced to finish a plate, knowing some had been poisoned.

"No, I—!" someone screeches, only to gurgle to an abrupt stop. The young woman, Era, tries to stem the foamy fountain coursing down her chin and chest, but she stumbles to the side. Justice catches her but Era slips to the ground. She's dead before her head hits the metal floor.

Fyve turns back to the Echelons, his breath frozen in his horrified lungs. They've been betrayed again!

Jiro spins to face Nole. "You poisoned them?"

"It's the Treasures we want," Nole snaps back.

Fyve glances down at the can he was just considering eating. The one he would've shared with Cloud or Halo or Tenn. There's no doubt in his mind it's been tainted with the same deadly poison claiming teens around him.

Another cry choked by blood has Fyve gripping Halo. "Did you eat any?"

She shakes her head, looking as pale as he's feeling. "No. I was saving it for Cloud, just like you were." Although Fyve quickly realizes Halo was safe all along.

She's a Treasure.

A glance down shows Tenn throwing her uneaten can away. It narrowly misses Abe as he works his way around the grizzly scene that's unfolding, moving toward the door.

Another teen drops, convulsing over and over as the foam progressively becomes darker and thicker. It pours from her mouth and nose, blooming across the floor to stain the hair of another dead teen. "Please," she gasps.

Then goes still and silent.

Justice appears by their side. "They're trying to trap us in here!" she shouts, pointing at the door.

Abe jolts when he realizes he's been spotted, then breaks into a sprint. Fyve does the same, adrenaline exploding through every cell, weaving through the teens as two more fall to the floor, poisoned.

Fyve crashes into Abe a moment before he can reach the door. He shoves the old man back with all the horror and disgust and fear he feels.

They were lied to again.

Teens are dying.

And they're about to be trapped, once more at the mercy of the Echelons.

Abe stumbles backward, his arms flailing wildly. Fyve follows, determined to finish it this time, when one of Echelons runs at him. Fyve whips out an elbow, driving it into the man's soft middle. He grunts and doubles over. Fyve grabs him by the tunic and shoves, sending him careening toward Abe.

The Raven was just regaining his balance when the Echelon barrels into him, propelling him backward again. Abe thrusts the man away, and he crashes into the pyramid of cans with enough force for them to explode in every direction.

Nole ducks as one sails past his shoulder. Another hits Jiro in the chest. Yet all he does is grimace. There's no cry of pain. No hand flying to the injured area.

The cans fall to the ground one after the other, but the unexpected sound has Fyve stilling. They *clang*, not *thud*. They *clatter* as they roll, rather than *thump* to a slow stop. They fly far too high and farther than a can should.

Justice confirms it when she picks one up, her lip curling. "They're empty."

The truth blooms through Fyve in the same sickly way the pools of blood are still expanding around each dead teen. The Echelons used their remaining food to try and kill anyone who isn't a Treasure.

"Fyve!" Halo gasps, breaking into a run.

Abe is sprinting for the door again. He's going to lock them in. Fyve launches after Halo, avoiding the slippery pools of crimson. Caddie's sightless eyes watch him as he passes, seeming to know what he's not willing to acknowledge. They won't be able to stop the Raven in time.

They're about to be trapped.

Another can flies past Fyve, hitting Abe in the shoulder, no doubt thrown by Justice. But the empty tin glances off. In fact, Abe runs faster, his head pulled low as if to dodge any other missiles. He yanks open the door.

"This is what will happen if you try to run!" Nole roars.

Something else flies past Fyve. The silver object spins through the air, then impales in Abe's back. He arches as he cries out, then tumbles to the ground. He turns over to look back at who threw it, even though it's obvious.

Abe's last thought is the realization that the Echelon he blindly followed is the one who's glaring at him from across the room, his lip curled with satisfaction. Fyve and Halo skid to a stop, trying to understand what just happened. Nole just used Abe to make a point.

Halo realizes what this means far quicker than Fyve does. "Quick! This is our chance to escape!"

She's right. Nole killing his Raven means exactly that.

"Get out of here," Fyve shouts to the others. "Now!"

Justice is already halfway there. She stops when she sees Iva staggering as she tries to help Dargo walk. Fyve just hopes it's because he's still weak, rather than Iva having fed him some of the poisoned meat. They exit the engine room, dragging the barely conscious Dargo between them.

"Don't let them get away!" Nole screams.

The Echelons lurch forward, only to be met by a barrage of cans. "Take that you fat bastards," Sica whoops.

The Echelons lift their arms to protect their face, stopping although they're still several feet away. Rhina even ducks behind Jiro, cradling her stomach.

"Cloud," Halo cries frantically. "Where is she?"

Fyve looks around, seeing Tenn pointing to a thick column off to the side. Cloud is cowering behind it, cradling Marvel and Miracle.

Fyve grasps Tenn's shoulders. "Go and help her. We have to get out of here."

Pale but determined, Tenn nods and darts away.

Fyve scoops up the tin he was given, his stomach constricting. This is one of the poisoned cans. The contents would've killed him or someone he cares about. With a roar of fury, he hurls it at Nole.

The leader of the Echelons ducks just in time and the can flies into the depths of the engine room. Fyve's about to pick another up, the need to make Nole pay a pounding pulse through his veins.

"Fyve!" Halo calls out. "Come on!"

He realizes he's the last teen left. Everyone else in the engine room is either an Echelon or dead.

"Fyve!" This time it's Tenn who calls out, a hint of desperation in her voice.

A slow, slimy smile spreads over Nole's face. It's a smile of victory. A self-satisfied one. One Fyve wants nothing more than to wipe off his smug face.

Instead, he spins on his heel and runs out of the engine room. The door slams shut behind him, propelled by Halo and Justice. The resounding boom is loud with no engines to drown out the sound.

Fyve collapses against the wall, a sick feeling slithering

through his insides. But the reality of their circumstances has even that stilling. The truth holds him immobile, a prison just as much as the dead Oasis is.

All that remains are the Treasures along with the handful of teens who hadn't eaten from the cans.

The engine room is still under control of the Echelons.

Nole's final glance is like a stain in Fyve's mind.

No matter what they've done, they've lost.

And ultimately, the Echelons have won.

HALO

*H*alo rouses in the morning light, the hard surface of the deck beneath her. She knows she slept. She must have. But the tiredness is still eating away at her bones, causing everything to ache.

She keeps her eyes closed. There's no point in opening them. She doesn't need to see the devastation on the faces around her. The loss. The complete and utter destruction of hope. Maybe this way, she can pretend none of it is real.

Fyve stirs beside her, perhaps sensing she's awake. She snuggles in closer, trying to capture some of his body warmth. She knows she shouldn't feel so cold while the sun is caressing her with its rays, but gooseflesh prickles her skin.

"I don't think I'm ready to go," whispers Tenn, from Fyve's other side.

"Go where?" Fyve asks.

"Up there," says Tenn.

Halo cracks her eyelids open to see Tenn pointing to the sky.

"To the real Terra," says Tenn. "We're going to die, aren't we?"

There's so much Halo wants to say in response. She wants to

tell her not to give up. That there's still a way out of this. That there's *always* a way out of a situation, no matter how bleak it might seem.

But she remains quiet.

Because none of that is true. There's no way out of this. Tenn *is* going to die. They all are. Including the Echelons. This floating ship of dreams, searching for a better tomorrow, will become their tomb as everything they were promised sinks to the bottom of the ocean. Perhaps that's why they'd chosen to sleep out on the deck. Halo had insisted she'd wanted to look at the stars. They're the only piece of home she has with her. The same constellations and planets watching over her. The same moon she's slept under all her life. There's some comfort in that.

It seems everyone else had felt the same, as those who'd survived the Echelons' final evil deception had come with them. A group that had once numbered a hundred is little more than a dozen now. Halo hadn't done a headcount. It would only strengthen the acuteness of the pain in her heart.

"Tenn," says Fyve, seeming to be struggling to form any words.

Halo waits for him to tell his sister not to give up.

"Everyone dies eventually," he says. "But whatever happens, I'm never leaving you."

If Halo had the strength, she'd let out a sob. But she doesn't even have the energy to cry. It seems that surviving without food was far more achievable when they were able to fuel their bodies with hope.

Perhaps that's why Fyve had chosen to be honest with Tenn just now. Speaking is difficult enough without dancing around the facts. Or perhaps he's had enough of lies. Tenn deserves better than that. There's not much left he can give her, except for the truth.

"I dreamed of Miracle and Marvel," says Tenn.

"Tell us about it," says Fyve, confirming he knows Halo's awake.

"They were old," says Tenn. "They lived in a house surrounded by trees. There were birds everywhere. Not just ravens, either. Blue birds and yellow and even some with every color on them all at once."

Halo smiles, bringing the image to her mind's eye.

"There were creatures that lived there," says Tenn. "Friendly ones like deer and crickets. There were humming noises and chirping noises and it was like the trees and the ground were alive. I couldn't just see Mother Nature, I could feel her, all around me."

"Tomorrow Land," breathes Fyve.

"Miracle called Marvel, Marv." Tenn giggles. "And he called her Miri."

"What did they look like?" asks Halo, not sure if her voice is strong enough for Tenn to hear.

"Miri had long silver hair like a moonbeam," says Tenn. "Marv didn't have any hair at all. Their faces were all wrinkled up and Marv was holding Miri's hand."

Halo basks in the warmth of this impossible image, feeling a little of her strength return. "Were they happy?"

"Very," says Tenn. "What do you think it means? Maybe they're going to make it to Tomorrow Land?"

"Maybe they will," says Halo, not wanting to lie to Tenn, but hoping she might be able to fool herself into believing her words.

"Do you think Cloud would like to hear about my dream?" Tenn asks.

"Definitely," says Fyve.

Tenn gets to her feet, moving more slowly than normal. She hadn't eaten her tin of food, although Halo wonders if it might have been safe to do so. But the risk had been too great. The Echelons can't be trusted. They never could.

Halo had taken her tin from the engine room. It was the only one they could be certain was safe, but even then, Cloud had gagged on it as she'd swallowed the contents down. It had helped her milk, though, which will hopefully give the twins a few more days to add to their tragically short lives.

A shadow crosses the sun, and Halo squints up, seeing Tenn hovering in front of them, looking uncertain.

"What is it?" Fyve asks, hauling himself to a seated position.

Halo stays lying down, the effort to move feeling too great.

"I just remembered something," says Tenn. "The birds in my dream reminded me of it."

"Go on," says Fyve.

"It's the Ravens," she says. "Not the bird ones. The people ones. Do you think we should let them out?"

These words have Halo sitting up. She groans as her whole body protests and her head spins.

"Do you know where they are?" Fyve asks.

Tenn nods. "Remember when you found me behind the hidden door? You said you heard me crying."

Fyve winces as he nods, the memory seeming to cause him pain.

"They're there," says Tenn. "They keep them there. The doors are locked."

"How many are there?" Halo asks.

Tenn shrugs. "A few."

"Why didn't you mention them earlier?" Fyve asks gently.

"I don't trust Ravens." Tenn pulls back her shoulders. "They're brainwashed. Abe was the worst."

"Then why do you want to release them?" asks Halo.

Tenn points toward the pool where Dargo is scooping out a pod and handing it to Cloud.

"Maybe they're not all bad," she says. "Besides…"

"What is it?" Fyve asks, getting to his feet and putting one hand on each of Tenn's arms.

"It's Viney," says Tenn. "I've been watching her and…"

"And what?" Fyve prompts.

"She's annoying," says Tenn. "But I think that's because she's sad. She lost her sisters, so Ajax was all she had left. Then Rhina tried to take him, too."

Halo shakes her head at the keenness of this small girl's observations.

"Are her sisters still alive?" Halo asks, dragging herself to her feet as she remembers Viney's sisters were taken at the same time as Dargo. "Are they Ravens now?"

Tenn nods. "I was lucky. I got to find my brother. I just thought maybe Viney needs her sisters, too. It might make her nice again."

Halo lets out a whimper as she loses her battle to hold back her tears. Here she'd been thinking she could teach Tenn all about the world when she'd just been handed a lesson in life herself. Of course, Viney's been upset about losing her sisters. It makes perfect sense that she'd latched onto Ajax like that. And that she'd be so pleased about having his baby. She'd already lost so much.

"We need to let them out," says Fyve.

Halo nods. Their situation might be helpless. They might all be about to die. But nobody deserves to perish while locked in a cage.

"Dargo!" Fyve calls, his voice echoing across the deck.

Dargo lifts a hand to show he heard and comes over to Fyve. Iva follows, as do Justice and Sica.

"What's the plan?" Justice asks. "Are we going to kill the lot of them? Because let me tell you, I'd rather die with my hands around one of those bastard's throats than to starve to death up here."

"Couldn't agree more," says Sica, cracking her knuckles.

"No more killing." Fyve holds up a palm. "As much as they deserve it. This is about the Ravens."

"You want to release them," says Dargo, biting his lip. "I wanted to talk to you about that. I'm not sure it's safe."

Fyve tilts his head, waiting for him to go on.

"They kept us fairly separate," says Dargo. "So, I never got to know any of them well, but from what I could tell, most of them think the Echelons are gods. Releasing them will just add strength to the Echelons' side."

"Brainwashed." Tenn nods. "Told you."

"We already lost our advantage with our numbers," says Sica. "We can't risk it."

"But Viney's sisters are there," says Halo. "They were taken at the same time as Dargo. We can't just leave them."

"I'm with Sica," says Justice. "It's bad enough with one Viney around here."

"Not everyone is like their siblings," Halo points out. "You of all people should know that. Viney deserves to see her sisters, before we all..."

"Die," Justice says when Halo fails to complete her sentence. "Honestly, do whatever you like, but count me out. I'll be over there in the corner if you need me. Dying. Like the rest of us. Let me know if you change your mind about killing those creeps in the engine room, though."

Sica nods, looping arms with Justice and walking away. Halo can't be upset with either of them. She understands why they feel that way. They barely have the energy to stand up straight, let alone release a group of prisoners. She just can't get Tenn's words out of her head. Viney deserves to see her sisters. And her sisters deserve to lie underneath the sky one last time so they can look up at the stars and pretend they're home.

"I'll help you," says Dargo. "You're right. We can't leave them there."

"Me, too," Iva adds.

Tenn jams her hands on her hips, reminding Halo of Sevin. "Me—"

"No!" Fyve cuts her off. "You need to tell Cloud your dream, remember?"

Tenn rolls her eyes. "I thought you said you'd never leave me?"

Halo suppresses a smile to see this defiant side of his little sister emerging.

"I didn't mean..." Fyve sighs. "Fine! But you need to be careful."

"Are you well enough to go?" Iva asks, and it takes Halo a few moments to realize she's talking to her.

"What do you mean?" Halo tries to stand a little straighter.

"You don't look well," says Iva. "Do you need a pod? When was the last time you ate?"

"I'm fine," says Halo. "Just a little tired. I'm not actually hungry anymore, anyway."

"Which is a sign of starvation," Iva muses. "Do you feel cold?"

Halo shakes her head. "I told you, I'm fine."

Tenn slips her hand into Halo's. "We'll stick together. We can turn back if Halo's sick."

"I'm fine!" Halo says more forcefully. She is fine. Well, not *really* fine. But fine enough. Certainly better than when she woke up. Perhaps having something to do is what's giving her strength. Maybe she needs to invent herself a list of jobs to fill her days until the lack of food eventually takes its toll.

Fyve nods, knowing when it's not worth putting up a fight, and the five of them step into the gloominess of the bowels of The Oasis.

Dargo leads the way as they wind their way through the ship, and Halo doesn't complain. The map she's been keeping in her head is too fuzzy to be of any use. It's taking everything she has just to hold onto Tenn's hand and keep her feet moving forward. But the thought of Viney's sisters spurs her on, and Halo remembers the Trial back on Treasure Island where she'd chosen Viney and one of her sisters to get on the ship, with Fyve selecting the remaining sister. Which in many ways, makes them responsible for what happens. If they'd chosen someone else, the three sisters might be safely back home right now. There's no way they can leave them locked in a cabin on a stranded ship.

"This is where I found your bracelet," Iva says.

"Still can't believe that." Dargo holds up his wrist with the strap of leather, and they come to a stop at the wall.

"How are we going to open it?" asks Tenn.

Dargo holds up his other wrist. "With this."

Halo's eyes widen to see he's wearing one of the Echelon's bracelets.

"Knew it would come in handy one day." He winks at Tenn, who nods, impressed.

Fyve pats Dargo on the back. "Far easier than breaking it down. Let's just hope it works."

Dargo presses his wrist to the hidden sensor in the wall and it slides back, revealing the corridor where Fyve had once found Tenn standing in fear. Halo lets out a breath. Surely, it can't be this easy.

Marching forward, Dargo opens the first cabin. There's a large hole in one of the internal walls, but the room is otherwise empty. Going to the next cabin, they find exactly the same thing, except there are two walls with holes this time. The next is the same.

"What's going on?" Halo asks Tenn, who shrugs dramatically in response.

"The doors are reinforced," says Fyve. "I think they tunneled through the interior walls to get to each other when they realized they couldn't get out."

"Over here!" shouts Iva when Dargo opens the next door.

Halo and Tenn follow, Fyve instinctively shielding them as they move forward.

Straining her neck to see, Halo catches a glimpse of four

terrified faces staring back at them from the cabin. Two males. Two females, both with red hair.

"It's okay," says Dargo. "We're here to help you."

One of Viney's sisters stands up. "Well, it's about time. We thought we were going to starve to death. Especially after the Echelons took their favorites and left us here to rot."

Halo swallows, not wanting to tell them that their prospects aren't a lot greater outside these cabin walls.

"We don't have any food for you," says Iva gently.

A guy with jet black hair steps toward the door. "We don't want your food."

"What do you want then?" asks Fyve, preventing his exit.

"We want our freedom," the guy says. "Now get out of my way."

Fyve pushes him back. "First, we need to know whose side you're on."

"Get out of my way!" the guy says. "We're running out of time. A storm's coming."

"Wait. One. Minute." Fyve pushes the guy back so that he falls against the bed and is forced to sit down.

Dargo and Iva block the door, while Halo and Tenn peer through the gaps.

The guy sighs. "Look, sorry man. I appreciate you letting us out and all that. It's just that we're in a hurry here. A storm's coming. A big one. We need to get on the water and clear the area before that happens."

"Water seems calm to me," says Fyve.

"Amet always knows when a storm's coming," the other guy says. "It's his thing."

"And my thing is to know what people are talking about," says Fyve. "Explain, or we'll close the door again. Who are you?"

Amet lets out a sigh and raises his palms. "Okay, okay. I'm Amet. This is Shade. We were captured by the Echelons in the Outlands. We've been Ravens since we were boys. But we're stronger in mind than the others." He taps his head. "There's no way we were going to worship them like the other Ravens. And they knew it. That's why they left us here and took the rest."

"How long have you been locked in here?" Fyve asks.

"Too long," says Shade. "A week. Maybe more. Easy to lose track of time."

"But now we're going home," says one of Viney's sisters.

"That's right," says Amet. "Shade and I are taking Holly and Misty back to Treasure Island. We're going to be free."

Halo gasps, hardly daring to believe what she's hearing. Viney's sisters look across at Amet and Shade in such a way that it's clear strong relationships have been formed in this small room.

"And how, exactly, are you going to do that?" Fyve asks.

"The liferafts," says Amet, trying to get up from the bed. "We've been getting things ready ever since this ship set sail. At least, we were until we got locked in here. We've been waiting for our chance. And that chance is now. I really don't have time to explain it to you. If you'd just step aside, then—"

"We'll let you go on one condition," says Fyve, his hands fists at his side. "You're taking us with you."

FYVE

*F*yve can't believe it. They can get off this ship of death.

Amet and Shade walk ahead, Holly and Misty at their sides, all four taking turns to glance back repeatedly the closer they get to the deck. Fyve can't blame them. He'd be nervous, too.

They'd found the rest of the teens huddled in one of the corridors complaining that the wind had picked up too much to stay outdoors. Fyve remains unconvinced this means a storm is on its way. They've experienced high winds on The Oasis before.

Viney had rejoiced at being reunited with her sisters, but everyone else remains as cautious as the two Ravens from the Outlands. No one knows who to trust.

Amet rubs his forearm as if shivers are dancing over it despite the warm, stale air. "This storm's gonna be a big one."

Justice steps around Halo, her lip curled. "Don't try and distract us."

"I'm not," Amet says, shooting her a look. "I'm telling you, I can feel it."

Viney hikes her hands on her hips. "We can trust them. I know we can."

Fyve doesn't answer. Viney also trusts Ajax and look how that turned out for her.

Halo holds up her hands in a conciliatory gesture. "We all want the same thing—to get off The Oasis—so I suggest we work together."

Amet nods grudgingly, his three friends slowly doing the same. It's the same fragile truce they reached in the cabin.

If the Ravens want freedom, they need to take the teens with them.

Shade pushes open the door to the deck and a gust of wind buffets into the corridor, tugging at their clothes. Fyve suppresses a frown as he acknowledges Amet's prediction may actually be accurate. This is more than just a little wind. A storm is coming.

The Raven steps out, quickly followed by Amet, Holly and Misty, and Fyve hurries to slip through after them. This is the chance for the Ravens to disappear. The deck of The Oasis is massive, with multiple doors leading to who-knows-where. And the Ravens are probably more familiar with the layout of all the floors Fyve and Halo haven't had a chance to explore.

Another gust of wind hits Fyve square in the face and he instinctively closes his eyes as if he was just slapped. He forces them open, not wanting to lose sight of the Ravens and finds the usual handful of seconds needed to adjust to daylight after the corridor aren't necessary. The world is shades of gray with dark, restless clouds looming above.

There are also four Ravens waiting for him only a few feet away.

He's also pleased to see that Justice and Sica managed to secure the net over the pool before they'd retreated indoors.

The last of the teens—all that remain after the Echelons' latest killing spree—exit and congregate around Fyve, some with hands up to protect their faces from the wind. It seems to burst from one direction, only to change and hit from another with the next blast. Fyve tucks Halo and Tenn even closer to him, figuring their joint weight will be a little harder to buffet. Hopefully the wind doesn't get any stronger.

Shade glances at Amet, whose mouth is set in a grim line. "Come on." Shade slips his hand into Misty's. "We'll show you where our lifeboat is."

Fyve glances back, taking note of Cloud and the way Iva and Dargo have flanked her. There are those who are far more vulnerable in their group and it's nice to see others taking care of the young mother and her babies.

Returning his focus to Amet and Shade, Fyve shoves his hair out of his face, feeling as agitated as the wind. They're making their way along the deck to a part he's never been to before. It could be a trap.

They pass the place where Halo set up their hideaway. Fyve glances at Halo, finding she's looking at it, too.

And she has her hand on her stomach.

He blinks, once more reminded that there could be consequences for those sweet moments of love and passion. His hand tightens around hers and she looks up at him, a soft smile playing at the edges of her lips.

It's a reminder that something precious and beautiful was born in all this danger and death.

And they need to get off this ship, no matter what.

"Here," Shade says, stopping closer to the railing and peering over.

Fyve and the others do the same, registering a row of large, faded-yellow boats. It looks like they used to run along the length of the ship, but every second or third one is gone. Yet judging by their size, their small group will only need one.

One lifeboat that will be their one chance at surviving this hell.

Amet bends over the railing and yanks open a door. Inside, barely legible in the gloom, are a stack of cans. "We've been stealing one at a time for months."

Which means they wouldn't be laced with the poison Fyve still carries in his pocket.

The same sense of shock and gratitude at having Halo in his life floods through Fyve, the question of whether he's worthy of all this right behind. He never chose to be a leader of this team. So many have died while he's fought for their freedom.

The wind blows Halo's hair across his shoulder, the ends touching his cheek. The sweet caress is a stark contrast to the bruising bursts of wind. To the weight that threatens to multiply in his chest.

Halo tries to tame her wild strands even as the wind tugs them the opposite direction. "We're going home," she says quietly. Hopefully.

"Not today, we're not," Amet says, glancing up at the clouds that seem oppressively closer. "This has to blow over first."

Justice plants her hands on her hips, still swaying slightly with the next blast of wind despite her stance. "We don't have that sort of time. The Echelons aren't going to stay in the engine room for long."

"Can we just get on and lower it, then wait?" Sica suggests, glancing over her shoulder. "I just want to get off this thing."

Shade rubs the back of his head. "The storm before last blew over without barely any rain," he says to Amet.

"This is a big one. I can feel it," Amet says stubbornly. "We're not going anywhere."

A droplet of water hits Fyve just below his eye, fat and heavy enough to sting a little. He's about to say he agrees when someone else speaks.

A voice that sends icicles through his veins.

"You're right, Raven," Nole growls. "You won't be going anywhere."

Fyve spins around, one hand clasping Halo, the other Tenn. He's about to tell the leader of the Echelons that they'll never cower before them again, but the words die in his throat.

Nole's grin grows as he hefts the flamethrower he's holding. Most of the Echelons spread out behind him are holding one, too.

"You liar!" Justice screams. "You never intended to have a truce!"

Throwing away a handful of their weapons was nothing but show. They clearly had far more hidden away.

Nole chuckles. "Does the lion make peace with the lamb?" The twisted grin falls faster than the air temperature around them. "Of course not. That would confuse the lamb. Upset the order of things." He takes a predatory step forward. "And it's the lion's responsibility to maintain balance."

Hatred burns low and hot in Fyve's gut. "You'll have to kill us to get to the lifeboat."

Nole shakes his head as if Fyve's an idiot. "We don't want the stupid lifeboat. We're staying on this ship and figuring out a way to get to Tomorrow Land. Just like we planned."

Fyve suppresses a sharp inhale. Nole doesn't know about the cans of food.

"Is that what you want, Echelons?" Halo says over the wind. "To stay on this ship and die?"

Rhina's hand flies to her stomach while a couple of other Echelons' brows twitch down. They've thought this themselves.

Halo straightens as she projects her voice even more. "When does a plan go from a daring dream to a desperate nightmare?"

"Shut up!" Nole roars and Halo winces.

He instantly lets out a breath. "I'm so sorry, Treasure. I didn't mean to shout at you. Please don't push me again."

Fyve's body is practically vibrating with anger. "You believe everything you say, don't you? That it's Halo's fault you shouted. That taking innocent lives was necessary." Fyve's gaze flickers to

Jiro, sickened that he's related to these men. "That you're doing this for the betterment of humankind."

Halo shakes her head. "When it's all for greed. Power. Your own selfish ego."

Nole draws back as if he was just struck. If anyone else said those words, he would be furious. But his Treasure said them as she unflinchingly looks at him.

Possibly with pity.

"That's the definition of crazy," Sica hurls out.

"Actually, the definition of crazy is following someone like that," Justice shouts.

Nole's gaze snaps to Fyve, glittering with hatred. "You've twisted my Treasure against me," he snarls. "I should've claimed you back on Treasure Island, just like your mother."

"It'll be your greatest regret," Fyve promises.

Nole brings the flamethrower to his front, his face twisting with sick glee. "I don't know what regret feels like, and I'm not about to find out."

A few gasps slice through the wind that's becoming a constant barrage. Nole must hear them because his grin grows as he adjusts the weight of the flamethrower in his palms. He sets his shoulders, his intent clear.

"You won't pull the trigger," Fyve grinds out, his heart thudding. A whimper escapes Tenn. "You could hurt Halo."

The flames those things shoot out are explosive. Anyone around Fyve would be burned, too.

Nole raises the flamethrower so it's pointed more squarely at Fyve. "The moment I do, the others will scatter." His gaze flickers to Halo. "And even if she doesn't, you'll push her away."

Fyve stills, knowing that Nole just spoke the truth, even as he hates him for it.

If the Echelon pulls the trigger, that's exactly what he'll do. If Fyve can't survive this, the least he can do is give Halo a chance.

"No," Halo moans.

"Yes," Nole hisses, clearly excited.

Fyve works to keep his breathing even though every molecule in his body has frozen. He's going to have to move fast to get Halo and Tenn out of the way. All before the flames devour him in a blaze of heat and pain.

Nole's hands tighten on the flamethrower. His finger constricts on the trigger.

Fyve realizes his life is now being counted out in seconds. That it's up to him to make them count.

"I love you, Halo," he says through his tight throat, hoping she heard him.

"No!" Jiro shoves past Nole, lumbering his round body toward Fyve, then spinning to stand in front of him. "You can't kill him, Nole! You promised my children would be safe."

Fyve's shock is only eclipsed by Nole's. Although Jiro's squarely in front of him, he's slightly shorter than Fyve, who sees Nole's face over his father's shoulder.

And Nole looks pissed.

He lowers the flamethrower and tucks it behind him again. "Move, Jiro."

"No," Jiro says, shaking his head vigorously. "He's my son. I won't let you kill him."

"He's Fyve's dad?" Justice says in disbelief.

Tenn slips in close to Fyve's side. "He's my dad, too!" she calls out, clearly proud.

"A father who let most of his children die on Treasure Island," Nole growls, his gaze on his brother. "Who left his other daughter behind."

Fyve still has no idea which of those are the true Jiro. The loving father? Or the blind follower…

Jiro's shoulders stiffen as he takes a step forward, widening the gap between himself and Fyve. "Because you had me believing in you. You said sacrifices had to be made if we were going to reach Tomorrow Land and make everything right."

Nole's face softens. "Of course I did. It's the truth. And you've been a role model to every Echelon as you've shown unfailing support."

Jiro's wince is apparent even from behind. He takes a step closer to Nole. "And what sacrifices have you made, brother? Killing Halo would end this rebellion as effectively as killing Fyve." He moves again. "My son."

Nole's features turn to stone. "Enough, Jiro. This is what needs to be done to move forward."

"No, it doesn't." Jiro stops a few feet away from his brother. "I won't let you hurt another of my children."

Fyve blinks, struggling to know how to feel about this. Jiro is saving his life. Again.

"Daddy," Tenn whimpers. She tugs Fyve's hand, looking up at him. "You need to save him."

Save him? Surely Nole wouldn't...

Fyve breaks into a run before his mind can finish the question he already knows the answer to. Of course Nole would kill his own brother.

And Jiro knows this.

He's risking his life so Fyve and the others can get away.

Fyve pushes his feet into the floor even harder as the wind tries to shove him back, having no intention of running away when his father's in danger. Nole won't take him, too.

Except the leader of the Echelons moves fast. Faster than someone of his fleshy weight should. Nole yanks something from his pocket and snaps his arm out toward Jiro. He yanks his arm back a second later, slipping the blade back in his pocket.

Fyve's father staggers backward several steps, clutching his chest. He turns slowly, his rounded face a pale backdrop to his wide, terrified eyes.

"No!" Fyve screams, registering the expanding red stain on Jiro's chest.

Jiro stumbles a few more feet, his gaze locked on Fyve, but

his legs give out. His knees collapse and he careens forward. Fyve leaps to catch him, but they both crumple under Jiro's weight.

Jiro lets out a pained groan as they hit the floor.

Fyve's own sound of anguish quickly follows.

He holds his father in his arms, the blood bloom now covering most of his torso. Shaking his head, Fyve desperately tries to figure out how he can alter the inevitability coming at him. "You shouldn't have..." he chokes, the knowledge that only going back in time will change what's about to happen.

The life that's about to be lost.

Pain is carved in the lines of Jiro's face as he struggles to breathe. "Unlike Nole...I have many regrets." He grimaces. "But this...isn't one of them."

"Dad..." Fyve chokes.

A ghost of a smile slips over Jiro's lips, then fades away as his eyes close and his body goes limp.

Fyve's lungs seize. His gut feels like it was just excavated. His heart is shredding as Tenn stands in silent shock beside him.

The low-hanging clouds open up, releasing a deluge of tears as he holds his father's dead body. They instantly soak Fyve's hair, his clothes, his skin. The water trickles down Jiro's still face, over his tunic, then runs in pale red rivulets over the deck.

"He was too soft," Nole's voice growls above. "The moment he got attached to Dee, I warned him. But Jiro wouldn't listen. It was his weakness and is what ultimately killed him."

Fyve's head snaps up, his focus narrowing on the Echelon's fat, self-serving face. He's the source of everything that's been inflicted on hundreds of lives.

And he'll never see it.

Nole lifts his flamethrower, the tip only inches from Fyve's face. "And your weak, foolish heart will be the end of you, too."

Fyve roars as he leaps forward, propelled by fury. Grief. And the drive for vengeance.

For his mother.

And his father.

For every sibling he lost.

For the Trials and the claimings and the cold-hearted killings.

He knocks the flamethrower away and rams his hands into Nole's chest. The Echelon stumbles backward, clearly shocked at the sudden attack.

He hadn't expected Fyve to retaliate.

It's just the advantage Fyve needs. He's going to show Nole exactly what Jiro's death cost him.

Lightning cracks, illuminating the Echelons as they lift their own flamethrowers, ready to protect their leader. Thunder almost drowns out Fyve's next words.

He spins to face Halo and the others. "Run!" he shouts. "We need to get below deck!"

The Echelons won't be able to use their flamethrowers there.

A quick elbow to Nole's face is all Fyve allows himself before breaking into a run, away from the Echelons, and toward Halo and Tenn. Jiro died so they could escape. No matter how much Fyve wants justice, he's not going to throw that chance away.

He leaps over his father's body, wishing his sacrifice could be honored, but knowing there's no time. He scoops up Tenn as he reaches Halo. "Come on!"

She nods, breaking into a sprint now that she's given Fyve time to catch up. The teens scatter, spreading out in every direction.

Yet all running toward one location.

The nearest door.

The rain beats with new ferocity, blurring the way ahead and more thunder rolls. Except the blast of light that follows doesn't come from above. It explodes behind them.

"The flamethrowers!" Halo screams.

Nole and the others are attacking.

Ahead, Justice slips to a stop on the slick deck as she reaches a door. She tries it, but it doesn't move.

The next blast of flames is so close, Fyve can feel the heat licking his back. They may be wet, but they won't stand a chance against the inferno contained in the flamethrowers. Even if it doesn't kill them, it'll do enough damage to ensure a slow, painful death.

With a curse and a shout, Justice tries again, her face twisted with desperation and determination.

The door slips open and she stumbles in. "Hurry!" she shouts, grabbing Cloud by the arm and yanking her to safety as she clutches Miracle and Marvel.

The small team pours in as Fyve glances over his shoulder. He intends to make sure every last teen is inside before he follows.

And Nole would know that. Would see it as a weakness.

The Echelon strides toward them, holding his flamethrower out. Water runs over his fleshy face, but it doesn't wash away the dark, violent mask he's wearing.

"Fyve!" Halo calls, grabbing him by the arm.

He's the last one on the deck. The others are running down the corridor the door led to.

Fyve leaps inside, slamming the sliding door shut.

He hears the roar of the flamethrower over the storm, but he doesn't stop to see what damage it does. Grabbing Tenn again, he and Halo run after the others. Deeper down the corridor. Down a set of stairs. Then up another according to Halo's instructions.

Clutching a sobbing Tenn, Fyve runs with the others as they descend into the bowels of The Oasis once more.

The ship of death.

Knowing their one chance of leaving just met the same fate as his father.

HALO

"We have to stick together," Halo says to the dwindling group of teens.

"Not much choice in that." Justice tilts her head at Sica, who's pressed against her left side, and Ajax, who's on her right. They're huddled in a random cabin on the fifth floor, hoping the storm will defy Amet's prediction and blow over without too much fuss.

Cloud is perched on the bed with Iva and the babies, while Viney and her sisters stand with their arms around each other, talking in hushed tones as they fill each other in on everything that's happened since they parted. Amet and Shade are by the door with their backs to each other, making it clear the only one they trust is each other. Dargo and a few of the others are sitting on the floor with their knees tucked up to their chests.

"Is she asleep?" Halo asks Fyve, who's cradling Tenn in a corner of the room. She hasn't said a word since their father was killed.

Fyve gives Halo a sad shrug. He knows as well as she does that it's likely Tenn is pretending to sleep as a way to block out the world. Which is such a huge shame, given she'd only just come out of her shell to show them her true personality. This will be a major setback.

The ship tilts violently to one side, reminding them that the storm is going nowhere right now. Halo is thrown onto the bed. Iva breaks her fall so she doesn't land on the babies.

"Thanks," says Halo, her heart racing as she holds her weight on her elbows.

Miracle wakes and lets out a whimper. Marvel doesn't seem bothered, which is even more concerning. The Oasis rights itself and Halo gets back on her feet, holding onto a shelving unit for stability.

A hushed conversation takes place between Amet and Shade.

"Talk to everyone," snaps Justice. "If you want to be part of this group, share what you have to say."

"We're talking about getting you some food," says Amet. "No offense, but you all look terrible. Those babies aren't going to make it if Cloud doesn't eat."

"I already ate," says Cloud. "The others haven't had anything for days."

"I'm fine," Halo says, although her stomach instantly betrays her by grumbling at the mention of food. Thankfully, nobody else can hear it over the sound of howling wind.

"None of you are fine." Amet slides open the door.

"Where are you getting food?" Fyve asks. "If there's anything left, the Echelons would've taken it for themselves."

Shade rolls his eyes and the lights in the cabin blink, threatening to give out. "The Echelons aren't as smart as they think."

"We've hidden food all over the place." Amet throws out his hands, hitting one of the walls.

"They called us Ravens to dehumanize us," says Shade. "But Ravens are smart, resourceful birds. They're scavengers. Some people believe they can see the future. It didn't take a crystal ball when we got dragged onto this ship to see it was all going to end in disaster."

"That's why we prepared the lifeboat," Amet adds. "And hid food. It's important to have options."

"How do we know you're not going straight to the Echelons and tell them where we are?" Justice asks.

One of Viney's sisters steps forward. Halo isn't sure if she's Holly or Misty.

"I'm trying to be patient with you," she says, flicking her long red plait over her shoulder. "But this is just too much. We *hate* the Echelons. They locked us in a cabin and left us for dead. They stopped us from trying to leave just now. What would possibly motivate Shade or Amet to tell them where we are?"

"Misty's right," says the sister who must be Holly. "Besides, Shade and Amet wouldn't let any harm come to us, and we're staying right here with Viney."

"I'll go with one of them," says Sica. "Then nobody has to freak out. This is really doing my head in, being cramped in here with the lot of you."

"Not necessary," says Amet. "But okay. Before that baby starts crying again. Then the Echelons won't need to be told where we are, it will be obvious."

"Hey," says Ajax. "That's my baby you're talking about."

Amet seems genuinely surprised about this, and Halo can't blame him. Ajax hasn't been near either of the twins the whole time the Ravens have been with them. Amet lowers his raised brows but asks no more.

Shade opens the door and steps back to let his friend out. Sica follows, leaning out first to look both ways before she exits.

"Be careful," says Halo, keeping her voice low.

Sica winks at her as the door slides closed again. Halo just hopes she sees her again. She's said goodbye to too many people since she set foot on this ship. It would be unbearable to lose anyone else.

There's a loud bang in the corridor as the ship is thrown

about on another wave and Halo holds onto the shelf to steady herself, her knuckles turning white.

Shade opens the door again, peeking out into the corridor then coming back in.

"It's okay," he says. "Amet was thrown into a wall but he's back up now."

Halo looks at Fyve, wanting to ask if he's sure they can trust Amet, but not wanting to cause any more of a rift in the group. He gives her a small nod and she knows that's all the reassurance she can get right now. Sica can take care of herself. She'll be okay.

"We need a plan," says Ajax.

"We have one." Fyve shifts Tenn to a more comfortable position on his lap and frowns up at Ajax. "We're resting. Soon, we'll eat. Then as soon as the storm passes, we get on that lifeboat and leave this ship forever."

"It's not that easy." Ajax lets go of the wall to put his hands on his hips but quickly returns them when the ship hits another wave.

"I never said it was easy." Fyve doesn't roll his eyes, but his voice does it for him.

"The Echelons will never let us get on that boat," says Ajax. "We have to outsmart them. Which is why we're lucky I have Rhina."

Viney elbows her sisters so hard that Misty doubles over.

Halo moves so she's standing closer to Fyve. He has her full support, even if Ajax is her brother.

"I know what you all think of me," says Ajax. "Three women having my babies at once isn't something you approve of."

A clap of thunder rattles through the ship as if agreeing with this statement.

"But it wasn't my fault," Ajax continues. "Cloud and I were in love. Then I was fooled into thinking I had to leave her behind forever."

"The plan was for you to come back to me, if you remember," Cloud mutters, not having the same restraint with her eyes as Fyve had shown.

"So, I had no choice but to seek comfort elsewhere." Ajax seems so sincere, despite the ridiculousness of his words. "I was broken."

"Comfort?" screeches Viney. "That's all I was to you? Comfort!"

Ajax lets out a sigh, barely audible over the wind that seems to be finding its way into every corner of the ship.

"Then I was chosen as a Treasure by Rhina," Ajax says, ignoring Viney's question. "Nobody here can hold me accountable for that. She chose me, not the other way around."

"But you didn't have to sleep with her!" says Misty, shaking her head. "None of the other Treasures did."

"Well, they weren't as strategic as me." Ajax pulls back his shoulders as one of his blonde curls falls into his eyes. Halo wonders how different his life might have been had he not been born so handsome. If his face had matched his heart, then maybe he wouldn't have caused so many women so much pain.

"Halo was strategic," says Justice. "And she managed to keep hold of her dignity."

"Yeah," says Misty. "And look where your strategy got you, Ajax! You're stuck hiding in this cabin with the rest of us."

Halo stifles a laugh. Misty may not have known Ajax for very long, but what she says is true.

"I'm not stuck," says Ajax, pushing his hair out of his eyes. "I'm here by ch—"

"What?" Halo tilts her head when Ajax abruptly stops talking and stares vacantly in front of him. "Are the Echelons talking to you?"

"Oh, that's right," says Justice. "I forgot that dimwit kept his chip."

The ship rocks violently again and Halo's glad they're not on the lifeboat. They'd have been no match for the anger of this storm. Amet had been right. Not that she necessarily feels any safer where they are.

"What did they say?" Fyve asks when Ajax's focus returns.

"It was Rhina." Ajax looks less certain of himself than he had a few moments ago. In fact, he looks slightly terrified.

Halo picks her way carefully across the cabin to Ajax, wishing she could let go of the remnants of feelings she has for her brother, even after everything he's done.

"What is it, Ajax?" she asks, putting a hand on his arm and presses the other to the wall beside them. "What did she say?"

"She wants me to come to the engine room." He swallows, glancing at Cloud.

"Then, go," says Cloud. "What are you waiting for? Not my permission, I hope. Because we've gone way past that."

"Yeah," says Misty. "Go. We don't need you in here taking up oxygen. Go and talk strategy with your new girlfriend, since you've just been telling us how good you are at it."

"No!" Justice is firm. "He'll tell them where we are."

"We can always move cabins after he leaves," says Halo, knowing there's no way they can trust Ajax, as much as she wants to. Not when their lives are at stake, including those of the babies. "We chose this one at random. It makes no difference where we hide."

"Sica and Amet won't be able to find us," Dargo points out.

Halo sighs. "Then he can wait until after Sica and Amet get back."

Ajax says something, but it's impossible to hear over the roar of the ocean. He waits for a lull and tries again, talking only to Halo this time.

"I can't go," he says, his eyes pleading with Halo. "You have to help me."

"What are you not telling us?" Halo asks. "If you want my help, tell me exactly what Rhina said."

He puts his hands to his ears and it's clear Rhina is talking to him again. His face pales and his fingertips rub the place on his temple where his chip is located.

"Is the chip giving you a headache?" Halo asks, well aware of the impact it can have when it's overused. She'd never had a headache on Treasure Island, but she'd also never heard any of the voices back then.

Ajax shakes his head and lets his hands fall. His mouth flaps at Halo, but no words come out.

"What did she say?" Halo lets go of the wall and grips his other arm. He pulls her close so he can speak directly in her ear.

"She wants me to choose between her and Viney," he whispers.

Halo pulls back to study his face. "Is that a problem?"

The ship lurches and both Ajax and Halo are thrown against the wall. They steady themselves and he hisses in her ear again.

"Terra has been speaking to me," he says. "The real Terra. I'm special, Halo. I've been chosen."

Halo frowns. He's either hearing voices that don't exist, or Nole is playing games with him. Both options are just as likely.

"Terra wants me to breed with multiple women," says Ajax. "To choose only one would go against Terra. She's pleased with the choices I made, even if I didn't know what I was doing at the time."

"We can hear you, Ajax," sneers Misty, while Viney weeps into Holly's shoulder. "Please, just get this over with and choose Rhina."

"If you heard me, then you'll know I can't choose," says Ajax, straightening his back. "My purpose here is different to yours. It's Terra's will. And Viney is playing an important part in that."

"If it's Terra's will, then why is Rhina asking you to choose?" asks Fyve, his disdain for Ajax clear.

Ajax shakes his head. "She's putting her needs above Terra's."

"What's the problem here?" Justice asks on a huff. "Then

don't go to her. Simple. Honestly, we have more important things to discuss right now. Like, how we're going to get off this ship."

"You don't understand." Ajax's fingers go to his temple. "She said if I don't go to the engine room in the next five minutes that she'll claim me."

Halo gasps. "We need to get your chip out. Justice, break the mirror in the bathroom. Hurry!"

"No!" Ajax booms. "You don't understand. You can't take out my chip."

"Then you have to go to Rhina," says Halo. "Please. Think of your children. All of them! You can't let her claim you."

"It's a bluff," says Ajax. "She won't kill me. She loves me."

"Then why do you look so afraid?" Fyve asks.

"I'm not," he says, although everything about him says otherwise.

"You asked for my help," says Halo. "And the best way I can help you is to cut out your chip. Then you don't have to choose anyone. Please, Ajax. Let me."

"But then I won't be able to hear Terra." Ajax shakes his head.

"That's not Terra!" Halo grips his arms harder, trying to get him to understand.

Another rumble of thunder rattles through the ship.

"You don't know that," says Ajax. "I'm special. Terra chose me!"

Halo's so exhausted, she doesn't know if she can continue to argue for much longer. But then Miracle lets out another cry and she knows she has to. The twins deserve the chance to grow up knowing their father.

There's the smash of glass and Justice appears with a long shard in her hand.

"Fyve," she says, waving the sharp glass. "You pin him down and I'll get it out."

Fyve repositions Tenn on the floor so he can stand. Halo

isn't sure if it's to help Justice or to convince her that what she's planning is outrageous.

"Leave me!" Ajax shouts. "Why do you even care? You don't even like me."

"We've lost enough lives around here," says Justice. "It has to stop. The Echelons have taken enough."

"Don't touch me." Ajax tucks himself behind Halo, holding his hands to his temples. "Keep away. Rhina won't do it. She loves me. Terra loves me."

Justice lurches forward.

"Stop!" Halo holds up her hands. "What you said is right. The Echelons have taken enough. We haven't been able to make any meaningful decisions for our future since we stepped on this ship. That's what has to stop. We need our power back. The right to decide what happens to us. Taking Ajax's chip by force makes us no better than the Echelons."

Justice stares at Halo for a few seconds then lets the glass fall to the floor. "Fine! Let him keep his chip. But you do realize it's suicide, don't you?"

Halo turns to her brother, her complicated feelings for him raging inside her. She can't bear to witness another death. "If you won't take out your chip, then you have to go to Rhina. Tell her you choose her, even if you don't. Buy yourself some time. Keep yourself safe."

"She won't claim me." Ajax pulls back his shoulders. "Terra will protect me."

Halo doesn't like any of this, but she nods, hoping her brother is right. Surely, Rhina wouldn't kill the father of her unborn child?

The door to the cabin slides back and everyone jumps. Fyve and Justice lurch forward, ready to attack.

But it's Amet and Sica, and there's a collective sigh of relief. Sica is holding half a dozen tin cans. Amet has two more. Both of them are grinning.

"Anyone ever heard of Santa Claus?" asks Amet as he slides the door closed.

"Nope," says Justice, answering for the rest of them as they shake their heads.

Amet rolls his eyes. "Doesn't matter then. He was just some old guy who bought children gifts. I was feeling kinda like him, coming back with all this."

Holly laughs as she lets go of Viney to kiss Amet on the cheek. "I'm glad you're back, Santa."

Sica sets the cans down on a bench and takes a metal tool from her pocket that she hands to Dargo. "You know what to do with this thing?"

He nods, taking it and getting to work, opening the cans.

Halo's stomach groans again as moisture pools in her mouth. She wants to let Cloud eat this entire stack of food, but she knows this time she needs to accept at least a small portion. To protect Cloud, she needs to stay alive. And to do that, she needs to eat.

Amet adds his cans to the stack and Shade distributes the open ones to everyone.

"One can between two," he tells them. "Cloud gets one to herself because she's already sharing with two."

Halo smiles, deciding she agrees with Viney for once. They can trust these Ravens.

Fyve jostles Tenn awake and they share a can.

"I'll share with you," Halo tells Ajax, knowing nobody else will want to.

It's a yellow-colored fruit, and Halo scoops a piece into her mouth and groans at the bliss it creates on her taste buds. It's such a relief that it wasn't that awful salty meat. She can feel the sugars instantly feeding her body.

Ajax takes a piece and swallows it so quickly she doubts his taste buds even got a chance to enjoy it.

"Don't go too fast," Fyve warns everyone. "Our bodies aren't used to it."

"Thank you," says Justice, looking directly at Amet as she licks the juice from her lips. "And I apologize for doubting you. We really needed some food."

Cloud is eating slowly, determined to keep this food down, despite how nauseous she's been since this storm took hold. She knows her babies' lives depend on her keeping this down.

"Should we save some for later?" Iva asks.

Everyone looks at each other, letting the howling wind speak for them.

"We might not have a later," says Sica between slurps.

A few eyebrows raise.

"What?" Sica waves a piece of fruit in front of her. "I only said what you were all thinking. Now isn't the time to save for a rainy day."

The pelting rain on the side of the ship intensifies, proving Sica's point.

They finish their food. Ajax and Halo pass their can back and forth. He takes the bigger piece each time, but she pretends not to notice. He's taller than her so needs the sustenance more. Then she glances down at Fyve and notices the way he makes sure Tenn gets all the larger pieces. Perhaps it's time to stop making excuses for her brother and accept he's his own unique selfish self.

Ajax takes the last piece of fruit and Halo drinks the juice, leaving some for Ajax at the bottom of the empty can. He takes it and slurps it down, only for it to come shooting straight back out.

"Ajax!" Halo cries, her first thought of what a waste of juice that was.

He drops the can, and it clatters to the floor as his hands fly to his temples.

Halo grabs him by the arms. "Is she talking to you ag—"

"Urgauh," Ajax mumbles. "Rhianaugh."

He drops to the floor and Fyve pulls Tenn back. Blood pours from Ajax's nose and eyes and Halo lets out a small cry. Dargo pushes Halo out of the way and forces Ajax's head onto his lap. He has the shard of mirror in his hand, his own blood seeping on the floor as it slices into his palm.

"I'm taking your chip out," he says. "It's not too late."

"No," says Ajax, although the word is barely audible through the gurgling of blood now coming out of his mouth. "Don't."

"This is ridiculous," says Justice, joining Dargo and pulling Ajax's hands from his head.

Halo whimpers, with no idea what she should do. Ajax clearly doesn't want his chip removed, but it's the only way to save him. At what point do humans get to make that kind of choice? Is saving someone who doesn't want to be saved as bad as killing them when they want to live?

Dargo slices into the side of Ajax's head while he thrashes on the floor. Justice is on top of Ajax now, straddling him as she pins his hands to his side. Blood spills from Ajax's temple as Dargo reaches into his scalp, searching for the chip.

"I've got it!" he cries, holding something in the air that's too small to see amongst all the blood.

"Yes!" Justice cheers. "Good work, Dargo!"

But there's something Justice hasn't noticed that Halo has. Something that has her frozen in much the same way Tenn had as she'd watched her father die.

Ajax is no longer struggling. Justice is pinning his arms but he's offering no resistance. Nor is that horrible gurgling sound continuing to pour from his chest.

"He's gone," says Halo quietly. She doubts anyone can hear her over the noise of the storm, but it doesn't matter as now they're all seeing what she had noticed first.

Her only sibling is dead. Killed by his own determined arrogance. Gone to join her father and her mother, leaving only Halo behind.

But then Miracle lets out a cry, and Halo remembers she's not alone. She has the twins. And Viney's baby. And Rhina's if she ever gets to see that baby born. Her family will go on.

Fyve is beside her now and he wraps his arms around her. She buries her face in his chest and knows that her family has stretched far beyond blood.

She has Fyve. And Cloud. And Tenn. And all the friends with her now.

Ajax has gone, but she's not alone.

The Echelons have taken so much. But she still has love.

Looking down at her brother's lifeless body, it's clear that the Echelons will stop at nothing to keep their control. Including taking the life of someone they cared about because he wouldn't do what they said.

Which means that hiding in this cabin together may not be enough. Now that they no longer have numbers as their strength, it might be time to take a different approach to ensure their safety.

Maybe it's time to split up.

FYVE

"I want you to stay here and look after Cloud and the babies," Fyve says to Tenn as he squats in front of her.

His little sister glances over her shoulder into the random cabin they found tucked away on the second floor. Cloud is sitting on the bed, holding Marvel and Miracle even though she looks like her arms could use a break. The ship's rocking is growing by the minute, meaning she's not comfortable putting them down, but at least she's kept her food down. Iva and Dargo are off scouting the rest of the floor to make sure it's empty.

Like Justice said, the Echelons aren't going to stay in the engine room forever.

Tenn looks back at him, her eyes wide and unblinking. "Okay."

Fyve's heart feels like it just got put in a vice. His feisty sister is gone, replaced by a scared little girl. One who reminds him of when she was forced to impersonate Terra. He cups her head, her stubble feeling soft against his palm. "I'll be back, I promise."

Her lower lip trembles. "Daddy said he could never make any promises."

"Because he couldn't," Fyve says, his voice hoarse. Jiro lived a life of divided loyalties, torn between his heart and everything he told was true. Fyve has always fought for one thing only—the truth that lies in his heart. "But I *can* make promises. I will always do everything I can to protect you, Tenn."

She nods, serious in ways no child her age should know how to be. "I believe you, Fyve."

He draws her into a fierce hug, already hating leaving her behind. It's just too dangerous. And Nole will be looking for Halo with the obsessiveness he's shown time after time. Fyve needs to find a way to end this before they can think of how to survive to tomorrow.

Tenn's thin arms feel both fragile and strong beyond her years as she clasps him back. "I love you, Fyve," she says, her voice muffled against his neck.

"I love you, too, Tenn," he rasps, pulling back. "Our family are protectors. That's why I'm leaving you here to look after Cloud and the babies."

Tenn straightens, then pulls her shoulders back as she nods resolutely. "We really are."

"Iva and Dargo are back," Halo says from behind Fyve as she rests her hand on his shoulder.

He pushes to his feet, wishing he could stay here and protect them all.

Hating the Echelons for making him choose.

Halo steps back, letting Iva and Dargo pass. They both look exhausted, but Dargo is particularly drawn and pale. The poisoning from Abe is still taking its toll.

"We couldn't see anything," Iva says. "None of the other cabins have been used, either."

Fyve nods, moving out of the way so they can enter. Dargo goes straight to the bed and sits heavily at the head, leaning back against the wall. Iva sits on the other side of Cloud, offering to take Miracle, who Cloud gladly passes over.

Tenn looks up at Fyve, who nods in answer to her silent question. Straightening her shoulders once more, she walks toward Cloud and offers to take Marvel. Cloud smiles and pats the spot on her other side. Tenn scrambles up and Cloud places the sleeping infant in her arms. The ship tilts sharply again and they move in close around the baby.

Tenn looks up and Fyve nods again, his throat clamped around a hard ball of emotion.

Halo slips an arm around his waist. "You're right," she says quietly. "You're a family of protectors. Your mother did what she could to give you a different life. So did Jiro, in his own way. Then Sevin made sure you left Treasure Island."

And now Tenn is holding a baby as danger surrounds them. Outside of The Oasis, the storm rages. Inside the ship, the Echelons want to enslave them. Or kill them.

The storm should blow over eventually. As for Nole and his followers—neither of those are options Fyve's willing to entertain. Not for Tenn. Not for Halo. And not for every other teen who entered the Trials, hoping for a better future.

Justice appears carrying one of her crutches like a spear, jogging from the opposite direction that Iva and Dargo arrived, Sica right behind her. "A few of the others are on the fourth floor. The Ravens wanted to go to the first floor, but there's water coming under the doors to the deck, so they're on the fifth."

"Thanks," Fyve says. "Let's see where we'll sit out the storm."

Halo's idea that they split up was a good one. If the Echelons go searching, they're less likely to find pockets of teens. And if they do find them, then they won't all be captured at once...

Fyve pushes the thought away. He's tired of death and loss.

Of living under the oppressiveness of fear.

"Stay quiet," he says to those in the cabin. "We'll be checking on everyone as often as we can until the storm blows over."

In the meantime, they need to find a way to ensure they get off this ship when the waters are calm once again.

A row of nods are his answer, Dargo's slower than the others, Cloud's little more than a timid twitch as she wraps her arm more tightly around Tenn and Marvel. Tenn's is touched with a heartbreaking mix of fear and determination.

Fyve closes the sliding door, hoping it's not the last time he sees any of them. He turns to Halo, Justice and Sica. "No more waiting for them to come to us," he says in a low voice, his gaze glancing in the directions of the stairs that will take them further into the bowels of The Oasis. "We're going to them."

Halo's face hardens as her eyes flare. "And do what?"

"Make sure they're no longer a threat."

"Yes," Justice hisses.

"About freaking time," Sica growls.

Silently, they stride away, wrapping their determination around them like armor. Fyve and Halo glance at each other. It feels good to be taking control. They won't be defined as lambs again.

They're taking the stairs that lead to the engine room floor, hands running over the walls as the ship sways erratically, when Sica speaks. "How are we going to kill them?" she asks, sounding like she's looking forward to it.

"We're not," Fyve answers. "We don't need to. All we have to do is lock them in the engine room and they're no longer a threat."

"You're right," Halo says, her brow scrunching in a way that means she's thinking. "Then the minute the storm passes, we leave."

Justice's fist lands in her palm with a *thwack*. "We'll lock them away just like they did the Ravens. They can rot in their own greed."

"Deciding whether they die of starvation, or eat their own poisoned food," Sica adds.

The stairs take a sharp left, meaning they're almost there. Not wanting to hesitate, Fyve's about to continue when he's forced to pause.

Voices carry up to them, faint but undeniable.

"He thought he meant something to me," chuckles a female voice.

Halo's eyes widen. "Rhina," she mouths.

"We wanted them smart, but not too smart," responds a male voice. Not Nole, so one of the other Echelons. "We're the ones providing the intelligence genes for the children of Tomorrow Land."

Justice snorts softly as she shakes her head in disgust. The Echelons still believe they're going to make it to the mythical Tomorrow Land.

The lights flicker as The Oasis tilts the sharpest it has yet. Halo crashes into Fyve, and he clasps her to him. Behind them, Justice and Sica mutter curse words, Justice's knees digging into Fyve's back.

"We have to find the Treasures before this storm is over," Rhina snarls. The sound of retching quickly follows. "Hopefully it's making that bitch Viney as sick as I am."

The male Echelon chuckles, then curses when another dip has him thudding into the wall. "Out of all the time we've been at sea, this is the worst storm so far."

Halo straightens, swallowing as they all listen intently. Fyve wonders if she's thinking the same thing he is. The hope to quietly lock the door and disappear is no longer an option. They're going to have to attack.

And Rhina's pregnant with Ajax's child.

"You're going to have to search on your own," Rhina says, retching again. "I'm carrying the future of humankind."

Justice makes her own retching sounds behind them. Rhina and Ajax aren't exactly who Fyve would like to see repopulate the Earth, either.

But at least this means they only have to fight the male. It should be easy enough to incapacitate an unfit, overweight Echelon.

"Fair enough," he grunts. "Send Art and Lear out, will you? These lights are probably going to go off permanently soon." As if to prove a point, they flicker, going dark for long seconds before returning.

Fyve tenses. They now have three Echelons to face.

Behind him, Justice hefts the crutch she's never stopped carrying. "I'll skewer their fat bellies."

"We have to stop them from leaving," Halo says in a low, hard voice.

She's right. They can't afford to have any of the Echelons wandering around The Oasis. It's the only way they'll be able to get off this ship.

Fyve glances at her. "Ready?"

She nods once. "Ready."

They simultaneously shoot to their feet and break into a run. A battle cry erupts from Fyve, one that's quickly echoed by Halo. Then Justice. And Sica.

It means it's four ferocious teens ready to wage war who bear down the corridor. The Echelon who was talking to Rhina's head snaps up, his eyes widening. Further down, closer to the open door of the engine room, is Rhina, two more Echelons beside her.

Rhina screeches and lumbers through the door, disappearing from sight. Fyve's glad. He wouldn't want to fight a pregnant woman, Echelon or not, nor would he want Halo to make the choice. Rhina killed Ajax, but she's also carrying his child.

Anger flushes over the first Echelon's face, bright and hot, and he breaks into an awkward jog. It's then that Fyve sees he's holding a flamethrower.

As if he means to use it.

Fyve doesn't stop, nor do the others. There's no way the

Echelon will use the weapon within the walls of the corridor. Self-preservation has always been their ultimate goal.

The Echelon stops as the distance between them closes. He hefts the flamethrower so it's pointing at them. "The walls are steel," he shouts. "You'll melt long before they will."

Fyve's stomach jackknifes into his throat. "Dive!" he shouts, taking Halo with him as he hurls himself down.

The burst of the flamethrower roars in the confines of the corridor. The heat is like an inferno. It explodes over the top of them, the smell of fuel and burned hair assaulting Fyve's nostrils.

But there are no agonized screams. A quick glance over his shoulder confirms it. Everyone got out of the way.

The blazing firestorm dies out and Fyve looks up to see the Echelon breathing hard, trickles of sweat running down his round face. He lowers his chin into his fleshy neck and drops the muzzle, clearly preparing to do it again.

Fyve breaks into a run. The fastest he's ever moved in his life. He propels himself straight at the Echelon, charred, metal walls on either side. All he has to do is get to the bastard before he pulls the trigger.

The Echelon's eyes widen, then narrow with hatred. His fleshy body coils. He aims the flamethrower right at Fyve.

Fyve ducks right, then left, using every spare inch of the corridor as he weaves his way toward the man. The Echelon jerks the heavy weapon too far as he tries to keep him in his sights, and it clangs against the wall. He snarls in frustration then stops. "The flames are wider than the corridor, you fool!" he screams at Fyve.

He'd already thought of that but was hoping the Echelon wouldn't.

With adrenaline injecting into his straining muscles, Fyve jams his hand into his pocket, rips it back out, and pretends to throw something at the Echelon. The man ducks, then flushes the brightest so far when he realizes nothing has hit him.

Fyve is using every trick he, Sevin and Coal used on each other when they'd play tag.

Except this time, he's playing for his life.

The Echelon bares his teeth as he hunches his shoulders, preparing to blast another inferno. Fyve's pounding heart stutters. He's run out of tricks in this barren, burned corridor.

He won't get to the Echelon in time.

A cry has the man's eyes widening with surprise. Footsteps sound behind Fyve.

"Are you going to shoot now?" Halo cries out. "With Nole's Treasure so close?"

The Echelon hesitates. But then he drops his chin again. "Nole's the one who's obsessed with you. Not the rest of us."

But those seconds are all Fyve needed.

He coils his muscle, crouches as he runs, and leaps.

The Echelon's eyes widen and he jerks the flamethrower as he tries to hit Fyve, but he was expecting that. Fyve knocks it out of the way, the barrel searing his hand, then plows into the Echelon.

The Echelon stumbles backward and Fyve maintains the momentum. He keeps his hands on the man's tunic and shoves as he continues to walk, herding him toward the door of the engine room.

The two other Echelons shout in alarm, and Fyve knows he needs to move fast. He pushes harder, only to find the two have joined their friend.

"No, you don't!" one screams.

"You're no match for us," the other shrieks.

"We won't be caged like animals!" shouts the one Fyve has his hands on. "I'm no Raven!"

There's a clatter of footsteps, and Halo appears beside Fyve.

Then Justice and Sica. They form a wall across the corridor, now pushing the Echelons back, too.

One at the rear falls over, but he quickly scrambles back to his feet. "I'm not going back in there!"

"You stay out here, and I'll rip you apart," Justice promises.

His face pales. He glances at his comrades. Then he spins around and runs into the engine room. The other who appeared with him glances between the teens and the doorway, then darts after the first Echelon.

Leaving the one with the flamethrower to be pushed inevitably back so he can join them.

The Echelon curls his lip, panting with the exertion. He scrabbles to grip the flamethrower jammed against his chest. "One flick of the trigger and I'll burn you all."

Fyve pushes his face close. "Do it."

The Echelon is bluffing. He would never risk hurting himself.

The man's eyes flicker with a dangerous mix of fear and fury. The lion doesn't like being cornered.

But it doesn't matter. They've reached the door and with a concerted effort, they shove him into the engine room. The moment their hands release him, the Echelon leaps forward.

"Get out of the way!" Halo calls.

Fyve steps back as the large metal door swings toward him. He tucks in his chin as it sweeps past his face, and he bumps into Sica.

"No!" the Echelon screams.

He jams the flamethrower into the door just as it slams shut. There's a *clang* and the door bounces open.

"Get back!" Halo shouts.

This time, the Echelon jams his arm through the gap, his fingers grasping at air. "Never!"

It's clear he assumes they won't try to shut the door again with his arm in the way.

The teens who first came aboard The Oasis wouldn't have. They were naïve. Hopeful. Filled with dreams.

But the Echelons stole each of those. Then took great pleasure in destroying them.

It means Fyve, Halo, Justice and Sica don't hesitate as they collectively throw their body weight onto the door. It slams on the Echelon's arm, bouncing on the rubbery flesh.

The Echelon screeches in pain, yet as a few precious inches open up, he pushes it out further, the flamethrower still clutched in his hand.

This time, Fyve grits his teeth, not looking forward to what has to happen. Halo presses in close to the door, the same determination etched on her face. Justice and Sica spread out and lock their arms.

Together, they push with all their might.

There's a squelch of tearing flesh.

A crunch of bone.

A hideous screech.

And the door slams shut, the Echelon's arm still protruding. The flamethrower he was holding clatters to the floor.

Fyve blinks, bile surging up his throat, bitter as it burns his tongue. Halo is pale and horrified beside him. He quickly spins the large lever on the front, closing the door.

"We have to lock it," Halo pants. She spins around. "Justice, I need the crutch."

Justice picks it up where it fell behind her. Halo takes it and jams it into the spokes of the round lever. Locking it.

"I knew this was going to come in use," Justice says, dusting her hands off on her trousers. "Serves him right," she mutters.

Sica shakes her head. "What an idiot."

Fyve swallows, tearing his gaze from the trickle of blood tracking its way down the door seal. "Let's get back to the others," he says hoarsely. "The Echelons are secure."

Halo nods, squaring her shoulders. "As soon as this storm passes, we're leaving this ship."

The ship lurches and Fyve grabs Halo as she's tilted toward the arm. The lights flicker, little more than a dim glow when they return.

A chuckle sounds behind them. "Silly Treasure," Nole purrs.

They slowly turn, dread filling Fyve's gut and weighing it down. The leader of the Echelons is standing at the other end of the corridor, a flamethrower pointed at them. Two more Echelons are behind him.

Nole takes an ominous step forward. "I'll never let you leave me, Treasure."

HALO

"Get out of our way," growls Fyve, picking up the flamethrower the Echelon had dropped. "You're not the only one with a weapon."

"Never," Nole spits back as the lights in the corridor flicker. "I'm not going anywhere without my Treasure."

Halo's eyes burn with fury. "I'm. Not. Your. Treasure."

"Yes, you are." Nole licks his lips, holding himself steady as the ship lurches on a huge wave. "And it's about time you realized it."

The lights turn off, plunging the corridor into darkness and Halo darts forward, positioning herself between Fyve and Nole.

"Halo!" Fyve calls desperately, not knowing where she is, but aware she's left his side.

The lights flicker back to life and Halo stands with her hands on her hips, glaring at Nole. She's a human shield, tasking herself with protecting Fyve, Justice and Sica. But it's a calculated risk. Neither Fyve nor Nole will fire their weapons while there's a chance she might get hurt.

"Halo! Get back," says Fyve, his voice panicked. He'd never have allowed her to get so close to Nole if he'd known.

She holds up a hand, not turning to look at him. He needs to let her handle this. If anyone can talk their way out of this situation they're in, it's her.

"Good, Treasure," Nole purrs as his two men stand at the ready behind him. "You decided to come with me. I always knew you were smart."

Halo tilts her head. "What is it exactly that you think you've done to earn my respect?"

The question throws Nole, and she sees panic in his eyes. "Lots of things."

"You *have* done lots of things." Halo puts out her hand to count the points she's about to make. "You stranded us on a ship with no fuel. You murdered my father and brother. I haven't eaten properly since you tied me to a chair and drugged me. My niece and nephew are most likely not going to get the chance to grow up. And now you have a flamethrower pointed at the person I love most. Would you like me to continue?"

"I did all that for you," Nole insists, his eyes flashing with anger. "For us. For our future. One day, you'll see."

Halo shakes her head, keeping her voice calm. "Right now, I'm not even sure there's a future. Not one with me in it, anyway."

"That's why you have to trust me." Nole keeps his flamethrower pointed at Fyve, but his eyes are on Halo. "I can keep you safe. Fyve can't."

Fyve huffs behind her, but to his credit, he remains quiet, the howling wind outside protesting enough on his behalf.

Clearly, he hadn't heard a word Halo had just said. She's never been more unsafe than since she met Nole. But pointing this out to him doesn't seem to be working. It's only enraging him more, when what they need from him right now is compliance. She needs to try another tack.

"How can you keep me safe?" she asks Nole, giving him a small smile.

He pulls back his shoulders, his ego sparking to life. "I'll protect you. I have a whole army behind me. I'll make sure you never get hurt. I have some supplies...I can keep you fed. Healthy. Satisfied."

He licks his lips on this last word and Halo's stomach lurches. She can feel Fyve fuming behind her.

She nods her approval at Nole, doing her best to look like she's considering his offer. "Actually, there's one thing you could do to win my trust..."

Nole narrows his eyes. "What is it?"

"You could step aside," she says. "Let Fyve, Justice and Sica pass."

"We're not going without you," Fyve growls.

"And me then," Halo adds. "Let us pass. If you do that, then I'll know I can trust you. Trust is so important in any relationship, don't you think?"

She keeps her eyes on Nole, wanting her lie to be convincing. She'll never trust him. Not ever. Too much water has passed under this ship for that.

He blinks at her, having clearly heard her request but not wanting to reply. But her words are working. She can feel the effect they're having on him. He's dreamed of her talking to him like this for a long time, which means he's choosing to hear exactly what he wants to.

"It's not like I can go anywhere," says Halo, trying to keep steady on her feet as the ship rears up over another wave. "Especially in this storm."

"You're not leaving me," says Nole adamantly. "It's important we have as much time together as possible."

"There's an ancient saying," says Sica from behind Halo. "If you love someone, let them go. If they come back, then you know they're into you. If they don't, then they never gave a crap."

Halo's brows shoot up. She hadn't realized Sica was so deep, even if she's sure these weren't the original words of the saying. The meaning is right, though.

"It's true," says Halo. "Let me go, Nole, and I'll know you love me. When I come back, you'll know I feel the same. Come on, it will be fun. Like a game."

The Echelons behind Nole stiffen.

"Don't trust her," one of them barks.

"And what if you don't come back?" Nole asks.

"Then you'll know she doesn't give a crap!" says Sica, sounding exasperated.

Nole smiles as he shakes his head. Halo's heart sinks, even though it was worth a try. She should have known it wasn't going to be possible to end this standoff peacefully.

Pointing his flamethrower at Fyve a little more directly, Nole shifts his gaze away from Halo.

"Give your weapon to Halo," he snarls. "Or I'll roast you all."

Halo turns to see Fyve has a thunderous look on his face.

"Do it!" Nole shouts.

"Why?" Fyve asks, hesitating. They all know in the time it takes to transfer the weapon, Nole could pull his trigger.

"Because if you give her the weapon, I'll let you pass." Nole rolls his eyes and the lights flicker again. "My Treasure won't hurt me. Even if she's insisting on testing my love."

The ship rears up and one of Nole's men stumbles to the floor. He quickly rights himself and resumes his position.

Halo slips in beside Fyve, pressing her back against his chest and placing her hands on top of his. There's a comfort in the close proximity, and she feels an aching emptiness the moment he lets go of the flamethrower and steps back. The weapon is heavy in her hands. If she hadn't had that half tin of fruit, she doubts she'd be able to hold it at all.

"Don't try anything stupid." Nole presses his back against the wall and nods at his men to do the same. "I'll be coming for you later, Treasure. And when I do, I expect you to show your appreciation."

It takes Halo a few seconds to realize what's happening. Nole has agreed to let them pass. Which means he'll release the other Echelons. But it also buys them time to come up with a plan. One that will enable Halo to show just how much she *appreciates* Nole. Which is somewhere in the range of not-even-one-little-bit.

Despite Halo being the one to hold a weapon, it's Fyve who remains Nole's target as they pass. Justice keeps her fists clenched as she walks. To Halo's horror, Sica is holding the severed arm with the bloodied end sticking out. There's no way anyone's going to make a grab for her like that.

Fyve remains behind Halo, as ready as always to protect her. Should he ever feel the need to let her go, there would be no need for her to come running back. Because she'll never leave his side. Their love is the truest thing she's ever known.

Halo gives Nole a nod as she passes him.

"See you soon, Treasure," he purrs.

"You sure will," she replies, meaning it.

There's a boom of thunder and Halo uses the distraction to get to a safe distance. Fyve takes the flamethrower from her and walks backward, making sure Nole doesn't decide to take one last swipe at them.

"I can't believe he let us go," says Justice from the front of the group as they take to the stairs.

"I can't believe Sica took the arm," says Fyve.

Halo laughs, despite the fact none of this is funny. The Echelon who'd belonged to that arm had been partly responsible for all the horrors they've experienced since leaving Treasure Island. If it were anyone else, their reaction would be very different.

"I thought it might come in *handy*." Sica waves the arm over her shoulder. "But now that you mention it, it's starting to give me the creeps." She lets the severed limb fall to the stairs and grimaces.

Justice seems to find this particularly amusing.

Halo turns to Fyve with more pressing thoughts on her mind. "Nole would never have let me go if we weren't trapped on a ship."

He nods. "I know. Which means he intends to get you back."

"He likes the game of it," she says. "That's why he started the Trials. For his own sick amusement. This is just like one of the Trials. He gives us a head start, then he comes to find us and kill us."

"Hide-and-seek," says Justice. "Zake used to make me play it with him. I didn't mind it so much, except when he found me, it was never any fun."

"It's not fun now, either," Halo points out. "Except maybe for Nole."

"What if he finds the others while he's searching for you?" Justice asks. "We need to find a better place to hide them."

There's silence as they step out onto the landing of the second floor. They all know what Justice has said is true. Just as they know this ship is limited in places where anyone can hide.

"Maybe I should have stayed with Nole," Halo says, on a long sigh. "Leaving him has only endangered everyone else."

"No!" Fyve turns to her. "That wasn't going to happen. We need to keep everyone safe. And that includes you."

"But how can we when Nole's obsessed with me?" Halo wrings her hands. "He said he wants me to show him my appreciation..."

Her words trail off as another realization hits her with force. Nole will stop at nothing until he gets what he wants. Which is the one thing he's never going to get.

Halo.

She draws in a deep breath as she accepts what she has to do.

He's left her with no other choice. If she doesn't, then the lives of everyone she loves will remain in danger.

"I'm going to kill him," she says, so quietly her words are swallowed by the raging storm. But somehow her friends seem to hear.

"About time!" Sica lets out a whoop.

Justice nods her approval. "I like this plan."

"No." Fyve shakes his head.

"You want him to live?" Halo is surprised by this.

But Fyve shakes his head again. "No. I'll do it. I'll kill him."

Halo puts a hand on his arm. "He expects it from you, Fyve. And he won't hesitate to retaliate. It has to be me. It's the only way. I have to outsmart him."

"Shouldn't be too hard," murmurs Justice.

Fyve stares at her for long moments, his eyes filling with tears before he eventually nods. "Okay. But I'm not leaving you. And I can't promise I won't jump in to help."

"With the idea I have, you won't need to. She runs her hand down his arm until she's holding his hand. "But okay. If I need you, you can jump in to help."

"You two are just too much." Justice rolls her eyes. "If I had anything in my stomach, I'd throw it up."

Halo pokes out her tongue. "Why don't you and Sica go and check on the others? Warn them to stay out of sight. We'll come and let you know when the deed is done."

"And miss the action?" says Sica. "No chance!"

But Justice is back to her serious self and nods her agreement as she turns to Sica. "Halo and Fyve have got this. She's right. We have to do what's best for everyone."

Sica groans. "Fine then! But hurry up about it. That asshole has used up more than his share of oxygen on this ship already. Get it over with already."

Halo watches the two of them disappear down the corridor, glad they've formed such a solid friendship. Back on Treasure

Island, Justice and Sica would have made the most unlikely allies.

Fyve loops the strap of the flamethrower over his shoulder so he can free up his hands and he embraces Halo, pressing his lips to her forehead. She doesn't want to think of this as a goodbye hug but knows it's very likely it could be.

"I love you so much," she tells him, slipping her hands around his waist.

"I love you, too." He pulls back so he can look at her. "So, are you going to tell me about this plan of yours?"

She shakes her head as she withdraws her hands and puts them in her pockets and steps away. She can't get distracted by him right now. He has a habit of making time cease to exist with just a single touch. If she's going to kill Nole, she needs to keep her focus.

"I can't, Fyve," she says. "It's better if you don't know. Please, trust me."

Fyve looks hurt, but there's no way she can tell him what she's thinking. Because her plan is risky at best. But if she can pull it off, then Nole will never see it coming. It's the best way. The *only* way.

"Where do you think he'll look for me first?" she asks, trying to distract him from pressing her further for the details.

"The wheelhouse?"

"That's too obvious?" She tilts her head. "He'll think I'm genuinely hiding and there's really nowhere in there to hide."

"What about that place you told me about where the Echelons first took their Treasures?" Fyve suggests. "There were tables and long curtains. Sounds like there are a lot of places to hide. Surely, he'd look there first before trying every cabin on this ship. Especially given he knows that you know about it."

She nods slowly. "Smart. But we need to make it obvious that's where we're gone. Leave some clues along the way."

"Lucky Sica dropped the arm." Fyve pulls a face.

"You're a genius," says Halo as they head back into the stair-well. She lowers her voice. "We'll leave him a trail of blood so he can track our movements."

Fyve looks surprised but then nods as he descends a flight of stairs to retrieve the arm. "He's so stupid, he'll think he's smart." With a look of utter disgust, Fyve drips blood as they climb up to the never-ending flights of stairs.

When Halo was first claimed as a Treasure and made this trip, it hadn't seemed so far up. But she had a full belly of food back then, rather than half a tin of fruit. A small half, if she's accurate. She can't regret that though, given it turned out to be the last thing Ajax ever ate.

They exit the stairwell and head into the large room, their feet disappearing into the plush black carpet as they walk. The ship tilts and Halo grabs onto one of the thick golden curtains to stabilize herself, while Fyve places the severed arm under-neath a table near the door. The crystal arrangements hanging from the ceiling swing wildly, making the dim light they're emitting move in dizzying patterns. If the tables and chairs weren't fastened to the floor, they'd be sliding all over the place.

Halo scans the room, looking for the perfect place to posi-tion herself.

"You really need to tell me what you're thinking," says Fyve, wiping his hands on his trousers. "Otherwise, I don't know how to help."

She walks over toward a long bar that's been built on a raised platform and ignores his question. Stepping up on the platform, she sees a space underneath the bar that should be just big enough.

"I'm going to hide in here." She points to the space. "If you hide behind one of the curtains, you can keep an eye on things and be ready to jump out."

She can tell Fyve is extremely uncomfortable with this idea, but before he gets to voice his concerns, there are the sounds of approaching footsteps.

Halo tucks herself in the hiding space and Fyve dashes away with no time to say goodbye or press her further for details. Which is exactly why she'd savored the hug they'd shared. Even if she'd used it for other, more sinister reasons…

The footsteps get louder, then pause. Halo readies herself for what she knows she has to do.

"Treasure!" calls Nole. "I know you're in here."

She remains quiet.

"Come out, my Treasure," he purrs, as he walks into the room. "Our little game is over. It's time now for you to show me how much you appreciate all I've done for you."

Steeling herself, Halo emerges from her hiding spot and stands on the edge of the platform. Fyve is nowhere to be seen. Nole freezes when he sees her, indicating for his two men to take a step back. A predatory smile spreads across his face.

Halo undoes her tunic and lets it fall to the floor. Doing her best to look seductive, despite wanting to throw up, she lets her hair down from its braid and allows her blonde locks to fall across her shoulders and cropped singlet top.

Nole's eyes widen as he takes in the sight of her. She positions herself in the flickering light to give him the view he so clearly craves.

"I've got this," he tells his men. "Wait for me outside."

Halo gives him a small smile to tell him she approves.

"Could be a trap," says one of his men.

"Get out of here!" Nole booms. "I said to wait outside. My Treasure and I need a little privacy."

His men scuttle out the door and Halo undoes her trousers and slips out of them. Now she's wearing only her underwear, which should make her feel vulnerable, except power surges through her veins.

"I knew you'd learn to appreciate me." Nole licks his lips as he stares at her bare flesh.

She nods, fluttering her eyelashes in the way she's seen other girls do when flirting with the boys they liked back on Treasure Island. She never has to do any of this with Fyve. All her actions come so naturally.

Letting his flamethrower sit at his back, Nole walks forward. The excitement emanating from him makes her nausea worsen and for a moment, she doesn't think she can follow through on her plan. But Fyve is yet to emerge from his hiding place, so he must believe in her, even if she's sure he won't approve of her tactics.

"My Treasure," says Nole. "You're so beautiful. Such perfect genes. I can see our children already. They'll be spectacular."

Halo indicates with her index finger for him to come closer.

He reaches her and goes to step up on the platform, but she pushes him playfully back so that he's standing on the floor, his head at the height of her chest. This doesn't seem to be a problem for him and he reaches out his hands to grope her. She knows she doesn't have long. Fyve isn't going to put up with much more of this. Nor does she think she can stomach it.

She puts her fingertips under Nole's soft chin and tips up his face to look at her. He parts his lips in anticipation and she bends down to bring her face to his...

And tips the vial of poison she's been holding between her teeth straight into his mouth.

Nole reels back, his hand coming to his mouth as he splutters out the liquid, but already knows it's too late. His eyes flare and he makes a choking sound. "You...you...but...my Treasure."

Halo spits out the empty vial and puts her hands on her hips. "I. Am. Not. Your. Treasure."

Red froth bubbles at Nole's lips and he clutches at his throat. She glares down at him as he collapses to his knees.

Never in Halo's life had she imagined she'd enjoy watching

someone die, and while she can't quite say she's enjoying this moment, she finds it disturbingly satisfying. This man destroyed not just her life, but the lives of an unspeakable number of teens to the point she can count on her fingers those of the original one hundred who stepped on this ship. He's a liar. And a creep. A murderer.

"Help me," Nole chokes out. "I'm...sorry."

"You're not sorry," says Halo. "You're only sorry that your own stupidity got you killed."

Convulsing on the floor, blood and foam spew from his mouth. The carpet eats up the red liquid, soaking it into its plush black threads, making it seem like it was never there.

Nole lets out one final moan and goes still. Halo lets out a long breath, trying to still the racing of her heart.

It's over.

It's actually over. She killed a man, but in the process now everyone she loves is safe.

The ship tilts and she accepts they're not exactly safe. But without their leader, the Echelons have never been weaker. If the ship can survive this storm, there's hope for all of them yet. Quickly re-dressing, she wonders why Fyve has remained hidden so long. But she dares not call out to him. There could be any number of people hidden in this room.

It's at this point that Nole's two men decide to investigate the awful noise that had come from Nole. They burst back into the room and rush to their leader.

"What have you done?" they shout, looking at Halo in pure fury.

Raising their flamethrowers, they point them at her. She puts up her hands, showing she's unarmed, but knows this won't make any difference to these heartless men. Her only hope right now is the one person she trusts without any doubt. The same person who trusted her, even as she was taking the poison from his pocket while she'd hugged him goodbye.

"You won't shoot," says Halo, doing her best to summon every ounce of courage she has. "You'll set this whole ship on fire if you do."

The taller of the men sneers. "Which is exactly why Nole had this whole room made fireproof. He was way smarter than any of you pathetic teenagers. He knew how to think ahead."

Halo glances down at Nole's body, letting the gory image do that talking for her. If he were so smart, then he wouldn't be dead.

"Any last words?" the other man sneers. "Before we roast you for our dinner. Maybe some words of regret? Nole did so much for you, you ungrateful bitch."

Fyve appears in the corner of her field of vision. He's creeping forward quietly, getting himself into the position he needs to keep her safe. She just has to keep these men distracted for a few more seconds.

"Actually, I do have something to say." She smiles as she pauses, hoping she's given Fyve enough time, but not daring to look at him directly. "I regret nothing."

Halo dives into her former hiding space and curls herself into a ball just as Fyve unleashes his flamethrower. Keeping her face buried, she hears the fire spew out at the two men.

The two Echelons scream. She doesn't look up. Fyve had trusted her. Now it's her turn to trust him.

He's got this.

The stench of burning flesh permeates every inch of the small space she's tucked inside, and she holds herself in a tighter ball, waiting for this to be over. All she and Fyve had wanted was to live in peace. They didn't ask for any of this. But once again, life has shown them it has other ideas. She can only hope that what the Echelons said about this room being fireproof is true.

Eventually, the hissing of the flamethrower ceases along with the howls of pain, and she's left with only the sound of the storm. Remaining curled in a tight ball, Halo's not sure she could come out even if she wanted to. Because she has no guarantees that the last man standing is Fyve.

There are footsteps and she holds herself still, not daring to move so much as her eyelids. Then there's the sound of the flapping of fabric as someone works to put out the flames.

Then, quiet...

"Halo," Fyve eventually croaks from beside her. "Come out. It's over."

She unwinds her body from the small space in an instant and throws herself at Fyve, wrapping her arms around him as he holds her tight.

"It's over," she repeats, avoiding looking at the carnage in front of her. The carpet is smoldering, with burned remnants of the golden curtains still smoking from smothering the flames.

There's another flash of lightning and they're plunged into darkness. Halo tightens her grip around Fyve, instinctively knowing this time, the lights won't come back on.

It's not over. They both know this. This ship is filled with enemies.

And right now, Mother Nature is the biggest one of all.

FYVE

*T*he smell of burning flesh still stings Fyve's nostrils as they fumble their way out of the dining room. The power cutting out was a small blessing because it meant no longer having to look at the charred Echelons. Although Fyve doesn't regret their loss, he didn't take any joy in their painful death or the way their screams were permanently seared across their faces.

But the loss of light also means The Oasis is now a maze of midnight corridors. One that's being tossed about as if it's little more than a toy.

The ship tilts sharply to the left and Fyve draws Halo closer to him as they crash into a wall. He grunts as his shoulder thuds painfully, but he doesn't get a chance to pull away. The Oasis continues to tilt, his stomach bottoming out as it plunges simultaneously.

"Fyve!" Halo gasps, her fingers digging into his side.

He holds her even tighter, wishing there were words of reassurance hovering on his lips. But there aren't.

The storm is only growing more violent.

The ship rights itself almost as sharply as it tilted, the floor seeming to rise up beneath them. Fyve locks his knees as his stomach shoots to his feet and he feels like gravity just multiplied.

The Oasis straightens, groaning as if it's being bruised and battered itself, a deep creaking reverberating through the walls.

"We have to get back to the others," Halo says urgently.

The same urgency is tugging at Fyve. Tenn, Cloud, the twins. They'd all be terrified.

"We'll need to stay close to the walls," Fyve says, his teeth gritted. The Oasis is already angling again, this time in the opposite direction.

Halo draws in a sharp breath as their world tilts once more. "I know which way to go."

Fyve squeezes her shoulder, hoping she understands what there's no time to put into words. In this world defined by darkness and upheaval, he'd follow her anywhere. Halo's his strength. His north star. His reason to hope when everything is so bleak.

Making their way to the second floor takes far longer than either of them would like. The Oasis is a giant see-saw as it rides waves that feel taller than the ship itself. Over and over, Fyve and Halo have to stop as gravity pushes them into the floor and The Oasis is propelled high into the air. They hold on to the walls, the railings of the stairs, to each other as they wait for the inevitable crash. Each time, there's a thundering boom as they slam into a trough, then a shuddering groan as the ship tries to right itself.

And never succeeds.

Fyve's shoulders are bruised from slamming into walls and his knees sore from dropping unexpectedly, and he guesses Halo would have to be the same, but they don't stop their unbalanced, frantic fight to get to the cabin.

"The second floor," Halo gasps as they descend another set of stairs.

The Oasis tilts again, but that's not why Fyve's own sharp inhale quickly follows. "No!"

Water gushes over their ankles, warm and faintly stinging, sounding like a gurgling stream as it splashes down the stairs behind them.

"Tenn!" Fyve shouts.

"Cloud!" Halo cries.

They run, hands skimming the walls, feet splashing through water, to the room their friends and family are hiding in.

"This door," Halo says, panting. She raps her knuckles on the smooth surface. "Cloud, Iva! It's us!"

"Thank Terra," Dargo mutters on the other side. There's a faint whoosh as the door opens, then the gurgle of water rushing into the room. "Whoa!" he exclaims. The sound of splashing reveals he just retreated. "There's more than we realized!"

Fyve enters, heart pounding. "Is everyone in here? Are you ok—"

"Fyve!" Tenn's cry is quickly followed by her small body crashing into his. "You're back."

He hauls her up into his arms, wanting her sensitive skin out of the sea water. "I promised, remember?" he says gruffly.

"Cloud?" Halo asks beside him. "Is anyone hurt?"

"We're fine. We're all on the bed. We haven't moved off since the water started coming in."

The tightness around Fyve's chest unwinds a little. He wishes he could see for himself that everyone's okay, but this is the next best thing. "We took care of Nole."

"That's the best news I've heard all day," comes Justice's voice, surprising him.

Almost as much as the blast of light that pierces his eyes. Fyve instinctively ducks, protecting Tenn from the assault.

Justice chuckles, moving the beam of light onto the wall. "It's a torch, Fyve. I found it rummaging in the cupboards."

Fyve blinks, trying to get rid of the bright dots at the center of his vision. "Good thinking." Somehow, just that one beam of light is enough to unwind the tension in his chest another notch.

He scans the room. Cloud is tucked into the corner of the bed, holding Miracle. Iva is beside her with Marvel. Dargo is in front of them, looking haggard but determined. Justice is to the left, holding a cupboard with one hand and the torch with the other. Sica's here, too, arms crossed as she stands in the ankle-deep water.

Justice shrugs. "I was looking for a weapon now that my crutches are gone." She waves the torch like a baton, the light swirling on the opposite wall. "Figured this will do."

The Oasis cants and dips, triggering arms to reach out to walls or anything they can find to steady themselves. The water rushes to one end of the room, slicing up Sica's legs and making her grimace.

Fyve puts Tenn down. "Hold onto—"

"Fyve!" she screams as the ship is pushed upward.

Justice drops the torch and they're plunged into darkness again.

The Oasis soars high and drops so fast, Fyve loses contact with the floor for precious seconds. He hovers in blackness, cries of fright and shouts of alarm the only thing surrounding him. Then he's crashing into the floor with enough power to crumple to his knees.

Justice curses. "Where the f—ouch!" A beam of light slices through the cabin. "Got it!"

Fyve pushes up, glancing around frantically then helping Halo up as she staggers beside him. Cloud and the others are a crumpled mess on the bed, but the babies are unharmed. Sica is already standing, now wet from head to toe.

Tenn is against the wall, still collapsed in the water.

Fyve rushes to her. "Tenn! Are you hurt?"

His sister looks up at him, blinking as she cradles her arm to her chest. "I hit the wall," she says, her voice small. "But I'm fine."

Except she doesn't look fine. Fyve scoops her up and she winces at the movement.

"Bring her here," Iva says, already shredding a sheet. "I'll bind it."

Nodding, Fyve braces himself as he walks, each step feeling dangerous on the flooded, shifting floor.

"The storm's getting worse," Cloud whispers, holding Miracle close. "How can it be getting worse?"

"They're called mega storms," Tenn says, her voice quivering as Fyve places her beside Iva. "There's a room on the ship with nothing but old books. I used to go there and read to get away from Nole and the others."

"Mega storms?" Fyve repeats, not liking the feel of the words.

"Much bigger than typhoons or hurricanes," Tenn says, glancing around as if the walls are about to cave in. "They're the reasons humans couldn't live too close to water. It's why the Outlands were the only place left for us to go."

And then Treasure Island.

What had felt like a prison Fyve would die on, turned out to be humanity's last haven.

He turns to Halo, noting the absence of color in her cheeks. She's just as worried as he is. With each increasing tilt, dip, or terrifying surge, there's the hope it's the crest of the storm.

Exactly how much worse can it get?

A fresh gush of water blasts past Halo, making her clutch the doorway. "We need to get to the lower decks."

"What?" Sica says, aghast. "I'd prefer a few feet of acid sea water than going back down there with the Echelons."

Halo shakes her head. "We have to risk it. That part of the ship is its lowest and most central. It'll be the most stable."

"We'll find a cabin," says Fyve, having no doubt she's right. "A small one. We'll keep each other safe."

Justice sloshes toward them, angling the beam of light from the torch past Halo and into the corridor. "Halo's brains and Fyve's blind, stupid-ass courage have kept us alive so far." She slips through. "Come on. Let's get to the heart of this beast."

His sides starting to get sore from constantly adjusting his center of balance, Fyve scoops up Tenn, her arm now tightly bound to her chest thanks to Iva. He remains silent as they exit the room, Justice at the front, him and Halo at the back.

They exchange another glance, and he wonders if her promise that the inner part of The Oasis is the best place to be felt as hollow as his promise that they'll keep each other safe.

Not when the truth is there's nowhere safe. The Oasis might be monstrous in size. Weigh more than he could ever imagine.

But against Mother Nature, the ship is insignificant.

"Terra's angry," Tenn whimpers as they slosh their way down the corridor.

"There's no such thing as Terra," Fyve says, wanting to banish that myth once and for all.

"Yes, there is," Tenn says, steely determination in her voice. "Not the Terra Nole and Dad used. But the real Terra. The one we need to honor."

Fyve braces himself against the wall as the ship angles forward. Tenn's talking about Mother Nature, herself. The ultimate power they overlooked. Dismissed. Underestimated.

In the same way humanity did centuries ago, leading Fyve, Halo and the others to this exact moment.

The beam of light is their guide as they stagger down the corridor and descend a set of stairs. They make their way to the next floor in a silent file, the walls and floor still angling and moving, but no one falls over.

It's Cloud who voices Fyve's secret hope. "Maybe the storm's abating—"

The Oasis rears up as if a hand just yanked it out of the sea. Fyve holds onto Tenn as they're helplessly, violently jerked up with it. He desperately tries to find Halo in the seconds they're soaring, knowing it's the landing that will be devastating, but the torch is gone again.

Then he's weightless once more, and this time The Oasis tilts while he's mid-air. Fyve crashes into the wall, the impact wrenching an agonized cry from Tenn. The floor they hit is hard and angled, sending them sliding into the others.

A baby's cry pierces the darkness, followed by a moan.

"Cloud," Halo gasps. "Where are you?"

The torch flicks on, revealing them in a jumbled pile against the wall. Fyve scrabbles away, looking down at his sister. Tenn's whimpering, her eyes squeezed tightly shut. She blinks up at him, her eyes frightened and lost before falling limp in his arms. Unconscious.

With The Oasis still on a dangerous angle, Halo crawls to Cloud, who's tending to a wailing Miracle. Marvel joins his sibling's cries, Iva looking dazed as she holds him.

Justice gets to her feet, keeping them wide apart. "We'll be dead before we get to the center," she says grimly.

She's right. They need to find somewhere to tuck in tight, not roam the corridors.

Halo nods, noting a door nearby illuminated by the torch. "This cabin is as good as any."

She slides open the door, clinging to it when the ship pitches sharply, drawing a cry out of Cloud.

"Quick," Halo says, indicating to her. "There will be furniture and shelves to hold onto."

Cloud lurches inside, spinning so her back slams into the doorframe when they're thrown in the opposite direction. Miracle screams even louder, giving voice to the fear they're all gripped by.

Another terrified scream joins it. Except it's not Marvel crying alongside his sister. Or Cloud.

Justice leaps into the cabin, sweeping the beam of light from one side to the other. Two sets of frightened eyes glint back, squinting in round, fleshy faces.

"Echelons!" Justice growls.

The next wail has her pointing the torch at the bed. Rhina writhes on the mattress, gripping the sheets with white-knuckled hands. "My baby!" she cries.

"Fyve," Halo gasps.

Rich, red blood pools between Rhina's thighs and down her legs.

"My baby," Rhina says again, this time her words a ragged whisper.

Iva steps past Halo, passing her Marvel. "Here. I'll do what I can."

Except there's nothing to do. Fyve saw this too many times on Treasure Island. Miscarriages were common, their mothers' fragile, malnourished bodies unable to carry another life.

The women used to say it was Terra's wish.

Fyve wonders sadly if that's the case now.

Justice reaches out to grab Iva's arm, stopping her. "Like hell you will. These bastards deserve nothing from us."

"Please." One of the male Echelons steps forward. "We need help."

Sica moves closer to Justice. "You have some nerve," she hisses. "After everything you've done."

The second Echelon sits heavily on the bed beside Rhina. "This was never what we wanted. It was never our vision."

Fyve glares at them. "Well, it sure as hell wasn't ours."

The man flinches, then falls over as the ship tips. He lands in a tangle, scrabbling to move closer to the wall.

Fyve strides over and stands over him. "Where are the others?"

"We don't know." The Echelon cowers. "Two died in the engine room when they were thrown against some pipework. We lost the remaining few in the dark corridors."

"And Sley was insisting we should go steal some pods while we could," adds the other. "We had no desire to try and find them."

Greedy fools. It'll cost them their lives.

The same greed that's now put them all at risk.

Rhina cries out, curling up around her stomach. "Please. My baby!"

Iva yanks herself from Justice's grip and walks over to the female Echelon, running her hands over the woman's shuddering body. She glances back at Fyve and Halo. "She's lost a lot of blood."

Fyve reads the unsaid words in Iva's eyes. Rhina could die along with her unborn child.

"All the more reason to find somewhere else," Justice spits. "Somewhere safe."

Halo moves closer to Fyve, pressing her side against his as she holds a now silent Marvel and he holds an unconscious Tenn. The ship rocks wildly, groaning and heaving. Every remaining soul in the room seems to turn their focus on them. To what to do next.

"We have to stay," Halo says, an unspoken agreement settling between them.

"If we leave, we'd be no better than their greedy, selfish souls," adds Fyve.

"Of course, you two would say that," Justice grumbles, shooting them a glare.

Iva nods in thanks, pressing her hand to Rhina's forehead. Dargo staggers to her side, and the Echelon on the other end of the bed reaches out to steady him. Dargo instinctively flinches back, but then grabs it when The Oasis pitches up.

He sits beside Iva, takes a sheet and starts tearing it into long strips. "We'll strap her to the bed," he says, passing the first length to Iva. "So she doesn't fall off. Is there anything else you need me to do?"

Iva glances at him with a soft smile. One that says she's glad he's here. One that says there's nothing left to do that could save Rhina.

Justice keeps the torch pointed on them so Iva and Dargo can see as she turns back to Fyve. "What do you want us to do?"

Fyve almost wants to hug her for the grudging show of loyalty. Justice may not agree with the decision, but she's respecting it. "Everyone, find somewhere to tuck into," he says. "Cloud, Justice and Sica, take the shower. Dargo and Iva, you should fit in there once you're finished with Rhina."

Which will fill up the small space, leaving Fyve and Halo in the openness of the cabin.

Halo looks around, then kicks open a cupboard door. She turns to one of the Echelons. "Take out the shelves."

The man's brows shoot up at the request and Fyve's lip curls. Less than a minute and he's already regretting the decision to stay in here.

But the Echelon crawls on all fours to the cupboard and does as he's asked, laying the shelves on the floor of the cupboard. He peers inside the space he just created. "You're going to hide in here?"

Halo nods, stilling as she holds Marvel. Is the Echelon about to take the small sanctuary she discovered?

The man nods, respect glinting in his eyes. "Smart." He crawls back to the bed where Rhina is now strapped down and picks up the remaining strips of cloth. "We'll find a way to secure ourselves."

Fyve turns away, knowing that's the best any of them can do right now. He indicates to Halo and she crawls into the cramped space, holding Marvel close to her chest. Fyve follows, his movement slow and ungainly as he clutches Tenn. Twice, The

Oasis lurches, slamming him into the edge of the cupboard and yanking a groan from him. But each time, he resumes the folding of arms and legs as he joins Halo.

Once they're both tucked in, the Echelon appears. "I'll close the doors." He hesitates. "Thank you," he murmurs.

The cupboard is shut, enclosing them in darkness. It feels like a tomb.

"Fyve..." Halo whispers. She doesn't finish her sentence, and he understands why.

"I know," he says, his fingers finding hers and twining them together.

There's too much to say.

And not enough time to capture it in a few sentences.

Weeks together, fighting to survive. A lifetime of hopes and dreams they never had a chance to explore. A connection that changed everything.

Their hands clamp tighter as another wave hits The Oasis. The ship plunges, then angles up as if it's a missile.

Then they're soaring up. And up.

And up.

The weightless moments are ones of realization. The further they rise, the further there is to fall. The greater the distance, the harder the crash.

And in the end, the Echelons were never their greatest threat.

It's Terra who held the ultimate power. She's the great equalizer. The one who will always overrule humankind.

The one who will decide whether they'll live or die.

The Oasis tumbles down, and Fyve and Halo hit the ceiling of the cupboard, clutching their precious bundles. A scream rips through the cabin.

Followed by a crash so loud, it's an assault on Fyve's ears.

Then nothing.

HALO

*F*ear. Pain. Shock. Relief. Confusion.

So many emotions flood Halo's consciousness as she wakes that she's not sure which one to grasp onto first.

She's still inside the cupboard, folded up on herself with Marvel cocooned at her core. He makes the smallest of cries and she lets out a breath to know he's alive.

The Oasis is perfectly still. After the constant movement during their days at sea, the permanence of their position on the Earth is unsettling. When the storm plucked them from the angry sea and tossed them into the air, they must have landed on solid ground. The Outlands, no doubt. It can't be Treasure Island—life back home never felt this still.

She becomes aware of another sensation. Her hand is clutching something. Something warm and familiar. She's still holding Fyve's hand. And if it's warm, it means he's alive.

"Fyve," she calls in the darkness. "Fyve!"

There's no reply, so she breaks contact to push on the cupboard door with her elbow. She forces it open and rolls out onto the floor, careful to cradle Marvel close to her chest.

Light streams through the cabin window and she looks

down at her nephew, pleased to see his eyelids fluttering.

There's groaning coming from the bed, but she barely hears it over her need to see if Fyve's okay. Settling Marvel on a pillow, she throws open the cupboard door beside the small space she'd just crawled out of.

Tenn tumbles onto the floor.

"I'm okay," she says before Halo even has the chance to ask.

She doesn't look okay. Her broken arm is bound to her body with a sling and her complexion is deathly pale aside from two dark rings underneath her eyes.

"Fyve?" Halo crawls closer to the cupboard and sees him stir. "Fyve!"

"Tenn?" He looks around, dazed. "Halo?"

Shaking his head to wake himself up, he climbs out of the impossibly small space and pulls Halo to his chest. She presses herself against him, wrapping both her arms and legs around him in her quest to get as close as she possibly can.

"We made it," she sobs. "We survived."

"The others?" he asks, not loosening his grip on her.

"I'm not sure." She savors his touch for a few more seconds before breaking away. She needs to get Marvel back to Cloud.

"Halo," says Tenn, pointing to the bed.

Rhina is lying there, still strapped down and moaning softly. The sheets have been stained crimson and there's no doubt she's lost her baby. Halo goes to her and unties the bindings. Surely, she won't try anything stupid. That storm was an equalizer if Halo ever saw one. They're all in this together now.

"My baby," weeps Rhina, bringing her hands to her stomach. "My baby."

"I'm sorry," says Halo. And she is. That baby had been her own flesh and blood.

Looking around the cabin, Halo turns her attention to the two Echelons who are crumpled in a corner. One is completely unconscious—possibly dead—and the other is staring blankly up at the ceiling, his breathing coming in raspy gasps. They're in far worse shape than Halo and Fyve. Crawling into the cupboard had very likely saved their lives.

"Help me," Rhina pleads. But Halo doesn't have time to help any of the Echelons right now. Not when she has no idea if Cloud and her friends have survived.

Or Miracle...

Scooping up Marvel, she goes to the bathroom door, which is blocked by a shelving unit that came off the wall.

"Fy—" She doesn't even have time to finish before Fyve is beside her, pulling the shelving away to free the door.

When the opening is clear, Halo surges forward, her heart stopping to see the glass of the shower cubicle has shattered. It's not in sharp shards like the mirror when Justice had broken that, but it's in thousands of pieces, still held together in one sheet. Nothing is visible beyond the maze of cracks and fragments.

"Cloud!" she cries.

The shower door slowly swings open, and Fyve puts his arm around Halo, ready as always to protect her from whatever horror they're about to witness.

Halo blinks, trying to take in what she's witnessing. Sitting on the shower floor with knees pulled up to their chests are Cloud, Justice, Sica, Iva and Dargo.

"You're alive," says Halo, her eyes going straight to Miracle, who's sleeping in Cloud's arms in the center of the group.

"Marvel!" Cloud cries as she struggles to her feet, handing Miracle to Iva. "Is he okay?"

"He's okay, but he's very hungry." Halo hands Marvel over and Cloud presses him instantly to her breast. Halo just hopes it's not too late. Marvel was already malnourished, and he's just spent who-knows-how-long without any sustenance at all. They can't have made it this far to lose one of the babies now.

Justice gets herself out of the shower and stretches. She

winces as she takes her weight on her damaged leg.

Sica is right behind her. "Are you injured?"

Justice shakes her head. "Wasn't much chance of that, the way we were jammed in there. Trust me, I learnt more about all of you than I ever wanted to know."

Sica laughs. It's a sound Halo never thought she'd hear again.

"Where do you think we are?" Dargo asks as he helps Iva to her feet.

"It has to be the Outlands," says Fyve. "We're definitely not floating anymore."

Halo nods. "I was thinking the same thing."

"I hope not." Dargo frowns as he takes Miracle from Iva to give her arms a break. "The Ravens told me way too many stories about that place."

"It can't be worse than this stinking ship," says Justice. "I can't wait to get off it."

Dargo shrugs, and Halo gives him a wan smile. She understands exactly what he's thinking. The Outlands is a desolate place where humans war over quickly diminishing resources. It will likely be even more dire than what they've experienced on this ship, as hard as that is to believe.

"Do you think the others survived?" Iva asks.

"Maybe," says Fyve, as Tenn slips in beside him and takes his hand. "Viney has a good survival instinct."

"And Amet and Shade are resourceful," Dargo reassures, still cradling Miracle. "They'll have known what to do."

They emerge into the cabin where there's a little more space. Rhina is sitting on the edge of the bed and Iva goes to check on her. The other two Echelons haven't moved.

Fyve goes to the cabin's window and tries to look out, but the glass is shattered, just like the shower, and he can't see out.

"I'm going to go to the deck," says Fyve. "See if any pods survived. And find out exactly where we are."

"I'm coming, too," says Halo, but her words are drowned out

by almost everyone else saying the exact same thing. Including Cloud, who's walking forward while feeding Marvel.

"I want to see where I'm raising my children," she says adamantly. "You're not leaving me behind."

"Let's go then." Fyve opens the cabin door and looks out into the corridor before stepping out.

"What about us?" Rhina calls after them. "You can't leave us here!"

"We'll come back for you," says Iva. "Once we know what we're dealing with."

Halo knows this isn't an empty promise. Iva has proven time and time again how caring she is.

"You'd better!" harrumphs Rhina. "I'm feeling very weak."

With fists clenched, Halo goes with Fyve down the corridor. The rest of the group follows in single file, many of them still holding onto the walls by habit after the storm. The ship seems to have landed upright. And although it's clearly suffered significant damage, unbelievably, it's still in one piece.

Most of the cabin doors have been flung open and the corridor is littered with debris, but they pick their way over it and head for the stairs.

The climb up is a slow one. They're injured and exhausted. And terrified of what they're about to discover.

With each step, Halo thinks back to the Trials that brought her to this ship. The Echelons had said they were testing for brains and strength, but she's certain they got that wrong. Because while intelligence is certainly necessary for survival, there's something they didn't test for that's proven to be a vital trait.

Kindness.

And there are examples of it everywhere Halo looks.

Dargo cradling baby Miracle.

Cloud feeding Marvel, while she barely has strength enough for herself.

Sica sticking to Justice's bad side, ready to catch her if she falls.

Tenn pretending her arm doesn't hurt, so Fyve doesn't worry.

Fyve climbing the stairs far slower than he'd like, so that everyone can keep together.

Iva promising to return to the Echelons, despite all the harm they caused.

This group has been kind to each other beyond anything Halo ever experienced back on Treasure Island. And the help they've provided each other is the only reason they're still alive. That can't be a coincidence.

That's what they need moving forward if humankind has any hope of repopulating this dying planet. *Intelligence and kindness.* If only there was a test that could determine what's in someone's heart. Because Halo's certain that everyone who's with her now would pass with flying colors.

Especially Fyve.

"Are you feeling okay?" he asks, proving her point as he loops an arm around her shoulders.

"Better than okay," she says. "I always am when I'm with you."

He kisses her gently on the lips, then pulls back so he can open the door to the deck.

Harsh sunlight floods into the stairwell, along with an oppressive heat.

"Are we dead?" asks Justice, wincing at the brightness. "I've heard about the light at the end of the tunnel."

Fyve and Halo step out onto the deck, their jaws falling open when they see where they are.

"This isn't the Outlands," whispers Iva from behind them.

Halo can't help herself. She leaves Fyve to run to the railing, tears streaming down her cheeks as her fingertips make contact with something she's been dreaming of all her life.

A tree.

A real one with an enormous branch reaching out over the deck, littering the surface with fallen leaves.

Looking around, she sees it's not the only one. There's a whole forest of trees, just like in the images she used to have stuck next to her bed in her tiny shack on Treasure Island. Branches of every shade of green form a lush canopy and Halo walks down the deck with her hands above her head, skimming leaves of jade, emerald, mint and sage.

"It's beautiful," she cries out. "It's so beautiful."

A bird with feathers like a rainbow squawks at her from a branch and Halo laughs, mimicking the noise and failing miserably.

"Halo!" Tenn cries as she points at something on the ground with her good arm. "Look Halo! It's a deer."

Halo rushes over and sees the majestic creature, which is standing with its head tilted up at their enormous ship, seeming to wonder where it's appeared from.

Fyve comes over, grinning. "A few of the pods survived."

"Trust you to check on that first." Halo shakes her head, unable to wipe the smile off her face. "Look, Tenn found a deer."

Fyve puts one arm around Halo, and the other around his little sister and together they stand at the railing, in total awe of their surroundings. The beauty of the forest may have been captured in the images Halo's seen, but never could she have imagined how it *feels* to stand in one. There are birds singing, insects buzzing and leaves caressing each other in the breeze. It smells like rain and sunshine and earth, with sprinkles of magic dust. She draws in a deep breath, unable to get enough of it.

"We're in Tomorrow Land," says Tenn. "It's really real."

"It really is." Halo can't believe she ever doubted it.

"Let's not call it that name," says Fyve. "That's what the Echelons call it. Let's find our own name."

"Terra Land?" Tenn suggests.

"Definitely not." Fyve laughs, then pulls a guilty face as Tenn pouts.

"What about Alaska then?" Tenn asks. "In ancient times, Alaska was covered in snow, but after the thaw it became a tropical paradise. This looks just like the books where I read about it, except…different."

"It's a good suggestion," says Halo, thoughtfully. "But I think it needs its very own name,"

"Askala then!" Tenn bounces on her toes. "Same but different."

Fyve and Halo both raise their brows, impressed.

"I love it," says Fyve. "Askala."

"Askala," Halo repeats, enjoying the sound of their new home's name on her lips.

As Halo looks out across the sheer beauty of the land, her mother's words come back to her.

If you want to leave your mark, first you must pick up your quill.

That's never been truer than it is now. If they're going to leave their mark on Askala, they have an enormous task ahead. Earth is regenerating, but the balance is fragile. One they can't take for granted, ever again. But if they're smart, it's possible. They can care for the land and make sure this is a place that thrives on intelligence and kindness for many generations to come.

Because ultimately the answer to everything in life hangs on just one little thing.

Love.

THE END

Ready for your next epic dystopian adventure?
The authors of The Thaw Chronicles bring you
The Sovereign Code.
Grab your copy of Book 1 now!
http://mybook.to/HarvestDay

River grew up in the Green Zone, a haven for those who are Immune. Bees are free to fly, pollinating their prolific crops. Echo was raised in the Dead Zone where bees are exterminated so vulnerable humans like her can live. Stealing from the heavily guarded Green Zone is a necessary part of survival.

River and Echo are both in their seventeenth year. They're both about to have their immunity tested. And they're both about to have their futures forever altered.

Ultimately, they're about to become part of the final fight for human survival. Are bees really the enemy they need to defeat? Or is mankind a far greater threat...

Prepare to be blown away. The authors of the best-selling series, The Thaw Chronicles, have crafted another unique dystopian adventure full of romance, twists, and page-turning excitement.

Grab your copy now!
http://mybook.to/HarvestDay

BONUS EPILOGUE

THE THAW CHRONICLES

Thanks for reading The Thaw Chronicles!

If you've enjoyed all fourteen books in the series (including the prequel), then check this FREE bonus epilogue.

Visit this link to download:
https://BookHip.com/QQDBDVS

WANT TO STAY IN TOUCH?

If you'd like to be the first for to hear all the news from Tamar and Heidi, be sure to sign up to our newsletter. Subscribers receive bonus content, early cover reveals and sneaky snippets of upcoming books. We'd love you to join us!

SIGN UP HERE:

https://sendfox.com/tamarandheidi

ABOUT THE AUTHORS

Tamar Sloan hasn't decided whether she's a psychologist who loves writing, or a writer with a lifelong fascination with psychology. She must have been someone pretty awesome in a previous life (past life regression indicated a Care Bear), because she gets to do both. When not reading, writing or working with teens, Tamar can be found with her husband and two children enjoying country life in their small slice of the Australian bush.

Heidi Catherine loves the way her books give her the opportunity to escape into worlds vastly different to her own life in the burbs. While she quite enjoys killing her characters (especially the awful ones), she promises she's far better behaved in real life. Other than writing and reading, Heidi's current obsessions include watching far too much reality TV with the excuse that it's research for her books.

MORE SERIES TO FALL IN LOVE WITH...

ALSO BY TAMAR SLOAN

Keepers of the Grail

Keepers of the Light

Keepers of the Chalice

Keepers of Excalibur

Zodiac Guardians

Descendants of the Gods

Prime Prophecy

ALSO BY HEIDI CATHERINE

The Kingdoms of Evernow

The Soulweaver

The Woman Who Didn't (written as HC Michaels)

The Girl Who Never (written as HC Michaels)

Made in the USA
Monee, IL
12 September 2023

42659034R00166